Voice of Innocence

Lindsay Detwiler

S

Published by
Satin Romance
An Imprint of Melange Books, LLC
White Bear Lake, MN 55110
www.satinromance.com

Voice of Innocence ~ Copyright © 2015 by Lindsay Detwiler

ISBN: 978-1-68046-059-9 Print
ISBN: 978-1-68046-060-5 EBook

Names, characters, and incidents depicted in this book are products of the author's imagination or are used fictitiously. Any resemblance to actual events, locales, organizations, or persons, living or dead, is entirely coincidental and beyond the intent of the author or the publisher. No part of this book may be reproduced or transmitted in any form or by any means, electronic or mechanical, including photocopying, recording, or by any information storage and retrieval system, without permission in writing from the publisher.
Published in the United States of America.

Cover Art by Angela Archer

To my husband, my first love

Prologue

~ Emma ~

You never forget your first love.
We've all heard that saying, probably more times than we care to. Whether he's the jock on the football team, the lead singer in the town's less-than-famous and less-than-talented heavy metal band, or the artsy "life is what it is" guy, the girl who falls for him is granted the eternal memories of him. For some, however, perhaps the better terminology is doomed—doomed with the memories, the connections, and the life-changing relationship.

Perhaps I seem bitter. Perhaps I am. I, Emma Ranstein, am the girl who lives in every small town. Maybe you even know a girl like me, at least to some extent. While debating between healthy and sugary cereals at the local food market, ladies in their World's Best Grandma sweatshirts whisper a bit too loudly, *"Oh, there's that poor Emma. Sweet girl. I remember when she was going places. If only..."* or *"Life has dealt her such a bad hand."* Perhaps, in many ways, they are right. However, I am not only that girl you know in town that everybody pities. The reasons behind my sorrow are probably not experienced by many, which is fortunate.

At forty-seven years old, I suppose I haven't done too badly for myself, at least from an external look. I've got the proverbial "American Dream"—sort of. Rosebushes swirl around a rustic picket fence, peeling and weathered, in front of my gleaming house. Its two stories and wraparound porch scream Americana. I've got a gorgeous husband named John, blonde-haired and blue-eyed. He's a doctor by day, and a wonderful companion by night, when he's not on an emergency call. Our life together is easy enough. We live comfortably, contentedly even. We don't have any children, but our one-hundred-and-thirty-pound yellow lab Hank helps fill this void with his oversized paws and heart. Every summer, we plop ourselves into two lounge chairs on the sands of the Outer Banks for a week. I go to my exercise class twice a week after work to sweat out my frustrations and attempt to fit into my skinny jeans, and I have a few friends I go out with on Friday nights to throw back a few Long Island's with. So, to an outsider, my life seems normal, maybe even good. Those who know me best, though, look at my life with a sense of loss, even though they won't admit it to my face.

You might be thinking that John, my husband, was my first love. Typical romance story, right? We met in college, perhaps an Ivy League. He swept me off my feet, we got married, he went to medical school, and here we are. A wipe-your-hands-off, neat and clean, predictable story, nothing exciting here to tell—might as well stop reading. Except this isn't how it happened, not even close.

First of all, we didn't meet in college. I never went to college. I know that in today's world where most high school graduates go on to higher education, you may be thinking I must have been a bad student. Maybe I was an aspiring actress or artist. Maybe my family was poor, or maybe I married right out of high school. I wish any of these alternatives were viable. They definitely beat the truth, at least in my eyes.

I had dreams of college, dreams of becoming a teacher. In the great scheme of things, this does not seem like such a grand aspiration to most people. After all, we know that a teacher's salary is not the six figures of a CEO or a famous singer. In a world where money rules all, why would one fantasize about such a career? I cannot answer this clearly or concisely. All I know is that in some deep part of me, I always felt that it was my purpose. School caressed me into my best self. Even with my less-than-supermodel-ish figure, my mousey-brown hair, the teasing glares of my popular peers and troubles at home, I didn't feel inferior in that desk. Don't get me wrong, I wasn't a total nerd. I had friends. I went to school dances and football games. Like every other teenage girl, I cried about the insurmountable inequities of the world, such as why I had to be a brunette when all of the guys wanted blondes. Still, my schoolwork kept me grounded in reality. Every *A* made me feel unstoppable, every answer made me crave more. Looking back, it seems like a no-brainer that I would choose a career in education. I never wanted to leave school. Moreover, I wanted to ignite the fire for education in others that was once sparked in me.

Why, then, am I going to a tiny cubicle, day in and day out? Why have I been typing letters and alphabetizing files in a dingy office for several decades instead of influencing our country's youngest minds? This is a story too complicated for the time being. It is my second biggest regret. I promise that I will get to the reason. Now is the time for other confessions and reflections. It is my first biggest regret that plagues my mind, and I cannot seem to get past the memory.

So, John and I didn't meet in college. The truth is, John and I met when I was forty-two. He crashed into my life when I had given up on everything, including love. He opened my eyes to new possibilities. I will always be grateful for that, no matter how my life's story plays out. I will always have love for him in my heart. However, he wasn't my first love or, if I'm being honest, my strongest love.

As I said earlier, everyone knows what first love entails—secret kisses, hearts palpitating with new emotions, and the floating dreams of what lie ahead. We all think our first love will be the "one and only," the person we grow old with.

Such is rarely the case.

Instead, we suffer the agonizing breakup. Our friends tell us, *"You'll find someone new,"* or *"He wasn't right for you,"* or, *"Single is better."* We try to believe these truths and for some of us, they eventually do ring true. Time, the great eraser of emotion, passes. We feel passive about the situation. Maybe we find someone new, or maybe we play the field for a while. No matter what we do, no matter how much time passes, we never forget. Yes, we forgive. Yes, emotions may not be so intense. Maybe we even convince ourselves that he truly wasn't the one; that we didn't know ourselves enough then to know what love was. But we never forget those fleeting moments of innocence, promise, and, in short, pure love.

Such is my curse.

Like most girls, I thought my first love was my soul mate. He understood me in ways no one could. All through high school we were an exclusive couple. We talked of marriage, houses, kids, and dogs. We talked about hopes, fears, dreams, and desires. He made me a more exuberant person, and I seemed to keep him on the straight path. Not that he was a bad kid, maybe a little rebellious. Detention halls, a few senseless pranks, and a bit of an aversion to homework flooded his character. Nothing I couldn't tame. Nonetheless, he came from an average family and had strong morals. He had a huge heart and would help anyone who asked, even if it meant giving his last bit of lunch money to a kid who came from a destitute family. Our love was strong, unwavering, and unbreakable…or so we thought.

It's been thirty-two years since I first laid eyes on him, the man who would change my life forever. He is also the man who plagues my life. For I cannot forget my first love. Even though our relationship has dissipated, the feelings live on. I know that our time has passed and that way too much has happened for any sort of rekindling. Today, however, on one of the most momentous days of his life, I cannot help but trace our past together. I cannot help but ponder what might have been if things had just been a little different, or if I had just believed. No, my first love is not like many others. It is an intricate, winding tale that doesn't necessarily end with our final good-bye twenty-eight years ago. It is a story that most girls cannot lay claim to, nor would they want to.

My first love was convicted of murder at the age of nineteen years old, during the prime of our lives.

My first love went to jail for twenty-eight years.

My first love told me he didn't do it and begged me to believe him.

And, most importantly, my first love *didn't* do it.

Chapter One
Miracles

~ Emma ~

With my baggy gray sweatpants and oversized T-shirt on, I slouch at the kitchen sink, peering out the window with glassy eyes. Hank pounces on his favorite tennis ball in the backyard, slobber flying as he shakes the ball to death. The neighbor's dusky gray cat languidly trespasses outside the perimeter of our fence, and Hank loses it. He darts back and forth along the peeling fence, angered at the cage that he cannot escape from, in order to annihilate this tempting creature. I have an inexplicable urge to open that gate and let Hank run.

A loose piece of hair traipses into my face, reminding me of how much of a mess I must appear. Blaring with a piercing tone, the timer on the oven startles me. John will be home any minute. I better pull it together if I don't want him to suspect something is up.

This morning I did something a bit ludicrous, at least for my rigid, square self. I called in sick at the office. I know my life must seem pretty dull. I get my kicks from calling in sick one day. Big deal, huh? For me, though, it is a step from the normal path. It's been my first call-off in three years. It's the first time *ever* that I called off sick when no physical ailment plagued me. After John left for work this morning, I just couldn't bear to stuff myself into that rigid black suit and pointy-toed stilettos, symbolic of the true professional. I couldn't bear the thought of mindlessly filing, typing, sorting, and answering phones—not on a day like today. So instead, I spent the day doing…well, nothing. I stayed in my frumpy sweatpants for the day, skipped the shower, and even took

Hank for a walk. Even though today is perhaps one of the hardest days, it was sort of wonderful to have nothing to do and nowhere to go. It was even more comforting not having to be anyone for the day.

I pull my domestic masterpiece, perfectly stacked lasagna accompanied by homemade bread, out of the oven. It actually screams edible, a unique feat for my handiwork. Considering my recent kitchen disasters, which include pancakes burnt beyond recognition and a blown-up microwave due to forgotten aluminum foil, John will be shocked. Now that I think about it, maybe the lasagna was too much. He will know something is up when he sees that I have been cooking all day. Without the familiar smell of Chinese or fried chicken from the local fast-food restaurant wafting through the kitchen, his body will probably slip into shock immediately. After he recovers, the questions will start.

I am wrong, though. When John walks through the door five minutes later, he seems happy for my efforts. "Looks great, babe," he says winking at me. He kisses me on the cheek, saying nothing about my less-than-gorgeous appearance. But that's John for you, always the sensitive one.

After he changes into some perfectly fitting jeans and an old, familiar T-shirt, he grabs his chair at the table. As I plop a piece of the lasagna onto his plate, he asks, "So, anything happen today?" He looks at me expectantly but hesitantly.

"Nothing much," I say, with a faked tone of indifference in my voice. He takes a careful, teeny-tiny bite, ponders over it, and nods in surprise.

"It's actually...delicious," he remarks, with true shock in his tone.

"It's *actually* delicious? What did you expect?" I poke.

"Well...this is the fire extinguisher queen we're talking about here. Seriously, Emma, it's great. Maybe you've missed your calling."

I smile with genuine happiness. It has always been this way with John and I; it's easy, comfortable, and familiar. He always knows just what to say to lighten a mood. Even if I don't want it to, a smile creeps onto my face when he is around. An inner warmth radiates from his every cell, tantalizing mine to do the same. I feel a glow in my cheeks and steadfastness in my bones with John, a feeling that usurped my body only one time before...

As I think these thoughts, I must wear my inner turmoil on my expression, because John asks, "Are you okay?"

"I'm fine," I manage to spit out.

"Is there something you want to talk about, Emma? You know you can talk to me about anything," he says. He has dropped his fork and reaches for my hand across the table, barely managing to avoid dragging his sleeve in the saucy mess on his plate.

"It's nothing, John. I'm fine. It's just been a long day," I stammer. I avoid his eyes with acute resistance. His eyes can always seek the truth in me, even if I don't want him to.

"Emma, you're not fooling me. I know what's going on. I know what today is. I've read the papers, you know," he says. He speaks quietly and slowly, as if he is afraid his very words will break me into a million little pieces. Usually, I am thankful for his immense sensitivity and empathy. Today, it just frustrates me.

"John, of course you know what today is," I spew. "Every damn news channel in the country has been plastering his face all over the place like he's some kind of miracle." I rise from my seat and jolt to the window, my inadvertent safe spot. I glance out at Hank, who is still pacing back and forth while the neighbor cat taunts him.

John saunters over to me and delicately pulls me into him. I feel his soft, warm breath on my neck and feel his need to make everything better. He holds me, silent and still, giving me time to cool off. There is strength in his arms and warmth that goes beyond just the physical heat from his body. I can feel him silently willing me to breathe, to relax, and to just be. Tears well in my eyes, and I feel a sense of regret. This can't be easy for him either.

"I'm sorry," I murmur. "I don't know why I'm so upset."

"It's natural. He was important to you."

My head shakes side to side as my eyes squint shut, trying to stop the incessant flow of moisture. "It was a long time ago. It doesn't even matter now. *He* doesn't even matter now."

"But yes, he does, Emma. He was your first. He was your only for a long time. You two went through some pretty intense things. Things you shouldn't have had to go through." He spins me around now and looks at me. Genuine concern glints in the depth of his eyes, cradling me with their concern. "You can talk to me about this. I know you love me. But I also know that you loved him for a long time. This can't be easy on you."

"John, honestly," I plea, breaking his grip on my arms. "I'm fine. It was so long ago. I'm sure he doesn't even think about me anymore. I'm sure he's moved on and forgotten all about me and what I did to him. I'm sure that he has much more important worries right now."

"Baby, trust me, no one could forget about you." John smiles, taking a step back to give me my space.

"John, listen to me. I love you. Yes, he was important to me at one time. But not anymore. You're all that matters. And yes, what happened to him was tragic. And awful. It shouldn't have happened, it wasn't fair. And yes, I can't help but wonder what it must be like for him, what he must be feeling today. But that's it. It's just…curiosity. No regrets," I say.

I speak with such confidence and assurance that the words seem true. Maybe a part of me believes they are true. Regardless, they do their job. John appears to be satisfied. He pulls me closer, and we embrace for a long time. He finally backs away, saying, "I better finish my lasagna. I have to be back at work in an hour."

"Tonight?" I ask incredulously.

"Emma, I'm sorry, but one of the new doctors called off tonight and there's no one in the ER. I have to go." Sincerity floods his eyes. "I mean, I could try to see if Jake could fill in, but he's having trouble with his wife and specifically requested tonight off and…"

I interrupt, "John, it's okay. Go ahead, I'll be fine. We have this weekend. It's fine." I utter the words calmly and, unlike other times, I actually mean them.

"You sure?" he questions.

"Finish your lasagna!" I order. "Maybe if you're lucky, you'll come home to an apple pie or something. This domestic thing is kind of growing on me."

"Let's not push it. I mean, I'll miss you tonight, but I don't want to see you in the ER later," he teases.

I grin softly. John always knows how to ease a tense subject. He stacks the last few bites of lasagna on his fork, gulps down a few drinks of water, gives me a sloppy kiss, and heads out the door. I'm so lucky to have this man in my life. I truly do love him. I love him in a way that I didn't think was possible. I stride over to the screen door and call Hank in. Reluctantly, he gives up his game with the cat and trots into the house, his nose whiffing in the smells of human food. I grab a seat on the couch. Hank glances at the remnants of dinner, drool dripping down his chin. He seems to consider launching himself onto the dirty dishes but decides that would be too much effort and follows me into the living room. As I snuggle with my only companion for the night, my mind wanders purposefully. No matter how hard I try to think about the coming weekend and the beach house waiting for our romantic getaway, I just can't. As guilty as it makes me feel, it is not John who marauds my thoughts tonight.

    I mindlessly rub Hank's ears between my fingers as my mind drifts back months, years, and decades. Like the floods of an unexpected tsunami, the memories drown me in their depths.

Chapter Two
Secrets

~ Emma ~

Memories

In my blinding, hot-pink shirt and denim jeans, I glided through the hallways. The first-day-of-the-school-year-exuberance and my new, sparkling sneakers had worn off. I had made it through my first four classes of tenth grade. I was now heading to one of the most dreaded classes of all—art class. For most kids, art was a place of freedom. There were fewer rules, the teacher was typically more relaxed, and there was virtually no homework. For me, however, art class promised the threat of embarrassing injuries and potential failures. Besides lacking creativity, I also greatly lacked any fine motor skills. Last year, I had sliced my finger so deeply on a penknife that I was rushed to the hospital for stitches. Covering everyone's art projects in blood splatters was not how I wanted to make my first impression.

 I walked into the classroom, glancing around at faces I had seen since kindergarten. Ruby's gleaming lime green headband, sequined and stunning, bounced the fluorescent lights aimlessly about the room. Noah had grown at least two inches this summer, and the giddy girls gathered around him didn't fail to notice. Everywhere, familiar kids laughed and joked, feeling a fresh sense of social status due to their newfound label as tenth graders. But then my eyes stopped on a new face. I slowly inventoried his body, making note of his chestnut hair, thick and disheveled, and his even deeper brown eyes. Although I didn't know his name, a sensation fluttered in the pit of my stomach. I hoped that my cornflakes and chocolate milk wouldn't spew onto the floor (also not a great way to make a good first impression). Some would call the sensation love at first sight. At fifteen years old, I was pretty sure the feeling was just some undigested food matter sloshing in my stomach. All I knew was that I was curious. I listened closely as roll was called and we were given seats. "Jenna Hansinger, Ashley White, Emma Groves..." And then I heard it for the first time. The teacher read the name of the boy who would be present in my life throughout its entirety, if only in memory. She assigned him the seat next to me.

My fate was sealed then and there.

I can't tell you much about the first half of art class on my first day of tenth grade. Yes, I sat rigidly in my desk while the loopy Mrs. Shire animatedly divulged promises about pottery and painting. I heard references to Picasso and grading rubrics but not enough to know what was actually going on. For the first time ever, class wasn't my focus; instead, my mind seemed glued to Corbin.

Corbin didn't seem too focused on the overly bubbly art teacher either. Instead, he mindlessly fiddled with his pencil, flipping it over and over as his brown eyes gazed ahead. I began to wonder why I'd never seen him before. Sure, I wasn't Miss Popularity. But in a town this small, every face was at least somewhat familiar. Then again, maybe statistics had been defiantly against us, preventing us from having a single class together in our ten years of schooling. What were the odds of that? Since math was never my thing, I decided to just accept the fact that maybe I had just passed over Corbin without noticing him. Then again, I became more certain than ever that he had to be new to the school district. I knew for a fact that even I, "Miss Nose-in-her-books," couldn't possibly have looked past that face...

Suddenly, a bit of chaos blasted through my thoughts. The previously silent environment bubbled over with the conversations and laughter of twenty students. What was going on? *Great,* I thought. The only time I decided not to pay attention, and I actually missed something important. Now what?

"It's Emma, right?" Corbin offered.

"Yeah…why?" I replied with more defensiveness than I had intended.

"Uh…the project…"

"What project?"

"The one Mrs. Shire was just talking about—you know, the collages?"

"Oh, right," I retorted with an air of assurance.

A smile gently spread across his face. "You weren't paying attention," he accused.

"Of course I was paying attention," I snapped. "You were the one flipping your pencil around like some sort of magician."

"It's called multitasking. I was still listening, unlike you," he joked. "Should I fill you in?"

I sighed. This was going just swell. "Please," I reluctantly uttered, swallowing my pride.

"Well, we have to work with the person beside us, hence, we're a pair," he began.

A pair. I liked the sound of that. Okay, I scolded myself. Pay attention this time.

"We have to get to know the person beside us, you know, the usual, what they like to do, where they're from, all of that. Then we have to make a collage that represents our partner and share it with the class," he said.

"Like from magazines?" I asked hopefully.

"Um…no, like drawing or painting it…you do at least know that you're in art class, right?"

"Are you kidding? I have to draw? This is just great. Why do I have to take a stupid art class anyway?"

"Okay, so you're a daydreamer and you hate drawing. And you like to complain. I'll write this down for my collage," he teased.

"I don't like to complain! You're getting me all wrong. I'm just not so creative, and I don't want to get a bad grade." The words piled on and on as my panic set in.

"Well, then we better get to it."

"When is this thing due?" I asked.

"Not until Friday. Which means we have all week to learn about each other."

All week to learn about each other. Which meant we would be spending a lot of time together. As long as he didn't already think I was a major freak and ask Mrs. Shire for a new partner. I grimaced at the prospect.

He mistook my expression. "You're still worried about the drawing part, huh? Don't worry about it. I can help you. I happen to be semi-okay at it," he assured me.

"That's kind of cheating."

"You worry way too much. Relax, it's going to be fine. This is art class. It's supposed to be fun."

"Great. Now you think I worry too much. Wow, can't wait to see how exciting my collage is," I sneered.

"Well, then you better start telling me some good things about you. There are good things, right? I mean, it's obvious you've got the looks down. But you do have some good personality traits, too, right?" he asked with a grin.

Wait, did he just compliment me? Or was he just joking? I opted for option two; no one ever noticed me for my "looks." After all, mousey-brown hair on a girl with a boyish figure wasn't exactly what all the guys were after, at least according to one of my mom's magazines that I carefully stole every month.

"Well, yeah, I might have a few good things to share. Let's see…I have a great memory. Like, I can remember any fact I hear in biology or history after hearing it just once. Oh, and I never forget an author's name of a book or poem or something," I said excitingly. Who didn't like a girl with a good memory?

"Okay, that's great. But tell me something that doesn't have to do with school. Like, what do you do for fun?" He seemed genuinely interested, to my surprise.

"Well, I don't have a lot of free time. I play the clarinet in the marching band. I guess that could be considered my hobby," I noted in a questioning tone.

"Okay, that's good, but it's still school related. Tell me something unique."

I racked my brain for a minute. Panic again bubbled. I wasn't yet ready to admit to Corbin how lame I truly was. I finally responded, "There's nothing unique about me, unfortunately. And besides, why is it all about me? What about you? I don't know anything about you. My collage is going to be blank."

"By the sound of it, you'd like to have an excuse to turn in a blank collage," he badgered. "We'll get to me. But first, I want to know something about you. I'm sure there's something unique about you. Some dream or something you've always wanted to do," he pleaded.

"Well...kind of. It's stupid, though," I abashedly admitted. Why did I even offer this as a possibility? I should've kept my mouth shut or made something up. I should have pretended to be studying karate or told him I wanted to go sky-diving or something. This social interaction thing wasn't going so well.

"Come on, you can tell me. Spit it out," he encouraged. "You can trust me."

"Um, I've only known you for like five minutes. And it's not like I can trust you to keep it a secret," I reminded him. "It's going to be on a collage."

"Well I won't put this on the collage then. I just want to know something about you that no one knows. So spill it!" His eyes pierced into mine, and I knew that I was doomed. I couldn't say no to Corbin Jones.

"Fine!" I asserted. "You asked if there's something I've always wanted to do. There is. I've always wanted to..." I paused, searching for courage "...to get a tattoo." There, it was done.

"Of what?"

"Well, I've always wanted to get a tiny dove, somewhere no one will see it."

"A dove? For like, religious reasons?"

"No, not really. I just always think of a dove as symbolizing innocence, freedom. I always thought that if I got a tattoo, it would have to actually mean something," I offered. Suddenly, it occurred to me how dorky this must seem. I waited for him to laugh. Instead, he seemed mystified.

"That's it? That's the big secret?" he asked incredulously.

"What do you mean, that's it? It's a big deal to me," I countered.

Voice of Innocence

"Okay, okay. When you mentioned a tattoo, I thought, well, maybe she wants something...naughty. But a dove isn't exactly what I would call rebellious." His face was plastered with that crazy-gorgeous grin. I started to think that his grin could get him just about anything he wanted.

"I told you it was stupid," I said sadly. I felt my face getting hot.

"No, Emma, I don't think it's stupid at all. You're missing the point. I think it's a great idea, really sweet. But that's the point. Most people have big secrets that aren't so pure," he remarked.

"Okay, well, if you knew me better, it would make more sense. I'm that girl who's always doing what she's supposed to. I never get detention hall, I get straight *A's* in every class. I never go out late or skip class. I never drink or smoke. I'm kind of a boring square, if I'm being honest. Maybe not your idea of exciting, but it's good enough for me," I explained. I tried to appear confident in my words, as though I actually believed them.

"Okay, fair enough. When I get to know you better, I'm sure I'll get it," he said seriously. "But I don't believe you. Yeah, you might be a great student, which is good. But I think there's a lot more to you than you're letting on. I don't believe that you're as simple or boring as you're letting everyone think," he suggested with a bit of intensity. "All I know is that I'm going to find out, Emma. I'm going to find out what you're all about."

"Yeah, for the project," I said. "I don't think you really have to get to a deeper meaning for it. It's just a dumb art project so we can learn the basics."

"Who says I'm just talking about the project? Maybe I want to get to know you *just* to know you."

My heart fluttered a little at the prospect that he could be serious. Even after this awkward conversation, he still wanted to know me. The real me. I hadn't scared him away yet. Maybe there was hope.

"Well, now you know my big, dark secret. It's time I find out some of yours."

Just then, the bell rang. I looked up in shock; the class was over already? Everyone started grabbing their backpacks. Mrs. Shire yelled something over the crowd, but I didn't hear. My attention was fixed on something a tad more interesting.

"What do you have next?" Corbin asked as he grabbed his black backpack from the floor. I grabbed my pink messenger bag, also brand new for the first day of school, hauled it over my shoulder, and turned to him.

"Lunch. You?"

"The same," he smiled. "Walk with me?"

"Sure. Maybe I can actually get to interrogate *you* for a change."

"Looking forward to it," he said as he followed me to the chaotic cafeteria.

As we glided through the people, I couldn't help but think that it just might be the best lunch period ever, even if lunch was Salisbury steak.

Chapter Three
White Promises

~ Emma ~

Memories

    Entering the cafeteria together felt like we had entered a war zone. As is typical on the first day of school, everyone was overly exuberant and loud. Friends who had a whole summer's worth of stories anxiously gabbed as they grabbed their food. Just like in junior high, tables were claimed by individual cliques. A group of five scandalously clad girls tossed their blonde hair in the corner of the room while the football team hungrily ogled them. Looking around the room, one could see all of the typical high school groups: the self-proclaimed science geeks with their fancy gadgets, the punks with their shocking clothing choices and purple/black/every-color-in-between hair, the quiet kids silently sipping on their lemonades, and every other group that exists within the strange world of teenagers. I glanced over at Corbin as he took in the room. I figured he was wondering where I would be sitting, what group I was associated with.
    Confused by the myriad choices of lunch lines that were now present in our school system, I slipped into a line and pretended I knew what I was doing. Potatoes splattered onto trays, and vegetables were discreetly discarded in a hidden corner of the lunch line. Girls grabbed single bags of chips in an attempt to seem dainty and skinny, pretending that the small bag would fill them up. I maneuvered through the chaos, grabbing a tray of mystery substances and some bread. At least

something would be edible.

Corbin followed. As we stood behind two girls anxiously chatting about some guy named Steven and their date that night, I turned to him. He was loading up his tray, already clad with a double lunch, and chips and cookies from the "extras" bin.

"So I'm guessing you're not from around here? I mean, I've never seen you before."

"No, I'm not. I moved here this summer from Arizona," he said nonchalantly while he grabbed chocolate milk. *Note to self, he's not a health nut.* That was a big check in my list of attributes. If we went on a date, at least we'd be going somewhere that there was real food.

"Arizona? Why'd you move to this crappy little town then?" I questioned.

"It's kind of complicated. Let's just say my family needed...change. My dad originally grew up here, so he thought it was a good place to relocate," Corbin offered, his focus purely on organizing his tray.

"Okay, fair enough," I added quickly. "Hobbies?"

"I played football back in Arizona. I wasn't very good, though, so I doubt I'll play here."

"That's too bad. At least I'd have someone to watch then on Friday nights," I said smiling. Where was this flirtatious side of me (if you could call it that) coming from? I usually couldn't think of two words to say to any guy, let alone a flirty line to a gorgeous one.

"Oh, yeah, that's right. You're in the marching band. Well, maybe I'll have to reconsider," he said, winking in a way that actually was cute. We moved through the line, aimlessly grabbing our plastic utensils and cardboard-like napkins. After we paid for our food, I glanced around the jumbled mess of a cafeteria. Finally, I saw my group and walked over, trying to remain confident that I wouldn't trip and do a face-plant into the gravy on my Salisbury steak.

From my peripherals, I could see Corbin following behind me. Feeling poised in his answer, I coolly asked, "Um, do you want to sit with me and my friends?"

"Well, yeah...I think it beats the alternative of sitting by myself or with *that* table," he offered, poking his shoulder toward the table of science nerds. At that precise moment, one of the kids at the table had slapped a piece of pepperoni on his forehead while the others took bets on how long it would stick due to its chemical properties. Lovely. As we casually shifted toward the open seats, Corbin added, "Plus, we have to work on our project, remember?" He glanced at me, and I almost forgot where I was going. I tripped, catching myself before I completely wiped out. I flipped my newly cut hair, trying to regain a bit of composure.

"I'll warn you. You're probably going to get hounded by my friends. We usually don't have any boys at our table," I muttered, slightly embarrassed, as we lowered ourselves into our seats.

The table, previously a chattering hubbub of emotions and shrieks, became completely silent at our arrival. Several sets of eyes glanced from me to Corbin and back to me with curiosity. Corbin gazed assuredly back at the girls, beaming as he looked across the table. My heart sank a little. I was sure that he would lose interest in me after meeting my friends. Out of the four of us, I always considered myself the least attractive. If he didn't lose himself in Katie's gorgeously sun-kissed blonde hair, he would find himself glued to Hannah's almost turquoise eyes or Jenn's super toned body. It was a hopeless case.

"Hey, guys! How was your first day so far?" I said, ignoring their obvious questions in an effort to seem normal.

I hadn't seen the girls since this morning; we didn't have any classes together so far. I wasn't quite ready to clarify the unexplainable presence that joined us at our table—I was still trying to figure it out myself. My tactic was ineffective as the girls ignored my question. Eyes glued to Corbin, they seemed ready to burst into pieces from curiosity.

"So who is this?" Jenn asked bluntly, dodging my formal niceties in favor of their true interest.

"Oh, right, this is Corbin Jones. He just moved here from Arizona," I offered, turning to look at him. He widened his perfect grin, and I thought for a second that the girls were going to melt right there.

"Hey, Corbin," they said in almost perfect unison.

"Hey, nice to meet you," he acknowledged while grasping his fork and stabbing his meat patty. I tentatively nibbled on the mysterious brown glob on my tray (a.k.a Salisbury steak) and decided it wasn't edible. I skipped right to the chocolate chip cookie. Meanwhile, the girls took turns asking Corbin questions as their food sat ignored and cold.

"So you're from Arizona, huh?" Jenn inquired. "Do you like it here in Pennsylvania?"

"Um...yeah. It's good so far," he answered politely, glancing my way every few seconds.

"Well, give it a few weeks. It'll get to you," Hannah chimed in. She was like the ying to Katie's yang—always pessimistic, always finding the darkness in any situation. But I guess our group needed someone to balance out Katie's enthusiasm and keep us in check with reality so that we didn't float away into the clouds of a perfect blue sky.

"Yeah, wait until winter," Jenn added. "It's so damn cold here that you'll be on the first flight back home. It sucks." The group nodded in agreement except for Katie, whose scowl was either directed at Jenn's "harsh" language, or at the prospect of a negative characteristic being noted about her hometown.

Katie gently leaped to the state's defense like only she could. "Oh, come on guys. It's not *that* bad. Besides, if it weren't for the cold, we wouldn't get to wear our awesome boots. That wouldn't be any fun, would it?" Coming from anyone else, this comment would edge on irritating. Coming from Katie, however, you couldn't help but smile. Her inner sweetness just effervesced through every word she said. Her attitude was so candid that you couldn't possibly get mad.

"I'm looking forward to the snow, actually," Corbin admitted. "I've never really experienced it, not in any notable amount anyway. I think it'll be fun."

"You've never been in snow?" I implored, not even trying to mask my incredulity.

"Well, there's not too much snow in the middle of the desert," he smirked. Everyone laughed while I blushed at my own stupidity. This blushing thing was becoming a habit.

"Oh, right," I said sheepishly.

"I've always wanted to go sled riding," he explained. "Or maybe snowboarding."

"Maybe you and Emma could go sometime," Katie offered with a mischievous grin. She peered my way as I murderously glared at her.

"Yeah, that would be great," he proclaimed. "It's a date." He beamed at Katie, then at me.

Voice of Innocence

"Whoa, wait a minute. I'm not going anywhere in the snow. No way. Not my thing," I blurted.

"Not your thing? The snow or the activities? Or me?" Corbin asked. At the last option, I had discerned a bit of worry in his eyes. His unabashed confidence, however, didn't let the worry creep too far into his unflinching psyche.

"All of the above. Well, not the part about you...the part about the snow. I hate cold. And sledding and snowboarding don't sound so great either. I'm not very coordinated," I admitted, looking at my plate.

Hannah started to laugh. "Well, I have to agree with the coordinated part." The other girls snickered, too, shaking their heads in agreement.

"What am I missing?" Corbin questioned, that grin still plastered to his face.

The group started chuckling, recalling their favorite story as of late. Jenn was the first to speak up.

"Well, last month we thought it would be a great idea to rent some kayaks for a day. Simple enough, right? Sit down, paddle a little, if you fall in, you swim to the surface, right? Well, Emma here, she got in her kayak like the rest of us. We're all paddling along just fine. After a little while, we're like, 'Wait...where's Emma?'" Jenn narrated. I put my head down. Sometimes I thought that the group of social rejects might be a better lunch table choice for me. I glanced over and noted, quite impressed, that the pepperoni was still in place. Interesting. Corbin's silent laughter snapped me back to the reality of my situation at the table of scientifically inept and socially humiliating girls I called my friends. Apparently Corbin was good at predicting, because he already knew what was coming.

"Guys!" I yelled. "That's enough...I'm still sitting here, remember?" But, as with most areas of my life, my thoughts were ignored. I started wishing I was like Jamie Rose, the head cheerleader. When she talked, people listened—even if it was only because she was a double-d with buttery blonde hair. Oh, and that her dad had more money than he knew what to do with. Jenn continued with her story, bringing me back to the unfortunate reality of the present.

"So we glance behind us, and there's Emma, stuck behind a rock. How she got stuck behind this boulder is beyond us. We all just steered right around it. She's there frantically paddling, going in circles, trying to get un-wedged. Finally, she gets loose, smiling at herself. We wave her on, telling her to catch up."

By this time the girls were all hooting, already knowing how the story ended. Corbin's melodious, deep laugh also echoed throughout the lunchroom, joining the chorus of traitors.

"And then she flips it! *Ker-Splash!* Right in the water," Hannah interrupted. "You should've seen her face. It was priceless." I darted my glare into Hannah's forehead, plotting schemes of revenge. I turned to Katie, the sweet one, hoping for some kind of support.

"I'm sorry, Emma, it's kind of funny," Katie added quietly. Great. Even Katie was on their side.

"Oh! What about the ice-skating story?" Hannah chimed in.

"Enough!" I bellowed. By this time, though, I was grinning, too. "I think he's got the point," I asserted, eyeing Corbin.

"So apparently I'm taking my life into my own hands if I take her out in the snow?" Corbin jested.

"Yeah, or if you walk down the hall with me. Or go to the produce aisle in the grocery store. Or sit beside me at lunch, for that matter. That's why you should definitely find another tour guide for your winter excursions," I said. A part of me thought that it would be kind of fun, though, frolicking in the snow with Corbin Jones.

"I think I'll take my chances," he decided, to my inner relief. "Maybe you'll fair better in the snow than the water. Sled riding doesn't require that much coordination, right? What's the worst thing that could happen?"

"She could hit a tree and die. Or have a traumatic brain injury that leaves her crippled for the rest of her life. Or there's always hypothermia," Hannah piped in without a moment's hesitation.

"Hannah! Enough!" Katie scolded.

"See, there's plenty that could go wrong," I said.

"It'll be fine. The first day it snows, I'll pick you up. It's a date. I'm not taking no for an answer."

"Oh, crap, it's almost time to leave," Jenn proclaimed. Everyone got up to dump their untouched trays. Corbin promptly grabbed mine in front of me.

"I've got it," he said.

"You don't have to," I argued, reaching for it.

"What are partners for? Besides, I better get practicing, just in case you hit that tree."

"Corbin!" I bellowed. "It's not funny."

"Yeah, it is," Hannah added over her shoulder.

I studied him from behind as he moseyed to the trash. His jeans were perfectly molded to his impeccably toned body. I couldn't believe this amazing specimen of a guy had sat with me at lunch. Of all the girls he could have latched on to, for some reason he ended up with me. Fate had dealt me a pretty sweet card, at least for the time being. I knew that he was new and would probably be thankful for any type of social interaction. Once he settled into the area, he would become more particular about whom he spent time with. Once people got to know him, his popularity would increase, a guarantee that his time with me would decrease. For now, though, it seemed I had Corbin all to myself. I would make the best of it while I could.

When he returned from his trash-dumping escapade, the bell rang and it was time for algebra class, my second-least favorite of the day. I waved goodbye to my friends, promising to get in touch after school if I didn't see them before the end of the day. Corbin walked me to my class, giving us time to chat alone.

"So, I was supposed to find out about you at lunch. And all we talked about was me again," I complained.

"You're more interesting," he said.

"I doubt that. And besides, my collage is going to suck. I don't know anything."

"You know I'm from Arizona," he offered.

"Yeah, well, that's not enough."

"Well, it looks like I'll have to sit with you again tomorrow at lunch." His face seemed to flash self-assurance, as if he knew that I couldn't say no. It's not that he was cocky; Corbin Jones had simply mastered the fine balancing act of having an appealing dose of ego without overdoing it.

"It's kind of hard to find out about you with my friends and their ridiculous stories about me," I observed sarcastically.

"Well, maybe we'll just have to find some time to spend together alone," he hinted. This time, his tone was just a slight bit hesitant, as if he wasn't sure how I'd react. I liked the fact that he didn't have me completely pinned down yet. I grinned at the prospect of alone-time with Corbin. *This was going to be a great year*, I thought to myself. I could feel it.

* * * *

The rest of the week flew by. By Friday, Corbin Jones and I knew each other well enough to make our collages. We had to present them to the art class. Mine, of course, was basic. I drew the state of Arizona in the middle and colored it green, his favorite color. I added a snowman in the corner because he wanted to see snow. I also drew a sled, the emblem for his favorite band, and a skateboard. I drew a picture that somewhat resembled a dog, although no one could tell it was supposed to be his Mastiff, Henry. In reality, it looked more like a wild-eyed llama mixed with a sad excuse for a squirrel.

Corbin's, on the other hand, was breathtaking. He actually made me seem interesting. In the center was a square with myriad neon colors, which he said represented my character as a whole. I was serious and square-like to the outsider. When someone got to know me, Corbin proclaimed, they would realize that I had many different colors to my personality. I laughed a little at the tiny kayak in the corner of the collage. It was capsized. The rest of the class, who had seen some of my clumsy escapades firsthand, laughed, too. Corbin shared little details about me—my favorite color (pink), book (*Wuthering Heights*), and food (chocolate). He put an apple in the corner for my desire to be a teacher. As he divulged my favorites and character to the class, the kids who had known me for years seemed a bit surprised to learn so many new things. To them, I had probably always just been the quiet girl with her head buried in textbooks. To many, I still was that fifteen-year-old girl who read classics just for fun. Corbin, though, made me seem like so much more. Even I was impressed by myself as represented in the collage. At the end of the presentation, the class clapped more enthusiastically than usual, meaning about four people clapped instead of two, and Mrs. Shire looked very impressed with both Corbin and me.

There was one emblem he didn't talk about with the class, but I

Voice of Innocence

noticed it. I smiled because he had remembered this tiny detail. Later, I asked him why he had included it.

"Because," he said. "I think it's important to who you are."

"What do you mean?" I asked, puzzled. It was just a tattoo.

"I think you like the idea of it because it's what you want more than anything. I think you want to be free. Free to choose for yourself what you will do. Free to just live."

That afternoon, I walked home from the bus stop thinking about how right Corbin was. How could someone who had only known me for a week know me so well already? I beamed to myself at my luck at being seated next to him. As I put my band uniform on for the football game that Friday night, I began to wonder how long it would be until the first snow. I hoped it would come early this year.

Chapter Four
Black and White

~ Corbin ~

The ever-familiar, yet ever-shocking blare of the door's buzzer snaps me out of my dream. Lying on my back on the neck-stiffening "bed," I glance at the peeling, drab ceiling. It blends perfectly with the four walls that rise to meet it, creating a feeling of emptiness and sameness without any effort. My eyes flicker to my desk on the farthest wall and to the tiny, worn picture taped to its edge. All day, my eyes have been relentlessly floating to that picture.

Fingers laced and arms outstretched, I yawn out of boredom and anxiety more than a craving for rest. Rest is something that overflows in this room. Despite the worries, the yelling, and the mind-splitting buzzer, the overflowing hours of tedium often lead to excessive hours of dozing. Luckily for me, my roommates over the years have also bought into this sentiment, leaving me to waste away many unwanted hours.

My knee joints crack as I edge off the bed and onto my feet. I pace over to my desk in my wool socks, reaching down to readjust them. A rip in the one toe allows my bare skin to touch the shockingly cold floor. I have grown used to always being numb, both inside and out.

I block out Frank's wet, gulping snores as I pull out the crudely made metal chair at my desk. I've lost count of how many other men have shared my room over the years—last time I counted, it was seven. As roommates go, Frank's been pretty decent. He spends most of his time sleeping or reading Steinbeck. Sometimes I dream of wrapping my fingers around his neck when he tirelessly speaks to me in the riddling quotes of the author, but I always refrain. I remember all too well what it's like to have a roommate whose only contact with you is a physical altercation. Frank and I have a workable situation as tenants of our room, and we respect each other's privacy as best as we can. We stay out of each other's way, and we don't destroy each other's shit. That's the most one can hope for in this place.

My fingers trace the familiar path along the picture's edges. At first glance, the picture isn't anything spectacular. It isn't even a professional picture. She's wearing a simple T-shirt in the picture, something you would wear around your house on a lazy day. She isn't even posing. It was a snapshot I took when she was unsuspecting, which are, in my opinion, the absolute best kind of pictures.

The picture's in black and white, so only the details of her facial expressions shine through. Her mouth is partially open in the early forms of a laugh. Her eyes squint with the promise of sheer joy that is so typical of an eighteen-year-old with a life ahead of her. She looks off to the side, to something that can't be seen in the photograph. Only I know what is to the side because I was there. When I look at the picture, though, I don't just see that moment with this eighteen-year-old-girl. I see a life. I see the years leading up to the picture and the years that were to come after the picture. I keep this image close because it is the best summary of my life before it went to hell. It was a life of excitement, of spontaneity, of joy. Of *her*.

As the clatter of doors nearby threatens to jar me out of my thoughts, I choose to ignore it. So much of life, whether it be a career or a relationship or a reaction, is up to choice. Here, there are few choices left. When I am faced with one, no matter how small, I grasp it with all of my might. I don't let the cursing or the fighting or the threats next door shake my concentration. I let the picture transport me to a different time, a time when unplanned snapshots and a beautiful, genuine woman were a reality and not only a piece of cheap photograph paper between two downtrodden hands. I let it indolently and aimlessly take me back to the memories that shaped me, the memories that led up to the picture, the memories that made me wish that this picture wasn't the last.

Chapter Five
Magnetism

~ Corbin ~

Memories

    Leaves scratched and swirled around my feet as the autumn air seeped through my thin sweatshirt. I stuffed my hand into my pocket, pulled out the required one-dollar student admission, and handed it to the kid working the ticket booth. All around me, groups of teens and adults alike chattered and scurried about, purchasing last-second snacks or just catching up about the new school year. I brushed past several groups, released a few amicable hellos, and headed toward the stands. The pre-game show was due to start any second.
    When I had told my dad where I was headed, he had offered a muffled "Really?" without looking up from the TV. He took another pull on his bottle of beer, shrugged, and asked if I needed a ride, although I knew that was certainly just a formality. There would not be a true ride to the game, despite the offer. Mom would be of no use in the transportation department, either. Feeling unwell, she had clambered up to bed before the sun had even set. I shrugged him off, told him I would be home later, not that he asked, patted Henry's head, and headed out the door to begin my two-mile walk.
    Most Friday nights, I was content just kicking back in my room with the TV and Henry as my sole companions. Back in Arizona, one of the crew would come over to listen to music or just hang out, but not here. It was okay, though. More often than not, I was content in my world, shoving cheese curls equally into Henry's drooling muzzle and my own

mouth as we lived vicariously through the television characters.

Not lately, though.

Only two short weeks ago, everything changed. Suddenly, those solar-system curtains and tiny TV seemed inadequate companions; I no longer wanted to sit in that room alone. Instead, all I could think about were ways to see her. Even if that meant braving the over-enthusiastic jocks and preps at the high school football game just for a glimpse of her.

It had been an ordinary day, really, the day that changed everything. I had rolled out of bed, rumbling and groaning at the blaring sound of the annoying alarm. The first day of school—a day of new sneakers, new haircuts, excitement—but for me, it was a day that I couldn't sleep until ten a.m. As I hauled myself off to school, I checked my class schedule again. Only one class from the morning schedule caught my attention—art. It was the one class that didn't drown me in monotony or endless, pointless paperwork. It was the one place where I felt like I could actually shine, maybe even excel.

Little did I know that it was the place where my life would change, forever magnetized around one girl. For when the teacher called that name to sit beside me, my whole world did an irrevocable backflip.

Not that it was love at first sight…no, such things didn't exist in my mind. Love at first sight was for either overly-dramatic girls or for overly-pussy guys. I didn't get a pitfall in my stomach. Angels didn't start singing when I saw her. There was no sappy love song playing as our eyes met. And yet, there was certainly…something. Something that told me I had to know this girl, see what she was all about.

Luckily for me, I got the chance during the first project. For the first time in my life, I was beyond jittery to talk to a girl. I still cringe at the thought of those first cheesy lines I fed her. Yet, despite all of that, something seemed to click for us. Within the first two weeks of school, we had developed a comfortable ease for which there was no replacement. We blended together perfectly on the artist's canvas, complementing each other's weaknesses and strengths. We found ourselves seamlessly finding each other at every possible opportunity in the hallway. We found each other yearning to learn more, to know more, about each other.

So there I was on a Friday night, joining the peppy crew of band moms and football parents to cheer on our school's team. Only a year ago, it would have been me on the field, running and tackling to the cheer of the crowd. Yet tonight I was less interested in the number of touchdowns as that brown-haired girl in the band uniform sporting the clarinet. As I climbed the bleachers, I quickly scanned for a seat. I finally spotted Logan, an acquaintance from my science class. He graciously asked if I wanted to sit with him and his family in the bleachers. He was there to cheer on his girlfriend, the star majorette. I nodded as I caught sight of Emma and clamored to my seat. Only three weeks ago, I wouldn't have recognized this girl if I walked right into her. Now, she was becoming a magnetic force in my life.

The cacophony of instruments marched in intricate patterns as they honked out the alma mater and the "Star Spangled Banner." With the height of my seat in the bleachers, Emma was barely a dot. Nonetheless, I could pick her out by her walk, her stance, by her hair gently lifting in the breeze. It would be the first time I ever appreciated the grace and beauty of any marching band member, certainly not something typically associated with a "band nerd" as they are affectionately called.

Once the pre-game show ended, the band members took their seats near the bottom of the stadium bleachers. I listened as Logan mumbled some comments about his hot girlfriend, but I was barely listening. All I could think about was what I would say to Emma after the game, if she had spotted me, and whether we would get to spend some time together. Outside of school, this would be our first "event" together, even if it just consisted of me watching her from afar. Still, when she had asked if I was coming to the game, I just couldn't say no. Those eyes could get me to say yes to almost anything.

Beside me, Logan's parents left to bring back some nachos. I felt a twinge of jealousy as his dad patted him on the back and asked if he wanted to come along or stay in the stands. Although most kids couldn't be paid to sit with their parents at the game, I thought he was lucky. His parents were a little nerdy in their almost-identical polo shirts and khakis, but at least they were there. At least they had given him more than a superficial, one-word response and a half-hearted offer to drop him off. At least they knew where he was and when he would be home.

Voice of Innocence

    The game continued rather uneventfully. A few touchdowns, an injury in which the player limped off the field, a few dozen songs from the band, and a mass exodus from the stands all took place before the moment I was waiting for. The band cleared the bleachers, filing out to head back to the school and hang up their uniforms. I headed to the gate where they were exiting.
    "Hey! You made it!" she shouted as she anxiously walked up to me, not even trying to hide her surprise and enthusiasm.
    "Of course I did. You didn't think I was going to miss that new, awesome routine to "Thriller," did you?"
    "Really?" she said, with a sarcastic tone and grin. "You're a marching band enthusiast?"
    "Um, yeah, why else do you think I came?" I offered unabashedly.
    "So that you could go for ice cream with the coolest band nerd there is," Emma declared with a serious tone, although a smile glinted in her eyes.
    "Oh really? Well, where is she?" I prodded, glancing around the crowd. She playfully shoved me.
    "Seriously, do you want to come? After we change, Jenn's mom is giving some of us a ride to get ice cream…band nerd tradition I guess."
    "You guess?" I asked.
    "Well, I'm apparently not the 'coolest' band nerd, so I'm not sure I have all of the inner workings down," she teased.
    "Well, this is true. But I guess for now I can trust your judgment," I added slyly. "But how will the other band groupies feel about an imposter joining in?"
    "We'll find you a triangle or something, and you can just pretend you're interested in joining," Emma offered.
    "A triangle? You think this much awesomeness is only qualified to play the triangle? I'm insulted," I implored.
    "Okay, okay. How about the cymbals?"
    "A little better. I suppose."
    I glanced around, noticing that the band had pretty much cleared out and were all animatedly walking back to the school. I figured that I better hurry up and decide.
    "Well, yeah, I'll come. But can I ride with you?"

"Of course," Emma retorted matter-of-factly. "Did you have someone else in mind?"

"Well, Mr. Ferguson does look like he could use a friend," I schemed about the less-than-spry band director.

"Keep it up and I'll go tell him you need a ride," Emma joked.

"Keep it up and maybe I'll go ask myself," I snapped back.

"Okay, seriously, I need to get moving or Jenn is going to flip. Want to walk with me?"

"Yeah, that's fine," I replied. I sauntered beside her as I reached for her clarinet.

"No way, buddy. No one holds Elsie but the pro," she said, pointing to herself.

"*Elsie?* Seriously?" I demanded, eyebrows raising.

"What's wrong with Elsie?"

I rolled my eyes, shook my head, and just sighed.

Emma laughed good-naturedly and said, "Yeah, I guess it's a bit pathetic. But hey, I'll have you know that my elementary band director thought it was a very cool name," she avowed in desperation.

"And how old was he? Eighty?"

"No," she replied coyly. "*She* was eighty-two. But still, she was pretty hip and 'in the know'."

"Oh, of course she was," I jeered.

As we approached the school, Emma playfully bumped into me with her shoulder. "Seriously, thanks for coming tonight. It was cool to have you there. My parents were so upset that they couldn't come tonight—funeral in Ohio for one of my dad's old high school friends. They left me with my grandma so that I could make it to the game. My mom is a sap for school events. Of course, she gave me a camera to bring with me so I could get lots of pictures for her. She'll be kind of p.o'd that I 'forgot' it at Grandma's." Emma giggled. "It was nice, though, to know that I had someone up there for my game. Lame as it sounds, I always get sort of nervous."

"Well, it was cool to watch you. Seriously."

"Really?" Emma asked, looking up at me.

"Oh, you thought I meant you? I was talking to Elsie. She did a phenomenal job tonight. Just superb," I responded, feigning an air of sophistication.

"You're an idiot," Emma said, stabbing my ribs with the mouthpiece.

"Go get ready so we can get this ice cream. I'm starving," I confessed, rubbing my rib from the jab.

"Okay, see you in a few. As long as Jenn didn't already leave us behind." Emma hurried into the school, taking off her hat as she did to save time. I waited on the sidewalk in front of the school, glancing up at the stars as I waited for Emma to return. It was hard to imagine that only a few weeks ago this girl was a complete stranger to me, someone I wouldn't even recognize on the street. Yet there we were, and I felt like we had known each other forever. A few minutes later, Emma and her friends came giggling out of the school as Jenn's mom pulled up in her minivan. Emma waved me over as she told Jenn's mom who I was. We hopped in, heading off for one of many ice cream trips over the next few years. My fifteen-year-old, immature self had no way of knowing it, but this was the first night of many that we would continue to grow together.

* * * *

Another buzzer jolts me to attention as I realize the picture is still in my hands. Frank is still snoring, although the buzzer momentarily causes him to rustle. A guard heads to our cell to check on us. It's time for inspections before we can go outside for some free time.

"How you doing, bud?" the stern guard offers. Ever since the news had spread, I've noticed a duller edge to the guards' normally blunt personalities. I wouldn't call it soft or even friendly, but just relaxed toward me. A sense of empathy radiates in their eyes even if their words don't say it.

"Fine, but I don't want to go out today. Don't want to risk any trouble, if you know what I mean. Can I just stay in?"

"Yeah, guess there'll be plenty of time for some fresh air soon, huh? Don't blame you. But poke Frank, and see if he has another opinion."

"Doubt it," I offer as I slowly rise from my seat and head toward the sloppy, drooling Frank. It's hard to believe that tomorrow this won't be my reality. But then, what will be? The prospect is almost unnerving.

Chapter Six
Hot-Chocolate Interrogations

~ Emma ~

Memories

"Emma! Emma, wake up!" I felt a warm hand shaking me as I groaned and threw my face back into the pillow.

"Emma! It's a snow day! Get your lazy butt up!"

I peeked up through squinted eyes at my mom's familiar face. After the morning fog cleared, I slowly sat up, rustled my hair, and directed my gaze toward the window.

"Snow? Already? What....it's like...October third?" I quizzed my mom.

"October fourth, but yeah, snow! School's cancelled."

"What time is it?"

"Time to get up. I made pancakes. So hurry up, then I have to get back to work," she ordered as she ripped the covers off my bed. Cold air abruptly slapped my skin, jolting me out of bed. I leered at my alarm clock.

"Seven-thirty! Are you crazy, Mom? I'm supposed to sleep in on a snow day!"

"You *did* get to sleep in," she articulated.

"Yeah, a whole hour! Wow. Thanks," I quipped. The smell of pancakes softened my mood a bit, nonetheless. I stumbled to the bathroom and then to the kitchen.

My mom had the habit of waking me up early on snow days ever since I was in kindergarten. She said when she was young, she always loved getting up early on snow days so that she could make the most of it. Apparently, she thought I would want to do the same. Although I loved the prospect of sleeping in until whenever, I begrudgingly appreciated her zest.

In the kitchen, I stared out our glass doors onto the deck. Overnight, we had gotten at least ten inches of snow. It was early in the season for this kind of snow, even for Pennsylvania. The forecasters had mentioned a storm in passing, but I don't think they predicted that it would hit us this hard. I smiled to myself, wondering if he would actually come today. I figured he would. He didn't seem like the type who would break a promise.

Sitting at the table, I doused my pancakes in syrup and shoved some into my mouth. My mom was also seated at the table, eating her pancakes as she talked.

"So, what are you going to do today?" she asked.

"I don't know. Maybe catch up on some reading or get ahead in my algebra book," I said nonchalantly. This was what I usually did on a snow day, being the overachiever that I was. I didn't say it, but deep down I hoped today would be different. Suddenly, equations and literary classics didn't seem like an exciting afternoon—at least not in comparison to those brown eyes I had already fallen for.

"Books? Homework? Emma, sometimes I think you're not my child," Mom mused. Mom had been a wild child, from the bits and pieces I could gather. She wasn't into drugs and never got arrested, but Grandma and Grandpa told me that she gave them their share of gray hairs when she was young. Although the motherly side of her was thankful to have a child that followed the "letter of the law" to a T, I think her inner teenager craved some excitement for me.

"Why don't you do something fun? Go outside in the snow or something. Or call up the girls and see if they want to come over," she said.

"I thought you had to work," I insisted.

"I do. But I don't like the silence. I work best with rowdiness. It helps give me...energy," Mom alleged with a grin. That was my mom for you—always craving chaos, even when she was working.

Mom was a novelist. She never "hit it big," so to speak, but she made a living. She always said she didn't do it for the money. She just loved being able to express herself and to have her voice heard. Plus, it afforded her the luxury of working from home. Unlike some children who found themselves in a day care from nine to five, my mom stayed home with me. Things had to be a bit crazy for her. She would squeeze in a chapter between a load of laundry and cartoons. When my dad came home from work at the law firm, she always had a hot meal on the table for the three of us. She always managed to get her motherly and wifely duties done and somehow still have time for her writing. She was one of those people who worked well under pressure.

"Actually, Mom," I began after chewing another bite of pancake, "there is someone who might be coming over…" I paused for a second, my stomach flinching from the adrenaline of my terror, and a moment of recognition dawned on her face.

"Oh, I see," she said mischievously. A broad smile gleamed on her face. "So do I know him?"

"No," I added curtly. Why hadn't I kept my mouth shut?

"What's his name?"

"Corbin."

"Corbin what?" Mom was way too good at this interrogation thing.

"Corbin Jones. He's new in town. He just came here from Arizona this summer."

"So when's he coming?"

"Why?"

"Well, I want to make sure I don't miss him. I don't want you running him out of here before I can get my hands on him," she smirked.

"Mom!" I shouted.

"I didn't mean literally, calm down," she added coyly. My mother was certainly a nut sometimes. This was going to be interesting.

"Mom, I know what you meant. I just don't want you…doing what you do," I added.

"And what do I do?"

"Overwhelm people," I observed, without restraint.

"Not me," she winked again. "I'll behave, don't worry. I don't want to scare him just yet if he's new here. I'll wait at least a few weeks," she laughed. It sounded more like a witch's cackle to me. "When's he coming?"

"I don't know. He might not even show up," I glumly remarked.

"He'll come. You better get your butt moving in case he shows up soon!" she exclaimed. "You're worried about me scaring him off, and here you sit, with baggy man pants on and hair that looks like 'jungle girl'." My mother always knew how to boost my self-confidence.

"You're probably right," I admitted. I cleaned off my plate and loaded it into the dishwasher, plodding to the shower afterward. "You better get back to work," I yelled over my shoulder.

"Yeah, yeah. But don't worry, I'll listen closely for the door…" she assured in a singsong voice.

"Great. Thanks," I uttered under my breath.

I took extra time to get ready, trying to figure out how I should look for a snow date. I supposed that smoky, runway eyes were a bit too much, not that I could achieve runway-worthy makeup, anyway. I opted for the more natural look, pulled my hair into a low bun, and added touches of makeup here and there. Of course, my mom interrupted me to add some extra eyeliner and blush. "You don't want to look like a corpse," she critiqued as she expertly painted my face. I had to admit, though, I looked pretty good when she was done.

I took an agonizingly long time choosing my outfit at the closet. After seven outfit changes, I opted for my favorite acid-wash jeans, some boots, and an oversized turquoise sweater. I also dug out my winter coat, hat, and gloves. Now there was nothing to do but wait.

Luckily, I didn't have to wait too long. About ten minutes later, the doorbell rang. My mom and I collided with each other in the hallway racing to the door.

"I'll get it," she exclaimed as she lunged at the door, beating me there.

"Hey! Corbin! I've heard so much about you! Come in, come in!" my mom offered with a bit too much enthusiasm. I could feel the color rising in my cheeks again. This was going to be a long couple of minutes.

"Hey," he said in his deep voice. "Nice to meet you Mrs. Groves," he addressed her in his perfect manners.

"Don't call me Mrs. Groves. I'm not an old hag yet. Call me Jill," she said, winking at him. *He must be thinking she's creepy,* I thought. *Or crazy. Or both.* I held my breath for what seemed a lifetime.

He strode through the door, and I felt myself finally exhale. "Hey," I offered as casually as possible. "I wasn't sure if you were still coming."

"And miss our first snow date? Are you kidding? I've been waiting for this since I moved here! It's fantastic!" he proclaimed, his smile giving me a glimpse of the adorable little boy he must have once been.

"That's right, you've never seen snow, huh?" my mom inquired. "Guess there's not too much snow in the desert, huh?" she laughed. I was reminded of my stupid comment at the lunch table. I guess Corbin was, too, because he snickered as he looked at me.

"No, not that I ever saw," he supplemented. "You have a beautiful home, Jill."

"Oh, please. This place is a disaster area. Who wants to spend time organizing and cleaning, though? I have better things to do," she declared. I looked around the house, noticing piles of clutter here and there. I should have cleaned the place up a bit. I forgot that he would probably come in. Oh well, it wasn't too bad…just…lived in. God, I was starting to sound like my mother.

"Okay, so are you ready?" I queried, anxious to get him away from the clutches of my mother before the excruciating photo albums or homemade cards or poems surfaced.

"Um, yeah, when you are," he grinned. "The sled's outside. I bought it this morning."

"Oh! Sled riding! Gosh, I haven't done that in years!" Mom exclaimed.

"You could come with us," Corbin suggested. Horror froze my face.

"Um, Mom, you have that chapter to finish? Remember?" I interrupted, urgency climbing into my voice like a cancerous cell.

"Yeah, I do," Mom sighed, depression leaking into her voice. "You kids have fun. Stop back afterward for hot chocolate. I have yet to ask my questions. You're not getting off this easy," Mom muttered, a light radiating in her eyes again.

"We'll do that," Corbin announced.

Why did he have to be so well-mannered?

Voice of Innocence

I threw on my coat, hat, and gloves. I fumbled with the zipper as usual. I felt a little ridiculous, since Corbin had foregone all of the winter gear. He had on jeans, sneakers, and a sweatshirt.

"Aren't you going to freeze?" I wondered as I shut the front door to my house. I noticed the sled sitting in my driveway. There was only one large sled...I guess we'd be sharing.

"Probably. I guess I'm not a detail-oriented person. Like, I forgot the detail that snow is cold," he laughed at his own weakness. "I'll be fine, though. I'll get some better attire before the next time," he noted. The next time. He was already planning a next time? As long as I didn't launch him into a tree or break a leg, things looked promising. Unless, of course, he couldn't handle my crazy mom. That was statistically likely.

"So, where's the best place to go?" he demanded, dragging the sled behind him.

"This way," I offered, following a path behind my house. "It's not too far." We walked together in silence, our only accompaniment being the frosty clouds of our breath and our crunching footsteps in the snow. It wasn't an awkward silence, though. On the contrary, neither of us felt the need to break the serendipitous peace of the setting. After a few minutes, we reached a clearing with a decent-sized hill. "Here we are," I proclaimed. "It's the best we can do without driving anywhere."

"It'll work," he approved. "At least there aren't many trees around," he poked.

"Shut up," I teasingly demanded, pretending to scowl at him. My eyes glimmered, though, at his teasing. We trudged up the hill, Corbin toting the sled. By this time I was just about out of breath despite my lack of cargo. I needed to start doing that exercise tape Mom and Dad had gotten me for Christmas.

"Okay, here we go," he declared.

"Drumroll please," I stated, "Corbin Jones's first sled-riding experience." I plopped on the front of the sled, my thick winter gear encumbering me, while he climbed on behind. He put his hands around my waist, delivering chills down my spine that weren't just the result of below-freezing temperatures. He pushed us off with his foot, jerking us forward. As we crested the curve at the top of the hill, we buzzed down faster than I had expected, but of course, I had never had the extra weight of a boy on the back of my sled.

I shrieked with sheer delight as Corbin chortled, not able to help ourselves. We weren't fifteen anymore—we were more like five-year-olds screaming in delight from the pure adrenaline of flying down the hill. At the bottom, though, things got a little out of control. I forgot how bad I was at steering. We veered left and right, spinning wildly at the bottom.

"How do we stop?" Corbin pleaded as the sled uncontrollably veered toward the lone tree near the bottom of the hill.

"Jump!" I dictated.

We rolled off clumsily, both somersaulting awkwardly in the same direction. We tumbled together in the snow, jumbling between the white flakes and each other. Snow slipped inside my shoes and up my back, shocking my skin with its icy pierce. The sled thudded against the tree, ricocheting toward us. After a few seconds of shock-induced paralysis, we creakily awoke from our stupor.

"That was awesome!" Corbin declared as we untangled ourselves. "Let's do it again."

"Are you crazy?" I blurted with astonishment. "We almost died." My heart was thudding against the wall of my chest, seemingly ready to crack a few ribs.

"Don't be melodramatic. We rolled off in time," he said, poking at me. "And we didn't almost die, you almost killed us with your horrible steering," he beamed.

"Oh, and you think you could do better?"

"I am a guy. Guys are *always* better drivers."

"We'll just see about that," I rebutted, my competitive nature kicking into overdrive.

For the next half hour, we followed the endless routine. Climb to the top of the hill, park your body, surge down the hill, and mesh at the bottom before crashing to our near death—on the times *I* was steering. In spite of my numb fingers and toes, I never had more fun in my life. And, to my disappointment, I had to admit that he was, in fact, much better at steering.

"You have to be frozen to death," I declared after our ninth time down the hill.

Voice of Innocence

"Yeah, I'm a little cold," he muttered, machismo in his voice. His shivering hands usurped his attempt at bravado.

"Well, I'm freezing. Let's go home," I commanded. "Oh, and I'm pre-warning you, you're about to get grilled by my mother. I apologize ahead of time. She doesn't have a sense of censorship on her thoughts. What she thinks is pretty much what she says," I added.

"I think your mom's cool already," he asserted with a note of validity that I simply could not fathom. We brushed the snow from ourselves as we stood up. He turned to gather the sled. Before he could turn around, I rolled a snowball and threw it at him. My horrific aim, however, resulted in a miss. It sailed by his head, launching itself onto the ground with a pathetic, soppy thud.

"Nice aim," he leered. "If you're going to start a battle, you better make sure you at least have some ammo," he supplemented. He dropped the sled and quickly gathered some snow. I bolted but tripped, as usual, over my own feet. I felt his snowball pelt me in the back, momentarily knocking the breath out of my lungs.

"Jerk!" I grunted. I scrambled to my feet and chased after him. Adrenaline bursting through my blood, I nabbed him.

"I win," I yelled triumphantly. We laughed together, wrestling in the snow like the inner children we were. He wormed his way out from under me with significant ease and pinned me down.

"I'm freezing!" I implored. By this time, he was looking into my eyes a little deeper than before. Gone was the immature young boy playing in the snow. The spirited smirk disappeared, replaced by a steady yet intense grin. I froze, not from the snow on my back, but from the inside out. Panic threatened to usurp my calm, but it subsided to a sense of wanting.

Slowly, steadily, he leaned down. Hesitancy looming, he brushed his lips over mine. Despite the icy cold of our bodies, a warmth buzzed between us. When it was over, I stared up at him with unrelenting eyes, knowing he had stolen more than just a kiss from me. I lay stunned for several moments, truly not expecting the afternoon to head this way. Neither of us said anything, basking instead in the realization that our worlds had flipped again, our present and future irrevocably linked by that simple moment. After a time, we stood up, the warmth from the moment radiating, despite the chilling temperatures. Corbin grabbed the sled and meandered toward the house, shuffling close to me, a sweetness grazing the air between us in silent reverie. Once we reached the porch, I paused.

"Are you sure you want to do this?" I asked.

"I can handle your mom, Emma," he affirmed.

"Don't be so sure. I just don't want her scaring you away," I teased. Deep down, the thought still worried me.

"Not a chance," he reassured. I believed him.

Inside, I took off my now useless cold-weather gear. Corbin took off his shoes and soaking-wet sweatshirt.

"Oh, good, you're back. I was getting a migraine from that damn chapter," my mom announced as she appeared in the hallway. At least she was out of her pajamas now. It even seemed like she had a bra on. It was truly a good day.

She offered Corbin one of my dad's shirts, which he graciously took. She made us some hot chocolate and turkey sandwiches while she amicably questioned Corbin about everything from sports to school to his parents. I noticed that anything about his family left him a bit...cold. Nothing too discernible, just a bit of reluctance that was not part of his exuberant character. My mom seemed to sense it, too, because she refrained from questions about them after a few moments.

For the rest of the afternoon, the conversation ambled effortlessly. We talked and laughed, sharing old family stories, and I found out more about him. Of course, there were the mortifying moments, too—like when the baby album magically surfaced on the coffee table. What a shock.

When he finally decided it was time to leave, Mom and I walked him to the door. As we watched him drag the sled down the block to his house, my mom turned to me.

"I like him, Emma. He's good for you." And that was all she said, turning to go back to the work we had torn her away from. It was uncharacteristically simple coming from my mom, which was how I knew she meant it. Even when things got rocky and many saw Corbin in a different light, my mom would never abandon this belief. She steadfastly believed in the positive contribution that Corbin made to my life.

Chapter Seven
A "Kind of" Christmas

~ Emma ~

Memories

Over the following months, Corbin and I became inseparable, falling into the routines of young love. Our weeks were consumed with classes and books. We walked hand in hand down the hallways, ignoring our teachers' threats at our inappropriate displays of affection. We didn't have a single class together, other than art class and lunch. I was on the accelerated track, while Corbin's lack of concern for his studies and horrible work ethic—not his intelligence—placed him in the standard classes.

"I've got more important things on my mind," Corbin grinned when I asked him about his lack of academic concern. I had a feeling that his poor habits had been formed long before me. So I was left alone, doodling his name and thinking about our days together during my intolerably long classes. Somehow, I managed to keep my *A's*, despite my complete inattentiveness. I guess miracles sometimes do happen.

Lunchtime became the glimmer in my day. We still sat with Katie, Jenn, and Hannah. Nonetheless, I couldn't deny that we were absent from most of their conversations. Our connection inevitably locked our focus solely on each other. Sometimes I would notice jealous glares from the girls who had once been my best friends. We didn't mean to exclude them. I suppose it is just a fatal consequence of young love. The intensity of the connection makes other relationships pale in comparison at times,

Voice of Innocence

just as the other stars must feel in comparison to Polaris. It's not that my friendships were inferior. They were just different. My relationship with Corbin clutched at my inner core, grappling at who I was and what I wanted to be. It was only with him that I felt life running through my veins. Katie, Hannah, and Jenn would all eventually fall victim to the same fate, finding serious relationships over the next few years. We remained friends, to an extent. Things, however, would never be the same. Amidst our relationships, we lost touch with each other.

Looking back, I cannot say I regret this fact. Certainly, any broken friendship or relationship is a loss. However, I have come to know that few relationships or friendships can stand the test of time. As we change, we sometimes outgrow our friendships. And, since we cannot change this fact, it is best to simply accept it for what it is in order to appreciate the power that the friend had in your life when he or she was a part of it. If only I could apply this rule to Corbin Jones.

* * * *

Every Friday night during the fall, Corbin would come to watch me at the football game. Ignoring the glares of my band instructor, he would sneak into the *band only* section of the bleachers to steal a kiss or bring me nachos. On rare occasions, Mr. Jones would even accompany him. Corbin said that his father had once played football on scholarship until he hurt his knee. Now the stern, rigid man was a real estate agent. I suppose that coming to the games stirred a sense of nostalgia that could not be found anywhere else. Mr. Jones was friendly enough, saying hi when he saw me in the stands and buying us snacks at half-time. Nonetheless, there was an aura of coldness that seemed to envelop the man.

On weekends, Corbin and I spent every possible second together. Sometimes we would do the typical teenager thing, going to movies or the mall. Whenever it was possible, we would go sled riding at our special spot. Other times, though, we were content to just hang out at my house. Despite my over-the-top mom and my somewhat firm dad, Corbin seemed to like spending time with my family. He actually craved our family dinners. My family brought out a new sense of vibrancy, of peace, in Corbin that he seemed to be missing from his own family.

In truth, his family remained a mystery to me. My impersonal interactions with Mr. Jones left me understanding little about Corbin's home life. Certainly, I sensed that there was tension in the family. I just couldn't discern where the tension sprang from.

I hadn't met his mother yet. Corbin rarely mentioned her, which seemed exceedingly strange. Despite all of our hours with my family, we hadn't spent any time with his. I hadn't even seen the inside of his house, even though it was only two blocks away from mine. I tried to play it down, saying that his parents were busy with work. His dad was always busy with house showings or property closings, and Corbin had said that his mom was a doctor back in Arizona. Nonetheless, I couldn't deny my concern over Corbin's placement of distance between his family and me.

The school weeks slid into one another until Christmas finally came. Corbin spent the holiday with my family, noting that his didn't celebrate. By this time, Corbin had become a permanent fixture in the family. My parents always included him in any activity, holiday, or trip. So, despite my curiosity, I refrained from questioning him about his own family. I figured that when he wanted to talk about it, he would.

For our first Christmas, I had bought him a much-needed winter coat, complete with hat, gloves and scarf. He had never gone out and bought appropriate winter attire, spending his money on music instead. Our sled riding excursions had become our snow day ritual, so I figured the apparel might come in use. Corbin bought me a bottle of my favorite perfume. It was the gift that he didn't spend a penny on, though, that would be my most treasured. While my parents were cleaning up the kitchen, he handed me a folded piece of paper.

"What's this?" I asked in surprise.

"Open it," he said.

When I managed to unfold and un-crinkle the piece of paper, I was startled that I recognized it—it was the collage he had made of my life during the first week of school. It had an addition, though. In the exact center, he had glued a picture of us that we had taken in a photo booth in the mall.

"Too...presumptuous?" he asked hesitantly. I looked at him with a huge smile.

"Not one bit," I uttered, simply.

Voice of Innocence

He peered at me seriously, stepping closer, and reaching out to wrap his arms around me.

"I kind of...love you, Emma," he said. His gaze demonstrated confidence, but I could tell from the slight pause that he was nervous about how I would react. For a moment, I stared blankly at him, not saying a word. I saw him go pale. Feeling bad about torturing him any longer, I finally laughed. Still grinning, I wrapped my arms around his neck.

"I kind of love you back," I said with assurance.

It was the best Christmas of my entire life.

Chapter Eight
Traditions and Truths

~ Emma ~

Memories

He wasn't ready to talk about his family until mid-June. Snowfalls had given way to warm, humid air and an occasional thunderstorm. With school out, we had nothing but empty days and firefly-filled nights ahead of us.

One lazy afternoon, we decided to forego our Wednesday tradition of walking to the local ice cream stand, Bob's Cones-n-More. Feeling adventurous, we walked to the local state park instead for a day outdoors. Nature was never my thing, but Corbin loved the prospect of open sky and desolate trails. Although I feigned enthusiasm for scampering critters, sweaty hikes, strange insects, and swimming in slimy water, it was the idea of being alone with Corbin that fed my tolerance. I begrudgingly splatted away the buzzing mosquitos and treaded carefully away from every weed that I could manage to avoid on the trail. I tried not to think about the risk of my bare legs contracting a tick or brushing against a poison ivy leaf.

Before I would agree to dip a single toe into the filthy Canoe Creek waters, I had Corbin agree to eat lunch first. We sat under the branches of a large oak tree. With my unicorn quilt, the only blanket I could scrounge up that my mother would let me out of the house with, spread beneath us, we rustled through my backpack of picnic foods. I pulled out all of the necessities—some peanut butter and jelly sandwiches, two sodas, a few snack cakes, and some potato chips. It certainly wasn't the best demonstration of female domesticity, but the Suzie-homemaker thing didn't seem to be in the cards for me, and still wasn't. I had inherited my cooking gene from my grandmother, who always either burnt Sunday dinners or gave the family a mild bout of food poisoning from accidental food safety violations. Corbin never complained, though, accepting the fact that homemade picnic lunches and romantic dinners from scratch wouldn't be in his future as long as he was with me.

As we gorged on our "lunch," I noticed that Corbin seemed a bit…off. He had been quiet since he knocked on my door an hour earlier. Silence wasn't in his vocabulary. Whether he was talking my ear off about a new rock band or asking me a million questions about my thoughts on a news story, he was an endless chatterbox. If his lips weren't moving a mile a minute divulging a detailed story, they were moving on mine in a stolen moment of passion. Today, they weren't doing either of those much-preferred activities.

Putting down my half-eaten snack cake, I turned to him. "Corbin, what's wrong?"

He kept on chewing. "Corbin! Earth to Corbin!" I announced, louder this time.

"Huh? What was that?" he inquired nonchalantly. He glanced at me with somewhat empty eyes.

"Okay, spill it. You haven't said two words all day. What's wrong? Did I do something?"

"No, it's not you, Emma. Everything's fine. I'm just tired." As he said it, he quickly looked at the ground. I may not have been an FBI special agent, but I knew a lie when I heard it.

"Corbin, just tell me or I'm going to think the worst. What is it?"

Corbin exhaled for several seconds, imperceptibly shaking his head. He knew it was no use; I wouldn't drop it until he told me the truth. Standing up, he slowly edged away from the blanket and stared off at the horizon with his back to me. After a moment, I rose to my feet and walked toward him. Leaning my head on his back, I wrapped my arms around his waist. I didn't say a word. For a minute, we stood like this, the only sound our soft breaths and beating hearts. When he had gathered himself, he turned around to face me. A chill edged through my spine, fearing that this dreamlike romance could be over too quickly.

"There's something I've been meaning to tell you. I just haven't been able to find the right words." He spoke so gravely that my heart stopped. This couldn't be good. I tried to suppress my tears.

"What is it?" I ventured, wanting to know the answer, yet not wanting to know at the same time.

"It's about why I moved here." After he spoke the words, he stood silent, a pregnant pause elevating the tension.

"Okay…" I said, breaking his awkward silence. "Go ahead."

"We moved here because of my sister."

The words didn't register right away. I must have heard him wrong. Squinting up at him with puzzlement, I implored, "Your sister? Corbin, what are you talking about? You're an only child."

"No, I'm not. Not really."

"But on the first day we met, I asked you if you had brothers and sisters. You said…"

"I said no. I know. It was wrong to lie to you. But Emma, I just couldn't bring myself to tell you the truth, not then. Not for a long time. The truth was just too hard."

"Okay, so what is the truth then?" I begged. Although I knew his reasons for lying must be good, I couldn't help but feel a little angry, a little betrayed. I thought Corbin told me everything. I didn't have any secrets. What else was he keeping from me? I quieted my inner questions, though. I knew there was much more to learn.

Corbin reached into his pocket and pulled out his tattered wallet.

"What are you doing, Corbin? You still haven't explained anything," I whined.

Corbin didn't say a word. He opened his wallet, reached inside, and pulled out a photograph. When he handed it to me, I saw a little girl beaming back at me. She was about four or five years old with brunette curls, glimmering and bouncing. Her cheeks were a bit pudgy, and she had familiar eyes.

"This is Chloe," Corbin simply stated.

"She's cute, Corbin. Why haven't you talked about her? Why haven't I ever seen her?" I asked, still a bit lost.

Corbin looked past my shoulder into the distance. His eyes were getting watery, something I had never seen before. As a tear started to roll down his cheek, instantaneous enlightenment washed over me like a hurricane. My heart stopped for a second time as I paused in pure shock.

My voice shook as I managed to whisper, "I'm so sorry."

Corbin just nodded, biting his lip and wiping away his tears. I wrapped my arms around him, careful not to bend the picture. He grabbed me, buried his head on my shoulder, and cried.

I had never seen any man cry. The men in my family were hard, sturdy. Their emotions were rarely discernible, especially not tearful ones. Although I found their rigidness in this department a bit ridiculous and saw no problem with tears streaming from male eyes, my inexperience with the event made me feel a bit uneasy. So, for several minutes I didn't do or say anything. I just clutched onto Corbin, feeling his tears moisten my shirt. Then he slowly looked up, wiped his eyes, and said, "Sorry. I didn't mean to lose it like that."

"Don't apologize!" I demanded. "I just...I don't know why you didn't talk to me about this sooner. It must have been hard holding all of this in."

"I'm sorry, Emma. I wanted to tell you. Please don't think that this was about you. It's not that I didn't trust you or think you'd be unsupportive. It's just...I wasn't ready to talk about it at all."

"I feel bad because there you were, going through hell, and I was dragging you sledding and yammering about some stupid pair of shoes. I just feel like everything must have seemed so insignificant."

"Don't even think that! That's not it at all, Emma. Being with you, going places, chatting about normal stuff, that's what got me through. You took my mind off everything. I felt like I didn't have to talk about it, because for the first time in months I was actually happy. You made me like life. And it's not that Chloe's death was the only reason I wanted to be with you, don't think that either. You know that I love you for you. But a part of that love stems from the fact that being with you made everything—anything—seem like I could deal with it, you know?"

I just nodded, smiling at him. Even when he was in the midst of grief, he was thinking about my feelings. I grabbed his hand and led him back to our blanket. We sat, facing each other, clutching each other's hands. I stared blankly past Corbin for a few minutes, trying to wrap my head around the shocking news.

Slowly, cautiously, I asked, "What happened?"

I turned my gentle gaze to him, wondering if this would be too much. Now that the gates had flailed open, however, the words gushed through.

He nodded, averting his eyes to the distant sky for a long moment before he began. "Chloe was the sweetest sister I could have ever asked for. When she walked into a room, she just lit everyone else up. She was always laughing or singing or dancing. She loved music. I think she would have been a dancer when she grew up. Anyway, she was so empathetic, even at five years old. I remember one week, I had gotten in trouble for coming home past my curfew. My parents stripped away my allowance privileges. Chloe was in the room when I was begging my parents to reconsider. I played football, as you know, and we were going to an away game. I needed money for dinner. Later, Chloe came up to me in my room and handed me her piggy bank. 'Here, Corby, take this. I don't want you to be hungry!' It was just little moments like that, you know, that made her who she was, even at five."

The moment of nostalgia gone, his face turned a bit harder. I could tell he was getting to the painful parts. "Anyway, one day last March, we were having a party in our backyard. The family was there, our friends, and neighbors. Things were sort of chaotic, with music blaring and people playing games and stuff. Chloe loved being around the people. She wandered from group to group, entertaining the guests with her exuberant stories and jokes. I guess it was easy to lose track of her. Our house was by a street. It wasn't too busy or anything, nothing my parents ever thought they had to worry about. Well, Chloe must have seen something across the street. We think it might have been the neighbor's cat. Chloe *loved* animals, and we had caught her more than once playing with it in their front yard. I guess that with all of the commotion, no one noticed her slip away. There were parked cars lining the streets because of the party. We think she must have snuck between two of them to get to the other side of the street. Just when she was edging out, a car came flying down the road way too fast."

By this time, tears had begun streaming down my cheeks. I hadn't known Chloe, but I could feel Corbin's pain. He started to cry again, too.

Pain stabbed my chest, crushing me from the inside out. He kept going, slowly but steadily, determined to finish the story.

"The driver said he never saw her until it was too late. From our backyard, we heard screeching tires and a sickening slam. Confused, we all ran out to the road, expecting to see a collision. What I saw on the road will haunt me forever—Chloe, lifeless, bleeding. My parents and I ran to her while someone called 911, but it was too late. She was gone."

I climbed into his lap and he wrapped his arms around me, resting his head on my shoulder. We rocked back and forth for a while, taking it all in. My heart ached for him, finally understanding his true burden. I couldn't believe I had no idea something like this had happened. Corbin was apparently good at blocking out difficult memories. His warm personality and bubbly nature were no reflection of the recent past he was forced to deal with.

He started talking again. "After her death, things were bad at home. My parents blamed themselves, as did I. We tried to get on with our lives, but it was just too hard. There were too many reminders of her and what had happened. After a few months, my dad decided we needed a change of scenery so that we could pick up our lives again. He decided to bring us here, to where he grew up. We moved here in June."

"Your parents must still be struggling with this," I noted, not knowing what else to say. Suddenly, Mr. Jones' stoic, off-putting nature made more sense. A pang of guilt stirred deep inside of me for thinking such wretched things about the man who was enduring so much.

"It's hard for all of us, but my mom's having the hardest time. Emma, I know you must have thought something was off since you've never met her or been to my house. I was afraid you would think I wasn't serious about you or something, but I just couldn't bring you into that environment."

"I understand. I'll admit, I did start to wonder. But I figured you'd talk about it when you were ready."

He kissed my hand and nuzzled against my face. "You're always so rational, Emma. You never jump to conclusions. That's one of the things I love about you."

"Don't jump to conclusions," I said, jokingly. "I have my moments. Is your mom getting any better?" I asked, turning things to a more serious note again.

"No. Not really, if I'm being honest. She spends most of her days and nights cooped up in her bedroom. Sometimes she'll read or watch television. Most of the time she just sits in the dark and cries. She's been to a psychiatrist, but it doesn't help. She can't get over the idea that it's her fault, that she was a bad mother. It's hard to watch. I've tried everything to pull her out of herself. So has my dad. Nothing seems to work, and we're both scared."

"I wish there was something I could do to help," I offered, truly meaning it.

"So do I," Corbin said. "But for now, I guess all we can do is give her space and hope that time helps." He turned my face to look at him.

"I want her to meet you someday, Emma. I know she'll love you."

"I want to meet her, too. But I understand why that can't happen right now. I'm patient."

"Yet another thing I love about you. Do you have any flaws, Miss Groves? I'm starting to wonder."

"Ha! Are you kidding? You just ate my horrid excuse for a picnic lunch."

"Okay, you're right, I forgot about your lack of cooking skills. But that's not so bad…I love takeout food anyway. I can settle for a woman who can't cook, I suppose," he grinned.

"Settle? You're 'settling' for me? Corbin Jones, you know how to woo a girl, don't you?" I poked at his ribs, tickling him into submission. He started to cry, this time from laughter. He managed, as usual, to use his strength and pin me down.

"No fair," I screamed as he tickled me back.

"Life's not fair, is it?" he said jokingly, easing up on his poking. But it hit me that his words rung true in so many ways.

* * * *

I would never get to meet Mrs. Jones. Life truly wasn't fair, as we would learn all too well.

Chapter Nine
The Universal Truth

~ Corbin ~

Head bobbing on the thinly veiled excuse for a pillow, I glance up at the bowing bunk above me. I have spent countless nights worrying I would die here, suffocated by Frank's mammoth body. Frank, though, has mercifully roused himself from his nap to hobble outside into the courtyard. Now I lie here alone, silence floating through the room like a familiar and comforting friend.

It is not the bend in the top bunk, nor the various profanities written there that catch my attention now. It is the picture, a different picture from before. A picture I stare at every night before bed—a picture that awakens a sense of remorse in my soul every morning, even in this clinical cell.

It is that same picture I shared with Emma during that picnic lunch that day so many years ago. The same warm smile, the same bouncing curls, the same gapped teeth that are imprinted in my mind. The same adoring cheeks that I only got to see for five short years.

I wonder what she would be like today. Would she have been that dancer I thought she was destined for, or would she have selected a more traditional path? Would she have stood by my side in that courtroom? Would she visit me here, offering me her piggy bank money to buy supplies at the commissary? Would she want nothing to do with her brother whose life was wasted in orange?

Lindsay Detwiler

It is her face that reminds me I have a gift. It is not easy to remember that in these surroundings of profanities and security checks, of murderers and stale food. But her face forces me to remain hopeful and to remain thankful that I am at least breathing. Chloe does not have that opportunity. Chloe's possibilities ended at five. I should at least be thankful for the years I have and, especially now, the chances that await me. I hope that in some capacity, Chloe has some wonderful chances that await her as well amidst the angels.

They say that everyone's life is riddled with both joys and sorrows. My first sorrow dashed into my life when Chloe died. My second sorrow stabbed even deeper into my soul when my mother chose to abandon this world. I know that she cannot be blamed. I know I cannot begrudge her the wish to dance with my sister and the angels instead of enduring the empty shell of a home that was left behind. At the time, though, I could not comprehend how Mom could be so selfish, how she could slap more pain onto the family. It was during that first set of evocatively morose days that I found the single, glowing star that would keep me focused and still. That same star would try to keep the faith glowing for me when even tougher times knocked at my door. That star, unwavering and true, would keep burning even when I thought it shouldn't. And now, when I lie here looking at this picture, remembering what a precious gift life truly is, I wish I had clung to that star with every ounce of strength in the universe.

Chapter Ten
The Light's Still Shining

~ Corbin ~

Memories

    The doorbell groggily pulled my refusing body to alertness, yet my limbs failed to move. Alertness brought remembrance, and remembrance only brought more despair. Loss had already become a constant in my life, depression an insurmountable fixture within those four walls where I kept myself contained.

    It had been a few hours since my world had yet again come crashing down around me, meteors setting fire to the only sense of stability I had known, even if that stability was shaky at best.

    I had gotten called to the office during ninth period. I knew I must be in trouble, although I couldn't recall committing any major offenses. I couldn't have an early dismissal, though. My dad never left the office early. Even though he was new in town, he already brought with him a solid reputation and, thus, a ceaseless rotation of clients. My mom was in no shape to schedule a doctor's appointment or dentist appointment for me or anyone else in the family, so I knew that was out of the realm of possibility as well. It was more likely that someone got struck by lightning. Thus, I clutched my books from my desk as Mrs. Dahlia continued yammering about mysterious formulas I had yet to decode. As I turned the corner by the water fountain to head to the office, I was greeted by a counselor. I had no idea what her name was, but she met me with those familiar, despairing eyes that I knew were a bad sign.

"Corbin?" she implored, her fraudulent air of confidence giving away her desperation to make everything okay.

"Yeah...am I in trouble or something?" I quizzed, stomach dropping.

"No, Corbin. But something serious has happened. You need to come with me." She led me toward the office as my heart plummeted into the depths of my chest. My feet suddenly morphed into sludge, not wanting to lose contact with the floor to carry my body forward. Devastated already by what I might hear, I traipsed beside the blonde-haired, haggard lady through the office. I was led to a back conference room and offered a seat. Our principal, Mrs. Sanders, was already there.

"What's going on," I spewed as I tossed my books loosely onto the table. "What's wrong?"

"We need to wait for your dad to get here," Mrs. Sanders offered gently. So it wasn't my dad, he was okay. But then...

I jumped to my feet. "It's Mom, isn't it? Did something happen? Is she okay?" I scrambled out questions and jerky motions faster than the adults in the room could react. Things were about to get hairy as anger started to build up in me. How could they stay silent? My agitation was broken by my father coasting through the door. His eyes were bloodshot, and he looked like he was in shock.

"Dad?" I pleaded, voice quavering.

"Son, sit down," he commanded. He glanced at the adults in the room with a gentle nod, as if to thank them.

I lowered myself into the chair beside the guidance counselor. My dad sat silent for a moment, sending my mind and stomach into another endless tailspin. He finally got up the courage to spit out those few words that would pitch my life into a familiar blackness once again.

"She's dead, son. She's gone."

I didn't have to ask who he was talking about, but the words hit me like a freight train blasting through a cement tunnel, and I realized I had been holding my breath. I waited for tears to start rolling down my cheeks, to drown me in their despair, but they didn't. I couldn't speak, I couldn't cry. I could barely breathe. I suddenly felt self-conscious as I noticed everyone was staring at me, waiting for some kind of reaction.

But I couldn't even muster one up.

It wasn't that I didn't love my mother or that I wasn't wrecked by the news. I guess a deep, inner part of me just wasn't completely shocked. The news had slammed me to the ground, but I had anticipated this pothole in the road. If he were being honest, so did my dad. My mom had been on a devastatingly fast spiral toward a cliff we couldn't bring her back from. No matter how many therapists and kind words we offered to her, time simply couldn't patch up the crater that Chloe's death had left in her soul. Or at least Mom didn't have the strength to wait around for the answer. As much as I had tried to avoid it over the past few months, I knew something had to break. I just didn't think it would be my mother, not so soon.

After a few difficult moments, all I managed to say was, "I need to find Emma. She'll be wondering where I am."

"We'll take care of that," the guidance counselor offered, reaching out to touch my hand. "You need to go home and be with your family."

"What family?" I sneered, shoving my chair back from the table and away from her touch. "Don't you get it? They're gone now. They're all gone."

"Son..." my dad consoled, rising from his chair to follow me.

I didn't respond. I just haphazardly gathered my books, headed toward the door, and then stopped. "Can you please make sure that Emma Groves knows what happened?" I asked, directing my inquiry to Mrs. Sanders.

"Yes, Corbin. And if you need anything, anything at all, you just let us know," she offered, a subdued smile backing up her weak words. This was clearly uncomfortable for her, and I felt a tinge of regret at being so harsh.

"We'll be fine," I mumbled as I opened the door and stormed toward the car, not saying a word as my dad patiently followed behind.

* * * *

When we had returned home, I refused to say anything to my dad. It wasn't that I was mad at him, I just couldn't find words that seemed appropriate or meaningful. Nor did I want to hear any hollow promises of "It's going to be okay." I had heard that before, not that long ago.

Things clearly weren't okay, and they never would be. With that in mind, I just wanted to sleep.

I climbed our stairs two at a time, heading toward my bedroom. On the way, I passed my parents' room. Turmoil and angst washed over me, bathing me in their irrefutable clutch. This morning, my mother had been lying in that room, breathing, dreaming, and thinking. Only an hour after we all left for the morning, she had ended it, right there.

I felt like there should be a dark cloud of fog sweeping over the room. A strange aura should be creeping through the small walkway around the bed. A voice, a whisper, should be reaching out to me. But this was no movie, and Hollywood couldn't give me the closure I needed. Strangely, there were no longer remnants of the "scene," so to speak. The police and other authorities had assessed and investigated the area, and cleaned everything up. To look into the room now would be to look into a blank canvas; it looked like nothing had happened in there at all. I think that this was what bothered me the most. It was symbolic of how life keeps going. A single death doesn't equate to much in the scheme of the vast universe. Yet to me, that single death had now detonated a newfound hole in my heart, a hole that I didn't even think there was room for. Chloe's death had left an empty shell. My mother's death now left me as a heaping pile of ash, ready to blow away with the first solid wind.

Something *had* happened in the room, despite its mundane appearance. Something life-changing, something devastating. Something potentially life-ending. My mother was gone. Glowering at the prospect, I finally passed by the room and hung a left toward my own. Shutting the door, tears finally started to fall. She was gone, gone like my sister. Both gone.

Even amidst the blunt force of my grief, I began to realize she had been gone for a long time. The mother I knew, the mother with the sparkling white teeth and a love for soap operas, was gone the day of that party. The mother who had studied ceaselessly to become one of the best emergency room doctors in the state of Arizona, yet still managed to pack my lunch every day for school, had disintegrated with the death of her only daughter. I knew it pained her that she couldn't be the mother I needed her to be, but the fact was, she just couldn't. That death—the guilt, the remorse, the regrets—swamped her entire being until all that was left was a skeleton of the woman she once was. Some days it seemed like even the skeleton was disintegrating right before our eyes, leaving nothing but a floppy pile of human flesh. When I looked into her eyes following the death, all I saw was a pile of blank slates, one after the other, lining the back of a masterpiece that had been destroyed. I no longer saw the joy or the drive that were so essential to my mother's person. Her life's painting had been wiped clean, leaving a gloomy backdrop where a once stunning portrait had rested.

Now, though, that blank slate had been emptied from my mother's soul and placed into mine. Now my mother was less than a slate. She was nothing. Despite my mother's lack of enthusiasm for life, she had still been there. I could see her face each day, tell her things even if she didn't seem to be listening. There had still been hope for recovery, that one day she would move past the death gently, carefully, back to her old self. Now that hope was banished, usurped yet again by the power of death.

I crashed into my pillow, not even bothering to take off my shoes. I just wanted to sleep, to fall into black oblivion where the realities of my life did not have to be faced. I just wanted to melt into my bed, a shiftless, formless shape of nothingness.

If I was being honest, I just wanted to be dead, too.

I had stayed in bed, shifting in and out of sleep, for several hours until the echoing doorbell roused me. I knew who it was even before that face appeared at my door. Despite the desire to fade into a state of nonexistence, I realized that in the depths of my being I was relieved to hear the doorbell, to know that her face would soon be in my hands.

She had eased into the room, watering eyes fearful of what she might find.

"Hey," she quavered.

I sat up, my back resting against the headboard of my bed. "Hey," I managed.

She sat beside me on the bed, facing me, shifting uneasily.

"I didn't want to intrude, but I had to see you, to see if you were okay," she apologized. I reached for her, took her in my arms.

"I'm okay now," I decided, willing the tears and emotion to go away.

She wrapped her arms around me, laying her head on my chest. She started to cry for a woman she had barely known yet genuinely felt grief for. She felt anguish, I knew, because I did.

"We're going to get through this," she whispered into my hair.

We held each other in silence for a long time until suddenly I believed what she said.

* * * *

That entire week was a hellish, wobbly blur. There were the viewings, the funeral, flowers, seas of black clothes, gloppy casseroles sent from friends and family. Tears, apologies, strange moments of not knowing what to say, cards, kisses, hugs from practical strangers. Most of all, there were awkward avoidances of the *how* surrounding my mother's death. The whole time, though, Emma stood right beside me, hand in hand, leading me through the darkness. There were plenty of days that my bed beckoned me to stay put, to not even bother facing the day, but Emma commandeered its power. She willed me on, willed me to breathe, to carry on. She became almost a permanent fixture in our household, helping with dinner and cleaning. Jill also became a frequent visitor at our home, helping in any way she could. There were many times that she would just stop what she was doing, hug me, not saying a word, then keep on with her task. She didn't try to make things better with kind, promising words; she seemed to know this wasn't what I needed. What I needed most right now was a hug from my mother, but since this wasn't possible, Jill figured she could offer me the next best thing—a hug from her. Together, those two women pulled my dad and me out of the black hole that had encircled our family. They helped throw us back into the orbit of everyday life, finding a new sense of rhyme and reason to the days. They helped us heal from two deaths that had scarred us, not only as individuals, but as a family. Even in the depths of despair, in the depths of loss and sorrow I thought I couldn't pull myself out of, the Groves proved to me that there was hope. There was hope for my life, even if the lives of my mom and sister were over. My life wasn't over, they seemed to say without saying a single word.

* * * *

Voice of Innocence

    Little did I know it then, but this wasn't the biggest test I would endure in my young life. Bigger, more arduous rocks lurked down the road, rocks that would fastidiously and unwaveringly overturn my life. Emma would be there for those rocks, too. She would again try to stand beside me, her hand in mine. This time, though, instead of letting her be my light in the darkness, I would snuff out her flame and flail her into an untouchable pit.

Chapter Eleven
The Plan

~ Emma ~

The phone's piercing ring echoes through the room, snatching me away from the memories. Hank grunts as I methodically roll him off my lap and stumble across the living room to the phone.

"Hello?" My voice has a distant, questioning tone to it that even I can detect. I probably sound hungover.

"Hey, honnie! How're you doing?" The overly chipper voice resonates through the phone cord, pounding against my brooding mood. I try to fake some enthusiasm.

"Hey, Mom. I'm fine. How are you?"

"Pretty good. Your dad and I just got home from our trip. I'm just unpacking." I quickly try to recall where my parents had traveled to. These days, they rarely stayed on the same continent, let alone in their hometown. Mom was always dragging them off to new lands, new experiences. Sometimes I envied her appetite for life and how she always threw caution to the wind.

"How was it?"

"It was *un-be-lievable!* India is fantastic! I think the best part was the elephant ride. You should have seen your father! It was hilarious! He climbs up on the thing..." My mother's voice becomes a buzzing mosquito in my ear. For the next few minutes, I tune out her mile-a-minute words about elephant poop and sand. Glancing out the window, I realize that the sun has almost completely sunk. The hour hand on the clock above the kitchen window is approaching the eight. Had I spent that much time reminiscing? What was wrong with me?

"He-llo? Emma? You there?" My mom screeches, snapping me back to the conversation.

"Sorry, Mom. I'm just tired. What did you just say?"

"I *said*..." she over exaggerates her words, "that I didn't call to talk about me. I called to see how you're doing."

"I said I was fine, Mom. Why wouldn't I be?" I offer a weak laugh, feebly attempting to convince her that my statement is valid.

"Oh, please, Emma. Who are you trying to fool? For God's sake, this is the woman that popped you out of her own body." That was my mother, so eloquent with her words.

"Mom, can we not do this? I don't want to talk about it, okay?"

"Well, what are we supposed to do? Pretend it's just another normal day?" she asks sarcastically.

"It is just another day. For us, anyway."

"Emma, come on. You can talk to me about this. I know you're going through hell. I know how you feel. You're not the only one who..." she trails off, not having to finish her sentence. We both know what we did.

"Mom, it's ancient history, okay? We can't change it. I'm fine. Honestly."

"It's just so unbelievable, isn't it? All this time, I thought you had done the right thing, that we had done the right thing. The evidence, logic, it all pointed toward the obvious. And now...it just doesn't seem fair, does it? I mean, why would God let this happen? It doesn't make sense." Her tone is serious now. I realize for the first time that this has hurt her badly, too. I had spent so much time wallowing in self-pity that I had forgotten how it had hit her.

After all, Corbin had become a big part of her life, too. It went beyond just you-could-be-my-future-son-in-law-so-I'll-be-nice-to you. No, their relationship had been forged out of tragedy and fostered by a true connection. After Liz Jones took her own life, Corbin sunk into himself. Losing a sister was hard. Losing a sister and a mother in a little over a year was unbearable.

I had tried my best to help him through it. I held his hand the whole way through the funeral and the weeks that followed. It was my mom, however, that gave Corbin what he truly needed. She had known the perfect words to say, the best casseroles to send over, and when to give Corbin his space. Over the next few years, she would walk a difficult balance beam. She played a motherly role to him without trying to be his mother. She offered him advice and nurturing without overstepping the jagged boundaries a teenage boy naturally puts up. She had grown to love him and care for him, and he had grown to need her.

And so, the tragedy had been felt by her, too. It hadn't been an easy decision for either of us to put him out of our lives. At the time, though, it seemed like a necessity. It seemed rational. Life had dealt all of us an unforgiving hand. It was now, with the cards on the table, that my mother and I could truly sense the guilt and regrets that we harbored within us.

I spoke now with a deep sadness in my voice. "I know, Mom, I know. It isn't fair. We both made mistakes. We did what we thought was right at the time. We didn't know what else to do. But it doesn't make it go away, does it? It doesn't make it right. I just can't help but think what he must have gone through. He was already falling apart and losing hope. And then, for us to walk out on him, both of us..." A tear lightly streams down my face. I hadn't meant for this to happen. I didn't want to admit how deep my wounds were, especially not to my mother. She had enough to worry about.

"Emma, do you want me to come over? Maybe it would help."

"No!" I yell more forcefully than I intended. This would be the worst thing. Seeing my mom's sadness would only foster a greater hurt within me. I soften my words this time, knowing I have to seem calm if I'm going to reassure her. "Its fine, Mom. I'm fine. John will be home soon."

"Emma…you're not just saying that, are you?" she asks, a hint of suspicion in her words.

"No, Mom, really, he'll be home soon." The second lie. I was certainly going to hell now, fingers crossed or not.

"Did you talk to John about this?"

"A little," I admit.

"Well, that's good. It's no good to keep it bottled up inside. Did you watch the news?"

Voice of Innocence

"God, no," I bellow. "I'm not a masochist."

"Well, I guess I am then," she replies with a hint of slyness. "It was all over the news, naturally. It's funny. Despite all of this time and tragedy, he still is as gorgeous as..."

"Mom! Enough! I don't want to hear it, all right?"

"All right, all right. I'm done." She pauses for a half-second. Before she even speaks, I know there is more to come. "Okay, not really. One more thought. Where do you think he went today? You know, on his first day of freedom? Back to his parents' house?"

"Mom, I have no clue. It's been years. I highly doubt, though, that after all those decades he's going to dream of going to his parents' house. Where would you go if you were him?"

"Hmm...well...he probably hasn't...you know...for a while. So probably Vegas. Yeah, I bet that's where he's going. A lot of partying, a lot of showgirls, a lot of willing...participants."

"Mom! For God's sake. I should have known better than to ask you that question!"

"Hey, I'm just being realistic. And just because I'm old doesn't mean I've lost touch with what men want." To my absolute horror, I can fully picture the cunning grin on her face as if she is standing right in front of me. My mother, the irrational lady with perverted remarks spewing out of her mouth in all situations. Some things never change.

"Well, Mom, on that lovely note, I'm going to say goodbye and let you finish unpacking. I'll call you sometime this weekend. "

"K, honnie. Love you."

"Love you, too. And try to stay out of trouble."

"That's no fun."

"Life's not always supposed to be fun," I remark, feeling, as usual, like the parent instead of the child.

"Toodles!" she adds before hanging up. What a tagline.

I put the phone back on the charger and shake my head. Despite her quirkiness, I have to admit that my mom does know how to lighten any subject.

I walk to the cupboard and pull out a wine glass. I usually need something strong to drink after a conversation with my mother. Today is no exception. I reach into our liquor cabinet and pull out some of my favorite wine. As I pour myself a brimming glass, Hank trots out to the kitchen, probably thinking he might score some kind of snack. He sits at my feet and begs me with his hopeful eyes. As I carry my glass toward the kitchen door, his eyes sink with disappointment. Nonetheless, he follows me out the door onto the deck. I slouch into one of our white Adirondack chairs and glance up at the perfectly clear sky. The sun has set and the first stars are making their dutiful appearance. I set my glass down on the tiny table between the two chairs. Hank lies down at my feet, and I reach down and pat him on the head. He sighs in delight.

As I look at the tiny specks of life, I can't help but reflect on my mother's question—how could God let this happen? Since preschool, I had been taught that God has a plan for us, that we aren't alone. And for so many years, I believed it. Looking up at the vast night sky, I would see the balls of light that shined from a distant part of an unimaginably large galaxy. There seemed to be no better proof of a higher power than the vastness of the great universe. There just had to be a plan. How else could one explain the complexities of life? Yet tonight, I look at the stars and planets and galaxies with doubt. Maybe they were nothing more than mere specks of light. Maybe we as humans try to read too much into them. Maybe we want them to mean more than they do. We want life to mean more than it does. We don't want to think that we are all just players in a pointless, endless game. How depressing and terrifying that seems.

Yet, looking at the sky tonight, I feel the true minuteness of man. In a galaxy with incomprehensible vastness, Earth is just a dot. In the scheme of things, then, a single life isn't even a blip on the radar. Sure, there is probably a higher power out there. It seems logical, and as a church-goer I do have some sense of faith within me. But maybe we put too much weight on God's shoulders. We are haughty enough to believe that he is watching our every move, planning our every step, listening to our every desire. Maybe he's just too busy with other things to strategically plan every breath for us earthlings.

I know that this is not what my mom meant. Hers was meant as a rhetorical question. For, despite her zaniness, her faith in God is unwavering. Although she may have regrets and sadness over Corbin, I know that deep down she believes all of this has a purpose. Maybe that's

Voice of Innocence

why she's unpacking from another trip while I'm sitting at home wallowing in pity and wine.

Perhaps long ago I, too, believed this whole thing had a purpose. But now, with decades gone by, I cannot bring myself to believe that this situation is anything but a horrible catastrophe, a symbol of the irrationality and unpredictability of life. No matter how hard you try to be a good person, to make choices that will lead to success, nothing is promised. Even the good and the innocent are damned from time to time. What good can come out of the loss that we have all faced? What positive message can surface from the damnation of an innocent man? How can we reclaim any sense of meaning when so much has been taken away? Maybe if so much time hadn't passed, things would be different. But time has passed, a lot of it. It's too late to redeem the situation, to redeem us.

And so, as I look at the sky tonight, I cannot help but think that there is no true meaning to the situation. The God I believe in would not, could not, be this cruel. However, this option leaves the situation in perhaps an even worse state. If there is no plan, if God is not to blame for this situation, then who should be blamed? Corbin? Coincidence? The police? No matter how long I sit here and stare at the stars, none of these choices will fit into my equation. For I know, deep down, the person I blame is me.

I look away from the star-filled sky. My mind plummets deeper and deeper into a murky sea of wandering, exhausting me to the point that it can't handle any more meaning-of-life considerations. Too many thoughts and feelings are already floating through my mind. I can't take any more. I sigh as I reach for my glass of wine and take a sip, hoping it will numb both the pain and my thoughts. As the grape wine sloshes over my tongue, however, a sense of familiarity creeps into my blood. What a mistake. For with this sip of the familiar flavor, more memories come sneaking up on me.

Chapter Twelve
Barnyard Antics

~ Emma ~

Memories

With my ringlet curls sprayed so stiffly that they felt as though they would crack off, I shouted at the top of my lungs down the stairs.
"Mom! Can you get up here? He's going to be here any second!"
I peeked down the hall, anxiously waiting to catch a glimpse of her. I felt like she was moving like molasses, which was totally out of character for my mother.
"I'm coming! I'm coming! Jeez, chill out, Emma. It's going to be fine."
I forced out an exorbitant amount of air in frustration. *It's not going to be fine*, I thought. With the hair salon running forty-five minutes behind and my black eyeliner being uncooperative, how could things be fine? I was already behind schedule, which equated to extra stress on an already taxing day.
My mom finally reached my room. She snatched the baby-blue, floor-length dress from its hanger, carefully slid it off, and handed it to me.
"Step in," she instructed. I obeyed in an overly cautious manner, careful not to trip over the excessive puffiness. When the dress was in place, she zipped me up.
I looked in the mirror, finally relaxing as I saw the finished product coming together surprisingly nicely. I looked…pretty… considering the

stress and all. Just one more touch.

"Mom! Where are my earrings?" I screamed in frenzy as I felt around on my dresser.

"Right here! I moved them so you wouldn't knock them off while you did your makeup." She reached for a tiny jewelry box on the corner of my dresser, clinking back the top to reveal my final accessories.

"Oh…" I sighed in relief. "Thank God. That would have been a disaster."

"Yes, a true, earth-shattering disaster," my mom teased. She smiled, though, looking serious for an uncharacteristic moment. "You look great, baby. Beautiful. See, it all worked out, huh? You need to learn to relax and go with the flow."

Just then, the doorbell rang. Ready with only seconds to spare.

"I'll get it!" my mom yelled, excitement gleaming in her eye like she was the one awaiting her date. It still made me nervous how excited she got to see Corbin. I always felt like she was on the verge of saying or doing something embarrassing. At this point, however, I guessed that Corbin was pretty used to my mother.

I took one last glance in the mirror as I heard my mother greet Corbin. I heard her make a fuss about how grown-up he looked and how handsome he was. It seemed corny to me, but I knew these simple words meant a lot to him. Without his own mother to make embarrassing spectacles of his big moments, my mother was an essential fill-in. She might not be the sanest mother, but she did have a big heart and an awesome sense of empathy.

I breathed in deeply, suddenly nervous to walk down the stairs. It seemed utterly ridiculous. Corbin and I had been a couple for well over a year now. We had been through so much—fights, kisses, jokes, secrets. We had survived tragedy with his mother's death. The winter and spring months had been hellacious, threatening Corbin's spirits and my ability to be strong for him. Corbin had endured the cycle of grief, all while trying to be resilient enough to keep what was left of his family together. Through it all, though, my mom and I worked hard to keep his spirits up and his visions of the future vivid in his mind. As we willed him out of the blackness of grief, we slowly began to see Corbin return to the vivacious guy he once was. He had grown a lot, been forced to mature due to weathering such tragedies, but he was back. In the midst of the darkness, we had also enjoyed small triumphs—Corbin's first semester of straight *A's*, and my first rollercoaster ride.

We had started to grow into the people we would become in adulthood, all the while growing together. Yet, we still hadn't lost that magic spark of adolescence. Looking back, I wish we had relished in the magic of those years a little more instead of constantly keeping our eyes on the horizon. We were always dreaming about the future and what would be instead of basking in the glow of our youth. We had no way of knowing, though, that we would be forced to abandon our carefree selves and grow up too soon. How could we? What teenager thinks that her life won't turn out as planned, won't be a stroll through success?

That day, though, wasn't a day for figuring out the future or strolling down memory lane. It was a day to celebrate, to dance, to simply *be*. Now, waiting to walk down those stairs for the final time, I couldn't calm the ridiculous butterflies in my stomach. I guess I just wanted him to think I was perfect. I wanted to be that girl with the flawless hair and airbrushed makeup hanging on his arm. I wanted to make him proud to be with me, even though I knew he was. On the other hand, I felt so ridiculous in my "princess" garb. I felt completely over the top.

All of the anxiousness and stress that I had put into my appearance had come down to this final moment. Although I didn't know it at this point, junior prom was a grandiose moment in itself, for it would mark a significant turn in our relationship. In many ways, it marked the transformation of us from two kids who were pretty serious about each other to two adults who were part of an unconditional, irrevocable relationship.

My thoughts were quickly interrupted by, you guessed it, my mom.

"Emma! What are you doing up there? If you're not drop-dead gorgeous by now, there's truly no hope for you! Get down here and see your hunk of a boyfriend!"

I rolled my eyes. Couldn't she ever just feign normalcy? No wonder my dad spent so many hours at the office. Even if he did love her, which I know he did, the office was a much-needed refuge from the total chaos that was my mother. After all, a person could only take so much of her intense personality before needing a break.

Voice of Innocence

I turned from the mirror and carefully treaded down the steps in my three-inch high heels, treacherous and wobbly. I prayed that I wouldn't roll down the steps and either rip the dress or break my ankle. Thankfully, and quite surprisingly, I did neither. Weeks of practice in my glittering heels had paid off, at least for the time being.

Corbin was waiting at the bottom of the steps, both hands resting in the pockets of his pants. He stood tall and strong in his black tux and perfectly straight bowtie. His tussled hair demonstrated a lack of fuss over his looks, but it seemed natural. It looked like Corbin. I smiled as I saw his reaction to me, and I felt nothing but sheer elation at my luck. Before me stood the most gorgeous, sweetest, and craziest guy I had ever seen. Most miraculous, that guy was looking at me with pure love. I guess all of the primping had been worth it.

"You. Look. A-mazing," he annunciated, savoring each syllable of every word. His face told me he meant it. I felt a bit silly, like we were in one of those cheesy romantic movies with third-rate actors. But a part of me was excited to have a romantic, Hollywood moment of my own, even if I looked nothing like a movie star.

"You look pretty good, too," I said with a teasing smile. As I got to the bottom of the steps, I reached out and wrapped my arms around him. He squeezed me back tightly after kissing me on the cheek.

"Okay, you lovebirds. Enough, enough. You're going to mess up her makeup and hair, and God knows we don't have time to go through all of that again. Now, get over there so I can take some pictures." She directed us toward the wall by the entranceway—our traditional photo op spot in the house because it was void of clutter.

"Some pictures" turned into what seemed like two hundred. My mother had us in every possible pose and even some impossible ones. When she had exhausted the possibilities in the house, she moved us outdoors for another series. At this rate, she could make thirty scrapbooks of this single day. And maybe even a few flipbooks.

"Is this necessary?" I whined after twenty minutes.

She pulled the camera down for a brief second. "Do you have to ask that, Emma? Did you expect any less?" she said, matter-of-factly. I sighed and rolled my eyes, knowing it was easier to go along with her demands than to fight them. Corbin graciously smiled over and over, never complaining. Finally, after one last pose, she said, "Okay, I think I have enough. You guys can go now."

I grabbed Corbin's hand and raced toward his white truck, not stopping to look back. "Bye, Mom. Love ya!" I shouted over my shoulder as I opened the door to his pickup and carefully slid in. I wasn't going to give her another second to deliberate.

"Wait! Take this so you can get some pictures at the prom!"

"Mom, really?" I whined as she approached the truck, flailing the camera through the open window.

"You have two choices. You can take lots of pictures and prove to me that I can trust you, or you can choose to not take any pictures and then for senior prom, I'll just have to show up and take my own. It's up to you," she sang in her oh-so-annoying "I've got you cornered" voice, eyebrows raised. The sad part was that any other mom would be joking, but I knew she would fully deliver on her ultimatum.

Knowing I had been beat, I grabbed the camera and an extra roll of film from her, shoving both on the seat beside me. "Are you sure I'm not adopted?" I asked, half teasing.

"Oh please, someday you'll be an exact replica of me," she beamed.

"God, I hope not," I said, directing it toward Corbin. He just shook his head and laughed.

Mom playfully poked at me, flailing her head with a disapproving look. "Anyway, sourpuss, try to have some fun, okay? Corbin, make sure she has fun! And take lots of pictures." She winked at Corbin, wiped at a smear of lipstick in the corner of my mouth, and skipped off toward the house, turning back every few steps to wave yet again. Unbelievable. This woman truly should be in some type of stupid comedic movie. Or maybe a horror film. Either would work.

Corbin, though, didn't seem to notice the ridiculous quality of her actions. He smirked back at her, waving her off into the distance, and finally jumped onto the springy truck seat.

"Finally! We're free!" I said to him as he started up the truck. "Okay, so where are we going?"

Most of the girls in my classes had planned their prom schedule itinerary to the millisecond, informing their dates of where they were to be and when. Corbin and I had done things differently. When I asked him where he wanted to go for dinner before prom, he simply said, "I'll take care of it." My controlling nature forced me to argue with him a bit, but I finally agreed to give up the reigns. "It'll be worth it, trust me," he had promised. Although I hated surprises, I gave in to the sensation, enjoying the prospect of the unknown. It had been driving me crazy for weeks. I guessed I would find out soon enough.

"Emma, do you think I'm going to ruin my surprise now after I've kept it secret for weeks? You'll see when we get there."

"Humph," I said, frustrated. Corbin just laughed as he backed up onto the road.

He had been right—the surprise was worth the wait.

At first, I was utterly confused at where we were going. I began to think that letting him plan our outing had been a mistake. After twenty minutes on a ridiculously long road, rutty and windy, we stopped at a ramshackle barn. This wasn't one of your bright, fire-engine red, picture-perfect, romantic-in-a-country-sort-of-way barns. What few swatches of paint were left on it were peeling off so badly that they were attached only by a centimeter. Weeds grew in the field, waist-high. No other houses or cars were around, highlighting the fact that it had clearly been abandoned for a long time. I didn't even move as Corbin unhooked his seatbelt and got out of the truck.

Usually, I was up for just about anything with Corbin, but now my stomach fell into a knot of disappointment. What would I tell everyone? They knew Corbin was surprising me, but how would I spin this to stand up to the anticipation and excitement I had expressed for weeks? What was Corbin thinking? I loved Corbin unconditionally, and I loved the simplicity of our relationship on a normal day. We could paint fences all day or sit and look at the grass for all I cared, as long as I was with him. This, however, seemed to be a bit much. Had I spent hours perfecting my look to wander around in some disgusting barn? I tried not to pout too much or to let the disgust mar my face. It was a battle, though. Finally, the words leaped out of my unconsciously pursed lips.

"Um, are you serious right now?" I asked him with true shock ringing in my voice. I could feel the whiny, high-maintenance girl in me bursting at the seams. This character was usually dormant, hidden away by my crappy T-shirts and clearance shopping. Now the valley girl within seemed to surface, horrified at this disgusting prospect. Corbin stayed calm, though, and just laughed.

"Just trust me, okay? It's not as bad as it looks."

"Are you sure about that?"

"Positive."

"Are you going to murder me or something? This is starting to look like one of those horror movies."

"Yes. That was the plan all along," he said, feigning a serious tone. He rolled his eyes and shook his head as he walked around the truck to open my door. I was still buckled in and hadn't even moved. He opened my door and looked at me just inches from my face.

"Are you done asking questions yet?"

"No. Where are we?"

"A barn."

"Well, I've figured that much out, genius," I spewed. "Whose barn is it?"

"It was my grandparents' before they died. It used to be an actual working farm. Now, obviously, it's just abandoned. My dad inherited the land but never did anything with it. So, for today," he said as he unbuckled my seatbelt, "it's our romantic prom dinner location." He raised an eyebrow at the word "romantic" in a sad attempt to be sexy. It looked ridiculous enough to make me laugh, if I hadn't been so peeved about the situation.

"Romantic?" I asked, trying to hold back his hand from my seatbelt in a desperate attempt to remain in the truck.

"Well, if you'd get out, maybe you'd change your mind. Besides, you are completely alone with your awesomely cute boyfriend. What does it matter where we are?" he said, jokingly. He flexed a bicep muscle in a mock attempt to seduce me inside. I rolled my eyes.

"You're a goof."

"And you love it," he said as he grabbed my arm and pulled me out of the truck.

"We can do this the easy way or the hard way," he said as I tried to resist getting out.

"What's the easy way?"

"You cooperate, trust me, and follow me inside before you make hasty judgments."

"And the hard way?"

"I drag you in kicking and screaming, leading to a potential rip in your dress or misplaced curls. Your choice."

I sighed, rolled my eyes for the umpteenth time—I *was* turning into a snotty valley girl—and said, "Fine. I'll follow you. But if it's nasty in there, I'm not promising anything."

"Why would I bring you somewhere nasty for prom? Am I that untrustworthy? Unromantic?"

"You do have me at a barn," I observed, annoyed. I slouched beside him, truly reluctant to see what awaited me.

"Just come on. You'll change your mind. You'll see."

"What about my dress?" I asked, eyeing the dirty pathway to the barn with disgust.

"Oh! Right! I've got it covered. But first, put this on." He handed me a blindfold.

"Really?"

"Yes. Really. Humor me."

I groaned, tied the blindfold in place, and crossed my arms. I felt like an idiot.

"Now what?"

He reached over and scooped me up in his arms, carrying me down the pathway. Despite my disdain, I couldn't hide how good it felt to be in his arms, whatever the circumstances. He set me down inside the barn. He walked away from me for a few minutes. I impatiently tapped my foot.

"Corbin," I whined. "Can I take this stupid blindfold off yet?"

"One second, almost ready." I heard rustling as he hustled around the room making his last-second preparations. Soft music resonated into the area.

"Ready?" he inquired as he reached for my blindfold.

"As I'll ever be," I said. Curiosity had gotten the best of me. He took off the blindfold, and I was shocked when I looked around.

The barn still was its rustic self, but it had been transformed into a sort of whimsical wonderland. Corbin had hung hundreds of soft, white lights all around the barn. A white runner, like the ones used in weddings, led from the entrance to a large, white carpet placed in the center. A tiny bistro table and chairs sat in the middle with candles softly aglow. A little table was positioned beside it with covered trays of food. A vase of roses also resided in the middle of the table. Rose petals were scattered on the floor of the barn, looking oddly picturesque on the dirt floor. I smiled in sheer delight. It may not have been glamorous, but to me it was oddly romantic, a perfect balance of old and new, of simple and chic. It was simply us.

"This must have taken you forever!" I exclaimed in true excitement and surprise.

"Um, yeah, it did," he admitted hesitantly. "Was it worth it?" He gave me an uncertain look as if he was finally wondering if he had made a mistake.

"Yes!" I shouted, wrapping my arms around his neck. "It's the sweetest thing anyone has ever done."

"I know it's not very sophisticated. But I wanted to do something different, something special that we would remember."

"It's perfect. It's us." I smiled, truly meaning the words.

Corbin led me down the "runway" to the table and pulled out my chair.

"The menu is somewhat limited due to cooking dilemmas, as you can imagine," Corbin said with a grin. He pulled out a tray of sandwiches, which had been crudely cut into the shape of hearts. He also uncovered two bags of chips, two sodas, and a few snack cakes. I smiled at the simplicity of it all.

"I'm starving, let's eat," I said with a genuine smile. To me, this was better than any stuffy dinner my friends were attending.

Corbin and I spent the next hour eating our "feast," talking about families, prom, graduation, and us. After dinner, he moved the table and we danced to songs on the radio, not caring if they were fast or slow, just holding onto each other and softly swaying back and forth. It was undoubtedly the most romantic moment of my life.

"Thank you," I whispered to him as I looked up into his soft brown eyes.

"You're so welcome," he said, pressing his lips to mine softly.

"Not just for this," I said, looking around. "Thank you for being with me. I don't know what I'd do without you."

"Well, I don't plan on you having to find out," he said.

At the time, his words echoed with truth in my soul. We both saw the vastness of the future, the promise of opportunities and time. What we didn't see, what we couldn't see, was the darkness, the drop-off that loomed not far ahead.

Chapter Thirteen
Hayloft Harmonies

~ Emma ~

Memories

"Emma! You look amazing!" Katie's voice screeched above the crowd. Her gorgeous blonde hair was perfectly swept up into an elegant French twist, a few golden tendrils falling around her face. In a hot-pink dress that fit her figure snuggly, she shimmered to match her personality.

Although Katie, Hannah, Jenn, and I still talked, it was Katie that I maintained a semblance of a close friendship with. We had all been pulled in different directions by different guys, lessening the time we spent together. Katie, however, always greeted me with a smile, her optimistic attitude allowing her to look past the distance between us.

"Katie! You look amazing, too!" I proclaimed, trying to match her enthusiasm, but ultimately failing. We hugged, and Corbin grabbed my mother's camera to take a picture.

"Hey, Corbin! Still handling the Pennsylvania weather, I guess?" Katie asked after the picture was snapped.

Corbin wrapped his arms around me, squeezing me to his chest. "I love it. No place I'd rather be." He smiled at me, and Katie grinned at his words.

"Gee...I wonder why," she said mischievously, looking from me to Corbin and then back. Katie's date, Thomas, pulled on her hand then.

"Well, we're heading to get some drinks. See you around!" she said, stumbling off with a smile still on her face.

Voice of Innocence

I looked around at the paper stars hanging from the ceiling and the glitter covering every inch of the gymnasium. I had to admit that despite the cheesiness of the starry night theme, the place looked pretty good. Or maybe I was just becoming a softy after Corbin's romantic escapade.

A huge crowd in the middle of the dance floor exploded with vivacity as the next song began to blast through the room. The group began to create the necessary formation for the electric slide. It felt like they were living in a ridiculously corny movie. Corbin grabbed my hand and yanked me toward the center of the crowd. "Let's go!" he said happily. I tried to yank back, but Corbin's strong physique prevented me from gaining much headway. "Corbin, no way! It's too crowded. And I can't dance."

Corbin disregarded my protests, pulling me closer to the dancing group.

"It'll be fine, Emma! It's prom. You *have* to dance."

"No, I definitely don't. I don't even know the moves."

"You're a fast learner. Plus, you have a great teacher," Corbin said, winking at me. He pulled me into a line beside him. I groaned in defeat.

"Oh, why not," I relented.

"That's my girl!" Corbin said. "Now follow me."

The next three minutes couldn't pass fast enough. I stumbled and tripped as the rest of my classmates, Corbin included, smoothly transitioned from move to move. I was constantly sashaying in the wrong direction. I tried to exit the dance floor a few times while I still had a crumb of pride left. Corbin grabbed my hand, encouraging me to keep going. When the dance was mercifully over, I said, "That's it, no more dancing."

"Oh, come on, Emma, that was just a warm-up. Besides, you can make up your moves to this one."

"Girl's Just Wanna Have Fun" resonated through the room. All of the guys in the room grumbled in chorus. I shriveled up my nose with them, annoyed by the squeaky voice singing about boys and who knows what else. Just before we could wiggle free from the crowd, a familiar voice yelled my name.

"Emma! Emma, over here!" Katie jumped up and down, her huge grin iridescent like the thousands of glittery cut-out stars on the walls.

"Come on, over here!" Beside her were Hannah and Jenn, swaying enthusiastically to the beat. It was like a reunion in the middle of the dance floor. I turned to Corbin.

"Go ahead! I'm going to make a pit stop, anyway. I'll stop and get us some drinks on the way back, and I'll meet you here." He leaned over to kiss me on the cheek.

I looked from him to the group. I guessed that it would be fun to spend a little time with the girls, considering I hadn't seen much of them this year.

"You sure you don't want to come?" I asked.

"As tempting as that may seem, I think I'll preserve my masculinity and sit this one out. Go, have fun."

Have fun dancing—right, like that would happen. But I kissed him on the lips and sauntered over to the girls. At least the song was halfway over.

"Hey, guys!" I yelled above the music with a little extra excitement.

"Hey!" they yelled in unison.

"Isn't this great?" Katie asked.

"Yeah, it is actually," I said.

"Where are your dates?" I quizzed Jenn and Hannah.

"They went to get drinks. They were worried about losing their masculinity," Jenn said, shaking her head at the prospect.

We all grinned. Despite the distance that had crept between us lately, it felt easy being there with them. It felt like nothing had changed. I guessed that events like prom did that to people, made them forget grudges and hurt feelings. We danced together, laughing at our clumsiness, joking about the girls who thought they were so "hot" gyrating ridiculously to the beat. I had to admit that I was having more fun on the dance floor than I thought I would.

When the song was over, Hannah said, "Well, guess I better go scrounge up Evan. I have to make sure none of the Miss 'Thangs' here stole him from me." We laughed some more and nodded, saying we were heading to find our dates, too. We went in separate directions as we had been for the past several months.

As I approached the edge of the dance floor, I spotted Corbin in the line for drinks. He glanced my way and waved. I smiled and started heading that way. Suddenly, however, I felt a tug on my arm. Thinking it was one of the girls, I turned around with a smile. It wasn't Katie, Hannah, or Jenn, though. It was Randy Clark, standing just a little too close to me with a grin on his face.

Randy Clark had lived down the street from me my entire life. I had known him since I was four years old. I remember that at the park in our neighborhood, he had pushed me off the seesaw so he could have a turn. And so our saga began.

As in all small towns, everyone in town knew Randy's story. Randy's mom had taken off when he was only two years old, feeling all sorts of urges, except the motherly ones. Thus, he was left under the care of his father, Joe Clark. Joe was infamous in our town for working too few hours and drinking too many drinks. As an only child, Randy supposedly spent many days and nights on his own. Although we had no proof or signs that Randy was abused physically, his personality certainly hinted that things were far from perfect under the hand of his drunken father. The town's hands were, in a way, tied just as Randy was tethered to a life of misery. In school, Randy was the average troublemaker. He picked fights, got suspended several times, harassed the teachers. He had been picked up for several infractions—stealing a candy bar at the local gas station, underage drinking, assault. Randy was about one step away from a juvenile detention center. Most kids and adults alike tried their best to avoid him.

Although I had my share of negative experiences with Randy, a part of me felt sorry for him. I couldn't imagine having a dad who didn't support me, let alone one that was downright neglectful. So, while others shunned Randy, I tried to be somewhat kind. I smiled at him in the hallways and talked to him at the bus stop. On several occasions, Corbin had also joined in my charitable cause, "loaning" Randy a few bucks for lunch when he attempted to beat it out of another kid in the lunch line. Randy repaid my kindness by not giving me too much grief—key words being *too much*. Despite a few nicknames he gave me and the seesaw incident, I got the feeling that Randy sort of liked me. Now, in the middle of the dance floor, I wished this weren't the case. I could smell alcohol on Randy's breath. I could also see it in his gleaming, heavy eyes.

His words came out slurred. "You look hot, Emma. Really hot."

I tried to shake off his grasp on my arm, but it was tight.

"Thanks, Randy. Maybe you should go home. You don't want to get in trouble. If they know that you've been drinking, they'll…"

Randy found this uproariously funny. He snorted with laughter, finally managing to choke out his words. "Oh, Emma, always worrying about getting in trouble. Ha! You think it matters for someone like me?"

"Randy, let go, okay?"

"Dance with me, Emma." He put his other hand on my waist, pulling me in too closely. The alcohol was even more pungent now as my face was forced against his chest. I glanced around, hoping to see one of the chaperones rushing to my rescue. With the music blaring and a large group of kids jumping up and down near us, we were probably out of the line of vision of the adults. I was on my own.

"Randy! Let go!" I started kicking and wiggling to get free.

"Emma, just dance with me. You know you want to. You've always wanted me. I can tell."

I continued writhing, trying to break free, afraid of what he might do. He was so drunk and so unconcerned with authority that it was hard to tell. A few kids around us started to look our way, wondering what was happening. Before anyone could go get an adult, though, Randy was ripped off me with such force and quickness that I fell to the ground, stunned by what had happened. People around me stopped in their tracks, gasping at a scuffle that was happening right above my head. I scrambled to my feet, recognizing the other participant.

"Corbin! Stop!" I yelled, trying to reach for his arm.

"Keep your hands off of her or I'll kill you!" Corbin snarled at Randy, true rage in his eyes and voice. I had never seen this side of him.

Instead of heeding the warning, though, Randy found it hysterical, guffawing crazily. "You're going to kill me, asshole? Let's just see about that," he taunted. Randy and Corbin danced around the floor in a sloppily choreographed show of strength and speed. Corbin got Randy into a headlock. Teachers started swarming the area, and the deejay had stopped the music. A circle had formed around the boys. Tears rolled down my face, praying that this would all be over soon—and that Corbin would still be in one piece.

Voice of Innocence

Randy was able to escape, despite Corbin's grasp. Once he was free, he swung and punched toward Corbin's face, his knuckles awkwardly landing near Corbin's eye. Corbin's head snapped backward as he fell to the ground. Blood spewed from Randy's knuckles and from Corbin's face. I leaped to his side.

"Corbin!" I screamed. Again, however, I was tossed aside as a teacher grabbed him. Another teacher had a hold of Randy. Corbin groaned, but calmly got back to his feet, holding his face.

"Are you all right?" the teacher asked. Corbin shook his head in a slight "yes" movement. Someone handed him towels to stop the bleeding.

Another teacher brought a pack of ice and handed it to Corbin. "Here, put this on it. Maybe we should call an ambulance."

Corbin did as he was told, and the teacher began to lead him toward the door. "No, I'm fine. It's nothing," he stoically stated.

"You're going to have to leave," the teacher said to Corbin, still holding onto his arm. "I'm going to have to call your parents."

"Really? What the hell? He grabs Emma, he is clearly drunk, and I have to leave?" Corbin shouted, slamming the ice pack to the ground. "If you were doing your job, there wouldn't have been a fight. If you had kept that dirtball out of here, there wouldn't have been an issue." Corbin had wriggled free from the teacher's grasp and was reaching for me.

"Mr. Jones, that is quite enough. I didn't see anything going on with Mr. Clark and Miss Groves, but if it was, fighting didn't solve anything. Now I'm sorry, but you will have to leave. I will be contacting your parents and the principal to see if there will be any disciplinary actions taken on Monday. Mr. Clark will be leaving as well," the teacher lectured. I wanted to punch him.

"That's ridiculous!" I screamed at the teacher. Everyone around us looked at me in shock. In all of my years of schooling, I had never talked back to a teacher like this. "He was just protecting me. Randy's the one who started it."

"No room for exceptions, Miss Groves. These two were both fighting, we saw it. They *both* have to go."

"But…"

"No exceptions," the teacher said with firm finality as I followed him and Corbin to the door.

"You go first," the teacher said to Corbin as the other teacher held onto Randy. "Are you okay to drive? I can still call an ambulance or someone to pick you up."

"I'm fine." Corbin's voice was gruff.

"Straight to your vehicle and out you go. If you come back, we'll call the cops. You're lucky we're not getting them involved now. Assault charges don't go away so easily, you know," the teacher harangued. I found myself completely disgusted with the teacher. This was ludicrous.

"Corbin, I'm coming, too," I added from behind.

I rushed out the door, not caring if the teachers had anything to say about it. We walked swiftly to the truck, climbing in quietly. Once there, I looked at Corbin's face.

"Corbin, are you sure you're okay? It looks pretty bad," I said softly. "Maybe we should call my mom..."

"No, Emma. I'm fine. I've already ruined your night with my damn temper." He sighed, a glassy look filling his eyes. He slowly turned the ignition on the truck, filling the parking lot with a dull roar of the engine. He still held the towel on the cut with his extra hand.

"Corbin, you didn't do anything wrong! You protected me from that slimeball. You didn't do anything," I yelled over the hum of the engine, hoping he would believe me. I felt horrible for the part I had played in the night. "If anyone's at fault, it's me," I added as my eyes shifted from his face to my feet with guilt.

"What?!" Corbin shouted in shock, looking over at me. I was afraid the truck was going to stall.

"What are you talking about? I saw that creep grab you, and I saw you pushing him away. You had nothing to do with this, Emma. "

"Well, I didn't play any smaller part than you. If I'm not to blame, neither are you. You stepped in when I needed you."

Corbin shook his head and sighed. "Regardless, I ruined your prom night."

"You didn't ruin it."

"How do you figure?"

"Well," I said hesitantly, "it's not technically over yet. Mom's not expecting me home for like three hours."

"And what do you suppose we do with those hours? It's not like we have many places we can go dressed like this."

I thought to myself for a second. "Well, there is one place that we are dressed appropriately for."

"Where?"

"We were there once tonight," I said, happiness in my voice.

"The barn? You want to go back to the barn?" Corbin asked.

"Why not?"

Corbin played with the idea in his head.

"Well, I guess we could. I had thought about asking you to go back there after prom anyway, you know, instead of going to the after-party. So I guess we'll just move the plans up a few hours."

"See, it's working out fine. Nothing's ruined."

"If you say so."

"Well, I'm with you. What else matters?"

He looked at me, a smile slowly spreading on his face. "You are missing out, though, you know."

"On what?" I quizzed.

"While you were dancing, I had requested the chicken dance. I figured it was a group dance you could handle."

I opened my mouth, gaping at him in mock horror. "Oh my goodness. What a shame I'll be missing out on that fun time," I proclaimed.

He laughed. I was happy that the mood was finally lightening up.

"Well, we do have a radio at the barn…" he said jokingly.

"I'll pass. I think there are better things we can do with our time," I offered.

"Like what?" Corbin asked with curiosity. His eyes flickered.

"You'll think of something," I flirted.

* * * *

I had no idea where this side of me was coming from. Sure, I was wildly attracted to Corbin. But sexy and flirtatious were not part of my vocabulary. I attributed this new confidence to the adrenaline rush from watching the fight. Corbin seemed to wrestle with the possibilities in his mind for the rest of the drive. After several miles on the now-familiar dirt road, his truck finally jolted to a stop.

"Here we are...again," Corbin said. His eye was starting to bruise, but the bleeding had at least stopped.

"Our own private prom," I added, laughing. "Mr. Jones, you are such a troublemaker. What am I going to do with you?" I asked, gently stroking his face near his injury.

"Oh, you'll think of something," he promised, winking at me. He leaned over and kissed me gently. It quickly turned into a more urgent, heavy kiss, his hand grasping the side of my face, crushing my curls as he cradled them. He pulled away gently, quickly got out of the truck, and walked over to my door, a man on a mission. He opened it, and this time I got out on my own volition. Not caring too much about the dress anymore, I followed behind him down the dirt path, holding his hand the whole way. He turned on the lights once we were in the barn and the magical setting returned.

"Much better than prom," I said, smiling up at him. His eyes were serious, looking into mine.

"Emma," he said, turning me to face him and putting his hands on my face. "I love you. So much. I thought I was going to lose it when I saw Randy touching you," he said, leaning in to kiss me when his words were finished.

"I love you, too," I softly muttered into the haven of his mouth. He continued kissing me, hands moving against my body in a claim of ownership, ownership that I was more than happy to submit to. I felt my heart start to race as the kiss got greedier. He darted away enough to look at me, his hands on my hips.

"I almost forgot. Wait here one second." I sighed in frustration. What horrible timing this guy had.

He jaunted across the barn, reached into a tiny cooler I hadn't noticed earlier, and pulled out a bottle and two glasses. I recognized the contents immediately. Despite my newfound carefree attitude this night, alarm bells started to ring. This was too much.

"Corbin," I said seriously, "this is a bad idea. I'm not going to risk..."

"Shhh..." he said, opening the bottle. "Relax, Emma. It's just grape juice."

Voice of Innocence

"Oh," I said, stopping mid-rant. I blushed at my blunder. Always the square. Or the killjoy. "Sorry, I just assumed…"

He handed me a glass of my bubbling grape juice. I took a sip. It was delicious.

"I think I know you a little better than to bring alcohol here. Give me some credit, okay?" he snickered, shaking his head.

"How about a toast?" he declared, raising his glass in mock sophistication. He put his nose in the air a little bit too high. I giggled.

"A toast? Are we the toasting type now?" I said, laughing at the ridiculous pretense that two people who ate potato chips and sandwiches in a barn would be toasting.

"To a prom night that we'll never forget," he announced, "and to us…and the long road that got us here and the long road that waits ahead."

"To us," I chimed in, clinking his glass and feeling somewhat silly. But I did like the pretense of the long road ahead.

I couldn't imagine my life without this crazy, romantic, sweet, gorgeous goofball standing beside me, making me laugh every step of the way. We sipped on our "bubbly." Corbin reached for my glass and set both of them on the table. He wrapped his arms around my waist again, his hands finding home on my protruding hips.

"You're so beautiful tonight, Emma. I love you so much. I want to be with you forever."

I blushed at the compliments and looked down at my feet. After the heat in my face had cooled, I looked up at him.

"I love you, too. Forever."

Corbin launched into kissing me again, his hands whispering across my back, igniting chills all over my body. I wrapped my arms tenderly around his neck and delved into the kiss completely. The kisses were initially languid and lazy, flowing gently like a dandelion seed in a breeze. Soon, though, the breeze intensified to a zealous gust. We kissed roughly, passionately, with a need that neither of us had recognized before but had become a welcome guest within these walls. I felt my mind drifting off into the twinkling white lights, floating into the whimsical setting itself.

The next few hours were filled with more joy, passion, and love than

I would ever experience again. We were two young kids treading into the waters of adulthood, neither one of us knowing what lay ahead or just how deep the waters were. And though we were clumsy and arguably foolish in our actions in the barn that night, our actions were guided by pure love and trust. Not a second of regret or hesitation flooded my mind as I followed Corbin into that hayloft. I had always considered myself a rule-follower and a moral stickler. Despite myself, though, it didn't feel wrong. It couldn't feel wrong when I felt so serene lying in the arms of Corbin, engulfed in his entire sense of being. For the first time in my young life, I felt fulfillment and contentment at their deepest levels.

When I awoke in Corbin's arms a few hours later, I smiled up into his face. My mind was soggy with the inevitable sleepiness that follows passion, but my mind still grasped that as a unit we were forever changed. The lightness of an adolescent relationship had been replaced with the heaviness of an irreversible connection. I knew at that moment that he would be a part of me at the deepest sense of my being for the rest of my life, and I relished in this fact.

When we knew it was time to return to the realities of the external world, we groggily treaded down the hayloft ladder. More kissing threatened to intensify, but we knew that my mother would hear about the fight and Corbin's expulsion from the dance. I would have some explaining to do for the last few hours. But I would worry about that tomorrow.

For that night, I had only wanted to revel in the beauty of our connection, in the strength of our desires. As Corbin hugged me to him and professed his love one more time, I glanced around the room, taking in the sheer magic of the atmosphere that would be gone come morning light. I knew there would be other nights and other memories, but I felt like there could never be another fairy tale night that lived up to this one.

* * * *

For the rest of my life, when I saw the stars twinkling in the night sky or lights at Christmastime, I would think of those lights that Corbin had laboriously hung in that barn. When I saw a rustic, peeling building claiming to be a barn, I would think of *that* barn, our barn, where we had eaten sandwiches and danced to the radio. And whenever grape wine or grape juice or grape anything tantalized my taste buds, I was transported

Voice of Innocence

back to that enchanted night when we first committed ourselves to one another completely and irreversibly.

Chapter Fourteen
Working Hard, Playing Hard

~ Emma ~

Memories

    The remaining weeks of our junior year flew with characteristic ease and swiftness. Before we knew it, the humid days of summer sat at our doorsteps, waiting to be filled with new memories and laughter.

    Thankfully, the only repercussions from prom night were my mother's uncharacteristic wrath. She had heard about the fight from Mrs. Pratt, our neighbor, who had heard from her son, and the teacher who had thrown Corbin out. Although my mother was gracious for Corbin's interference between me and Randy, she was curious about where our extra hours of time had gone after leaving the prom. We left her in the dark as much as possible. She eventually dropped it, probably because she thought that not knowing what happened may have been better than facing what truly happened. As a precaution, though, I found myself facing a "birds and the bees" talk only a few days later. With my mother, that was certainly a trip I wouldn't ever want to sign up for again.

    The weeks that had passed since that night deadened the intensity of the situation, and things went back to normal. Randy Clark, of course, glowered at Corbin every chance he got and went out of his way to flirt with me at school. Other than that, the situation seemingly dissipated. And so, with hot, empty days ahead, Corbin and I both decided to take summer jobs. I took a job in the mall in an attempt to save up some money for the exuberant expenses associated with college.

Voice of Innocence

Corbin took a job at the local amusement park, which afforded him the simple luxury of being outside all day. After much persuasion, he decided that he would apply to the Art Institute of Pittsburgh. A typical desk job just wasn't his cup of tea, and his amazing artistic abilities made it seem like a perfect fit. Corbin wasn't so confident in his abilities, but he agreed to humor me and apply, admitting that if he got in, it would be a dream come true. He knew, however, that his dad, Mr. Practical in every sense of the word, would never go for four years at an art school. He would deem the endeavor a complete waste of time and resources. Unless Corbin was going for a "real" career, such as a lawyer or a real estate agent, Mr. Jones probably wouldn't be supportive. So Corbin needed to save as much money as possible. He would borrow the rest. Of course, Corbin wasn't too concerned about it. His motto was *"worry about it when you're standing right in front of it."* Too often than not, his small paychecks from the park were spent on music or day trips for us that summer. I, on the other hand, saved every single penny I earned. I tried not to hold his laissez-faire nature against him, but sometimes it was hard. I knew that come fall, he would be scrounging for cash.

Nonetheless, we both worked away our days and laughed away our nights together. We still visited "our" oak tree on a weekly basis and visited "our" barn as often as we could. With his sense of freedom found in his driver's license, our possibilities for exploration were opened up tenfold. We visited the zoo, a water park, and even drove to the beach on our days off. We spent Memorial Day and the Fourth of July picnicking with my family at the local lake. My mom invited Mr. Jones to our picnics on both days, and to everyone's surprise, he came with us on the Fourth of July. To Corbin's true surprise, Mr. Jones actually had a good time.

The summer passed with an ease that is typical of the sunny days of the season. Merriment was plentiful, especially on the days we spent with my mother, who was more often than not in her hot-pink string bikini in a lounge chair on the front lawn. *"If you've got it, flaunt it!"* she would say while a chocolate ice cream cone dripped down her chin. Poor Corbin saw more of my mother that summer than he had bargained for.

As the end of August loomed and the first day of our senior year threatened to end our summer fun, dread started to pang within me. One more year, and then it was off to the real world. Bills, distance, and major life choices loomed ahead of us, threatening to come between us. Although I hoped, even prayed, that Corbin would get accepted to the Art Institute, a part of me feared what it would mean for us. Would we start to grow apart if he was three hours away? What if I only saw him once a week or once every few weeks when we were busy? Although I tried to quiet these fears and convince myself our love was strong enough to survive, I couldn't calm the uneasiness I felt deep down.

    I felt like a black cloud was looming in the distance, waiting for graduation day to pass. I knew that if I mentioned it to him, Corbin would quickly dismiss the application for the Institute and pass up on his dreams. Thus, I kept quiet. I knew that I needed to suck it up. It would be worth it in the future when we both had careers we loved. I would have to deal with some distance in the short term to ensure our happiness and solidity in the long run. So, on the last day of summer, as we sat entwined under the oak tree watching the ducks swim on the creek, I decided to relinquish my fears and doubts to the universe. What was meant to be would work out, I told myself, trying to believe it. Just then, Corbin leaned down and kissed me. All was well. It seemed that all would work out.

Chapter Fifteen
Wings

~ Corbin ~

The cell door clinks open as Frank trudges back into his familiar place on the top bunk. I think nothing of it until a guard yells, "Jones." I sit up from the bed and glance over toward the bars. It is time.

I exhale audibly as I head toward the gate. Despite the recent developments, I still must be searched. While those in the outside world would shudder with humiliation at the depraving search, I have grown accustomed to it. In here, nothing is sacred or private. Humiliation and inferiority are a part of life.

I am led down the corridor to a room in which I have spent hundreds of anguish-filled hours. Hours spent hoping for a change, hoping for news, hoping for the truth. For so many years, that hope dwindled until it finally became nothing but a bug stomped into the cement floor. Now it has been resurrected, against all odds. The hope has grown wings again and is ready to sail out of this prison, carrying me with it. Overjoyed shouldn't even begin to describe it.

I had dreamed of this meeting, dreamed of the day I would be exonerated from that crime, when I would hear those final words that would set me free. Yet, as I walk down the hallway to meet with my lawyer, the warden, and the prosecutor, I feel nothing of the sort. Instead, feelings of confusion, fear, and anger swarm my soul.

For years I sat in here, an innocent man labeled a criminal. For years, I spent my days in the company of true murderers and rapists, living the life meant for them. Solitude and sorrow became fixed entities in my day to day life. Yet now, after twenty-eight years of buzzers and clinking bars, of cardboard-like nourishment and monotony that can kill, of years of letters and pleas that fell on deaf ears, of appeals and disappointments, they decide I am truly innocent. One dedicated foundation, some fingernail scrapings, an overlooked hair, and some DNA testing helped the suppressed truth to finally surface, but it took twenty-eight years. Twenty-eight years. What is one to make of that? Clearly, I have known all along that it wasn't my fault, that I wasn't a murderer. It is no surprise to me. Yet, shouldn't it be more surprising to them? The guards, my lawyer, the judge, the warden, they all act so formal and nonchalant about the news. I mean, yes, they seemed apologetic, but how can a "we're so sorry," make up for twenty-eight years? How can they give me back those years that I lost? How can they make up for oversights and mistakes that should have never happened, that cost me my life? How can they explain away their overzealous prosecution of an innocent boy based on how a situation appeared? How can they reign in the ships that have already sailed from my harbor and sank, their treasures obliterated in the crash? No settlement can possibly give me back the life that I lost, the part of my life that would have probably been the best years of my life.

No one can bring her back to me, either, which, if I'm being honest, is what this true rage is focused around.

For of all the things I have lost—the freedom to choose my life, a career, a house, children—she is what my heart aches for the most. The what-ifs plague my mind relentlessly until I can barely stand to breathe.

When I thought all hope was lost, when I thought this would be my life, it seemed somewhat bearable. I knew I had done the right thing, that she was better off.

Yet, when the lawyer from the foundation approached me upon my dad's request and said we had a real shot at proving my innocence, old, familiar anger refurbished itself in my cell. Why now? Where was this proof for the nineteen-year-old boy, facing the potential loss of everything? Where had this voice of innocence been then, when I needed it, when it could have made a difference? Where was it when it could have saved the life Emma and I had been planning, when it could have ensured a life worth living? And more importantly, was this voice even worth anything now? What life did I have to return to? What could possibly be left for me except disappointment and reminders of all that was lost, archaic symbols of a past that would never transpire into a future?

Some might say that I am overreacting. Sure, I should be pissed and regretful of all that I lost, but shouldn't I also be appreciative that I am getting out now? I am forty-seven, true, but I'm not dead. I still have choices and chances ahead of me; the possibilities are just waiting for me. My name has been cleared, the battle has been won, even though it took longer than expected. I am free. Some unlucky souls would die for this opportunity, no matter how long it took.

Certainly, the potential for sunshine warming my skin outside of these bars, the chance to eat real food and decide what I do every day, has lightened my spirits. I can't wait to be able to simply drive to a fast food restaurant just because I feel like it or get in the car and just go anywhere I want. It will be great to leave my house without being patted down for weapons, to share a meal with people other than a burglar and a true murderer. I can find a job, find a purpose to my daily life, other than just surviving. I can go to sleep in a bed that isn't underneath a guy I barely know. I can wake up and walk out of the door of my room, free to encounter the day. I can buy a house, meet new people. I can choose my destiny. Maybe I'll even get a dog or go on a vacation. In some ways, I can't wait to get out there and make up for all of the things I missed, to just explore and experience. I can't wait to fill my life story with more than just a jail cell.

Despite these lists of things I can't wait to do, a part of me knows that all of this will be somewhat pointless. I can go to Hawaii for a month, I can go skydiving, I can eat the biggest burger in America, but I'll never be happy. Things will never be okay. I have been tainted by a lie, ruined by circumstances, forever changed by the drop of the gavel. I cannot go back to that fearless, free boy I once was. I cannot grasp that enthusiasm for life I had before. I can pack hundreds of experiences into the next few years, but what for? What will it all mean? I have been hardened in some ways that are irrevocable. I have lost faith in much of humanity. I have lost faith in higher powers as well. How could a just God allow this to happen? What was the purpose of this? Why me?

These questions battle with my mind and heart every day, wrestling with the peace of my soul. In prison, time is the only thing you have too much of, so I have had a lot of time to do soul searching and to wonder what will happen if I ever get out. I have come to the conclusion that life can never be the same and that my faith can't either. Some men in here find a stronger sense of faith due to the circumstances. For many, like me, though, God becomes as distant a figure as freedom. Especially those in my boat, those who are truly innocent. Yes, God tests us, but isn't this a bit extreme? Why are some tested more than others? What did I do to deserve this?

Amidst all of this inner turmoil also lies confusion. Where do I go from here? My résumé only has laundry-folding in the correctional center. True, I will be exonerated, my criminal record wiped clean. But will this matter in the real world? In a perfect world, I would be treated with pity. Society would feel somewhat of a debt to me for the wrongdoing against me. In the real world, though, I can't help but think that I will be shunned even though I haven't done anything wrong. The stigma of prison will stamp itself on me, even if this isn't where I belong. I will be outcast with the rest of the criminals, if not for my record, then for my lack of skills and contribution to society. What's the best that I can possibly do out there without training, experience, or a degree? Is hamburger-flipping in my future? Has it all come to this?

A part of me can't wait to sniff the air of a free man, but a part of me fears that the air will quickly turn polluted.

I walk into the meeting, my face heavy with grief and worry.

"Mr. Jones," the District Attorney says. I nod silently toward him in acknowledgment of his greeting. "On behalf of the state of Pennsylvania, I grant you exoneration from all counts held against you. I also grant you a settlement determined at an amount of $400,000 for your pain and suffering over the past twenty-eight years. You are free to gather your things and go."

And with that, I am finally free to walk out of the prison for good. I sit for a while in silence, disbelief leading to hesitancy. *It's over*, I say to myself. But in the back of my mind, I wonder if it really is.

Chapter Sixteen
Rust Bucket Road Trip

~ Corbin ~

After my things are gathered and I change into the outfit my dad brought for me, I am free to walk out of the prison. It's an odd feeling to be able to walk out of the gates. They slam shut behind me as I finally reach the outer gate. I look over my shoulder, almost expecting to be detained for escaping. Yet no guard comes after me. Instead, I am almost detained by another type of authority—the media. My story has apparently become a news sensation in the past few weeks. I dodge flashes and questions, just wanting privacy. I walk beside my dad toward his station wagon, my face down. We manage to shove away some pushy media outlets. My dad starts his car, yells a few harsh words out the window, and threatens to run down any SOB who doesn't get out of the way. Coming from his frail figure, the words seem misplaced. Apparently, the camera crews sense this, too, because amazingly they obey him.

Age has not crept up on my now seventy-five-year-old dad; it has almost bowled him over. He uses a cane, arthritis threatening to steal his ability to walk. His hands are shaky with the onset of Parkinson's, and his mind isn't always one hundred percent on. Yet, when the time came to turn to someone for the details of my release, he didn't hesitate to take the reins. Even though I knew it wasn't easy, he made arrangements and answered all types of questions. He has dodged the media at his home for weeks since word got out about my release. When the day finally arrived, he sat in his car for the three hour drive to pick me up.

Sitting beside my dad is, in some ways, like sitting beside a virtual stranger. It's not his fault, though. He never abandoned me or gave up on me. The harsh realities of physical distance, nonetheless, have strained our connection, despite his attempts at letters and phone calls. I know that he has done his best. My dad did not visit me often during my sentence, but he came whenever he could manage. It was not an easy affair with his ailments, but he always managed to make it to see me at least once every few months. Although his visits weren't frequent, his letters were. Written words cannot substitute for face to face interaction, but they have helped. We may be on the verge of "stranger" status, but I know there is hope for a rekindling of our father-son relationship.

Many weeks, my dad's letters were the only letters I received, and they helped keep me out of the grips of complete isolation. His words weren't gushy or overly optimistic. They were often quite simply details of his everyday life, which had become almost as monotonous as mine in prison. He had never remarried after my mom, choosing a life dedicated to his work over any personal relationships. In the early days, he was my staunchest supporter in the battle for my life. Even years after the verdict, he continued to do everything he could to turn things in my favor. It was he who wrote to various foundations and groups repeatedly in the past decade, hoping against all odds that his letter would be picked out of the thousands they received. It took a lot of time, but his pursuits finally achieved success about a year ago when a group agreed to fight for my cause.

It was an understatement to say that I owed my dad a lot for all that he did over the years. In a way, it wasn't just my life that was ripped from me—it was his, too. He was robbed of the chance at seeing his child become successful or have children. He was robbed of a family because I was robbed of a family. I could see that we had a lot in common because of the droning lives of seclusion we had been forced to live.

Yet here we were, rising from the ashes together, ready to embark on a new era. Who could be sure what that era would hold, but at least we would now have each other. My dad wouldn't be all alone, left to care for himself and the house in his condition. So the trusty station wagon squeaked along the road, heading into the distance, speeding

Voice of Innocence

away from the nightmare that had ripped our lives from us.

Since I didn't have a license, my dad was forced to drive us home. We sat in silence for a few minutes, both stunned that this was truly happening. It seemed surreal and anticlimactic. After all that had happened, here's where it ended. A rust bucket station wagon with oldies tunes belting in the breeze, windows down, taking us back home. When my dad finally spoke, I was shocked by his words.

"So are you going to go see her?" he asks, eyes not leaving the road.

"Who?" I question, looking over at him.

"Emma, of course. I thought you'd be anxious to see her."

I sigh, shaking my head at the mention of her name.

"I don't think so. It's been so long. I don't think it would be good," I mumble, staring at the trees passing by.

"Son, what do you mean? You don't think she's thinking about you? Your story has been on every news station for the past week. I'm sure she's expecting you," he says, glancing over at me for the first time. We are stopped at a red light.

"She's married. I don't think she'll want to see me," I mutter.

"Son, she's still living in town. You're bound to run into her at some point. You might as well make it on your terms," he reports, and then reaches over to turn up the radio.

We spend the rest of the ride in easy silence, both lost in our complicated thoughts. I had been considering the idea of seeing her for decades. Yet, now that it is a possibility, I am reluctant. How would I feel about seeing her again? What would it do to her? How could I face her after that meeting so many years ago? How could I admit that I was wrong? Questions dizzy my mind until I drift off in the passenger's seat, not ready to take over the driver's seat just yet.

Chapter Seventeen
Imperfections

~ Emma ~

A gusty chill shivers through my spine as the once-gentle breeze gushes with newfound intensity. The threat of an incoming storm crashes into my thoughts like a sailboat careening into an undetected rock. The brewing storm creeps through my bones, prompting me to face the present day and head for cover.

"Hank...Hank, c'mon, let's go inside," I say as I shake the mammoth-sized dog awake. He snorts and groans, stretching to his feet with a sense of lethargy still ricocheting through his bones. I reach for my almost-empty glass and stumble to my own two feet. Hank follows behind me with painfully sluggish movements. At this rate, we would drown in the rain before we spanned the whole ten feet to the kitchen door. Maybe it was time to stop feeding Hank so many hot wings, pizza, and peanut butter sundaes. Then again, I think as my empty hand absentmindedly feels my ever-growing stomach pooch, maybe I could afford to eat some celery and carrot sticks, too. My mother's voice rings in my mind like a nightmare.

"All of that wine you drink is either going straight to your ass or to a disgusting, blubbery pooch on your stomach. And trust me," her nagging voice echoes in my brain, *"no one's going to want to jump your bones when that happens. No one."* Great. Now the woman was torturing me without even being around.

Sighing, I slide open the kitchen door and glide inside. Hank groggily follows, groaning in agitation at the prospect of moving locations yet again. My restlessness was ruining his nap. After finishing the last sip of the alcohol (I'd worry about the stomach pooch tomorrow and do a few extra sit ups), I strategically stack my glass in the myriad dishes overflowing from the sink. I decide to retreat to the couch, pulling out a magazine on the way. I hope that celebrity gossip and makeup tricks will numb my overworked mind. Hank, sick of my inability to sit still, plops down in the middle of the living room floor. He is snoring in about two minutes. I envy his lack of worries and thoughts. I wish I could succumb to mindless sleep so easily.

As I flip the pages of the magazine, I note two things. One, none of the models have any resemblance of a stomach pooch. I guess they never sip wine. Or down a few dozen hot wings. Oh well, I guess someone has to sacrifice in order to be in the magazine. I'm just glad it's not me. The second thing I notice is that the models and the "life-changing" beauty products advertised are all streaming together into a pile of pointlessness. No matter how hard I try, I cannot focus my mind on anything tonight—anything except for him.

Plopping the magazine into my lap, a new thought claims my mind. Why were only the happy moments of our relationship floating relentlessly through my mind? True, our love had been hopelessly idealistic. We had been, as cheesy as it seems, the center of each other's universe. There were zillions of ridiculously romantic moments in our book of memories. The majority of our days, I had to admit, began and ended in a dream-like state of ecstasy. Just being together, talking to each other, or even thinking about each other electrified us. In Corbin I found a seemingly unattainable joy, comfort, and a vivacity equivalent to an adrenaline rush. Unlike other couples, we had not endured the rocky roller coaster of many typical teenage relationships, at least not for the most part. I watched friends endure breakups and reconnections with only a few hours separating the two "life changing" events, while Corbin and I stayed steady on an even, Zen-filled road of joy. In short, we were the couple that everyone would love to hate out of sheer jealousy.

Nonetheless, our love wasn't always easy or perfect. Like all couples, we had our shaky moments. We argued. We gave each other the silent treatment. I cried, and he swore. We pushed painful buttons, and we pushed each other away.

Lindsay Detwiler

Our worst fight lasted two agonizing weeks. It was during September of our senior year. Looking back, I had been ridiculous in my stubbornness. I had let my trust in others outweigh my trust in Corbin, my trust in us. I had let doubt and self-consciousness cloud my faith. Looking back, I would do anything to have those precious, wasted moments back.

* * * *

Memories

It began on a Friday. Corbin was out sick. It was a genuine illness this time, unlike the "Friday Flu" he sometimes got. I glumly walked into the lunchroom alone, counting the hours until I could head to Corbin's house with some chicken soup and *Jaws* to cheer him up. After claiming my less-than-delicious-looking chicken patty and fries, I grabbed my usual seat across from Jenn, Hannah, and Katie.

"Hey guys," I said, the melancholy in my voice hard to disguise.

"Oh, hey," Katie said. "Where's Corbin?"

"Sick."

"Wait, you mean he's not attached to your hip today? A whole day apart? How will you ever survive?" Jenn said, rolling her eyes.

"I don't know," I glowered. Lately, she had been a little edgy toward me and especially toward Corbin. I didn't understand it.

Katie sensed the tension. "She's just kidding, Emma." She shot Jenn a warning look.

"Well, I'm just worried about her. She can't live for a second without him. How will she handle it if he leaves her or something?" Jenn said, feigning concern.

"Well, he won't," I declared, staring across the table at Jenn. What was her problem today?

"Don't be so sure," she muttered under her breath as she plunked a fry into her ketchup.

"Jenn, don't," Hannah said, speaking up for the first time.

"What's that supposed to mean?" I half yelled across the table. "Okay, Jenn, cut the crap. What's your problem?"

"It's not my problem, Emma. It's kind of *your* problem." Katie and Hannah just stared at her, as confused as I was. They didn't say a word,

Voice of Innocence

curiosity goading them into silence.

"What are you talking about?" I murmured, a little softer this time.

"Let me ask you this. Where were you and Corbin on Tuesday night?" she interrogated. I felt like she already knew the answer.

"Tuesday?" I stopped and perused my recollections. "Tuesday...Corbin was with his dad. We didn't hang out. He had to help him paint their bathroom. Why?"

"Wrong," Jenn said, matter-of-factly, not even bothering to look up from her French fry.

"What do you mean 'wrong'?" I retorted.

"I mean...I saw Corbin on Tuesday," she revealed without even looking up from her sandwich. She took a bite as if the conversation wasn't even worth her attention.

"Where at?" I asked, humoring her. So she saw him out somewhere. Maybe he had run for more paint brushes or something. Big deal.

"I saw him at the diner," Jenn asserted, hesitating to gauge my response, looking up from her tray with somewhat of a smirk.

"Okay..." I stammered, still not seeing the big deal.

"I saw him at the diner...with Bridget Hodges," Jenn said, wincing a bit on the statement as though she could feel my pain.

"Shut up," I spewed at her, ready to pounce across the table.

"Well, believe me, don't believe me, I don't care. You'll be the idiot when everyone else finds out," she revealed, continuing to stuff her face with food. She shrugged her shoulders and pursed her lips, staring off into the distance like she hadn't just dropped a bombshell on me.

I felt my stomach drop with a whoosh and tears start to sting my eyes. As a knee-jerk reaction, though, I tried to dismiss the accusation as false. Bridget Hodges lived down the street from us. Although she was a nice girl, we had never been close. I had never even seen Corbin talk to her.

I finally gave in to Jenn and asked, "What time?" as though more details would help me disprove the theory.

"Five o'clock. My family and I were eating there. They stayed for an hour or so, and then they drove off in his truck. I'm sorry, Emma, I didn't want to tell you. But I thought you should know the truth," Jenn assured, seemingly genuine remorse filling her face. Katie and Hannah's mouths fell open as though they were shocked, too. I guessed it was the first time they were hearing all of this.

Tears threatened to stream down my face. I squinted hard, trying to hold them in. Surely there was a mistake. Corbin, lying to me? Out with another girl? Things had been great, beyond great lately. He had even picked me flowers on Monday. This had to be a mistake. But why would Jenn lie? She had a boyfriend, and she barely ever spoke two words to Corbin. It wasn't like she wanted him for herself.

"Are you sure it was him?" I implored, convincing myself mentally that she had made a mistake.

"I'm positive," Jenn added. "I had a perfect view of him."

"Did they see you?"

"No, I don't think so. They didn't seem to notice me," she reported. "Look, Emma, I'm sorry. I mean, maybe there's an explanation," she included, trying to reassure me.

"Yeah, I'm sure there's an explanation," Katie declared hurriedly. She reached over and put her hand on mine. "Emma, it's going to be fine. I'm sure of it."

"Yeah, and besides, if he's a cheating asshole, you'd rather find out sooner than later, right?" Hannah observed with nonchalance.

"Hannah!" Katie scolded, shaking her head.

I couldn't hold it back anymore. Tears rolled down my face. "I'll talk to you guys later," I managed to whimper over my shoulder as I gathered my books and headed toward the bathroom, not even bothering to throw out my trash.

"Emma!" Katie yelled to me.

"Give her space," Jenn said to Katie and Hannah.

I didn't hear the rest. I rushed to the bathroom, swiping at my tears and trying not to fall apart. Once there, I locked myself in a stall and tried to pull it together. How could he do this to me? Bridget was undeniably pretty, her golden-blonde hair bouncing in beautiful curls around her face. She was on the girls' basketball team and was perfectly fit. But still, how could he do this to me? Things had been perfect between us, especially lately. I wanted to dismiss it as a lie, keep going as if I hadn't heard this. I didn't want to break the connection we had. I didn't want to lose the easy days of laughter. But how could I just ignore

Voice of Innocence

what I'd learned?

Sure, maybe Katie and Jenn were right, maybe there was an explanation. But what could possibly explain this away? What could possibly justify Corbin lying to me and going out to dinner with another girl alone? I thought about the possibility that Jenn was lying, but she had no motive. Sure, we hadn't been exactly close lately, but I still considered her a friend. It's not like she wanted Corbin herself. She and Rodger had been going together for the past four months, and from the looks of it, they were doing great. I had to face the facts. Things between Corbin and I weren't what they seemed.

I emerged from the stall and peeked in the mirror. I was a wreck. I grabbed a paper towel and wiped off my tears and running mascara. I still looked awful. "Pull it together," I said aloud to myself. Great, now I was going crazy, talking to myself. I took a few minutes to calm down. I would push this out of my mind until later. I had to get through the day. After all, I couldn't skip my afternoon classes. My schoolwork was all I had left now. This thought threatened to send burning tears down my face, but I resolved to tough it out. After a few minutes of calming down, I walked out of the bathroom. The bell rang, signaling the end of lunch. *Thank God,* I thought. At least I wouldn't have to face the girls again. It was humiliating.

I attended my last three classes of the day, focusing hard on cells and Hemmingway and volleyball. On the bus ride home, I thought about how I would handle the situation. Clearly, today wasn't going to be a great day to confront him about it. Although he deserved no kindness on my part, I thought it best to wait until he was at least feeling better. Yet, I couldn't face him without bringing it up. So I decided to do something I hadn't done in the years that we had been together—I went an entire day without speaking to Corbin Jones.

On Saturday, he called the house. My mother handed me the phone.

"Hey, Emma. What happened to you yesterday? I missed you!" he proclaimed, sounding as if he truly meant it. I almost gagged at the prospect. He still sounded nasally from his cold.

"Um, I was just busy. Homework, football game, you know the drill," I sneered, faking nonchalance. It was hard.

"Oh…well, I'm feeling better today. What do you want to do?"

I hesitated. This was going to be painful. But I had to do it. I couldn't keep going on like this. "Oh, well, we can do whatever you want. As long as you don't have other plans," I snarled, hinting at what was to come.

He densely paused for a minute. "Why would I have other plans?"

"You tell me," I demanded, huffiness filling my voice.

"Okay..." he said, confusion underlying his voice. "Well, anyway, why don't we go to our tree and have a picnic? It's going to be getting cold soon, so we might as well enjoy what nice weather we have left. I'm not feeling great, but I'm a little better and I still want to see you. I'll pick you up in fifteen?" he said, ignoring my coldness. He probably attributed it to school stress or moodiness.

"Okay. See you then," I added with coolness. I hung up. I said goodbye to my mom and headed to my front porch to wait for him.

He was there, right on time. He kissed my cheek and grabbed my hand, pulling me in for a hug. I tensed against him.

"Hey, I missed you!" he declared. I didn't reply.

"What's wrong?" he asked. "I'm not contagious anymore..." he added jokingly, but I did not smile.

"We'll talk about it when we get to the tree," I mumbled, pulling away from him and looking at the ground. I started walking in the direction of the park.

We walked in a tension-filled silence, something that never happened between us. I guessed that Corbin sensed what was up. I wondered if he knew that I knew.

We got to the tree, and I turned to him. Pain again panged in my stomach, threatening to overturn my calmness. I had promised myself that I would preserve my dignity and be strong. I wouldn't cry. Now, I wasn't so sure if I could fake the strength.

"I know about Bridget," I professed, jumping right to the punch. I couldn't bear to prolong this.

Corbin crinkled his eyebrows, looking at me in confusion. "What...what are you talking about?" he inquired, reaching for me. I pulled back, not letting him touch me. I didn't want my emotions to usurp my rationale.

"I know about last Tuesday. Jenn saw you. Game's over," I stoically snapped.

"Emma, I don't know what you're talking about," he said reservedly. Befuddlement careened with his expression, almost convincing me that he was truly confused. He was a good actor.

"You at least could be honest with me now. I know the truth. Stop lying," I rambled, verging on the edge of hysteria. Anger overthrew my calmness. "I thought what we had was real. And now I find out it was a lie. How long's it been going on, Corbin? How long have you been going out with her?"

"Emma, slow down. I don't know what you're talking about," Corbin inched closer to me. I looked him square in the eye.

"Last Tuesday, when you said we couldn't hang out because you were painting the bathroom. Yeah, well, apparently not. Jenn saw you with Bridget," I yelled.

"Emma, I *did* paint the bathroom. I don't know what you or Jenn are talking about. You can ask my dad," he said calmly, still perplexed.

"It figures. You can't even tell me the truth now. You're a coward. You're a bastard. You're worse than a bastard. Leading me on all these years. *Years.* Wasted. With you. I thought we had something special. Here, I've been thinking about weddings and houses and kids, and you're off with Bridget. And that's fine, if I'm not what you want," I screamed. Corbin stood perfectly silent and still, letting me finish my monologue. It hurt, but it felt good to get it off my chest. "But you could at least be man enough to tell me instead of sneaking around behind my back. God, I'm an idiot."

"Emma, listen to me. I swear to you, I don't know what you're talking about. I painted the bathroom last Tuesday with my dad, just like I told you. I never even speak to Bridget, let alone go out to dinner with her. You're the one I love, the only one. You know that," he demanded, walking toward me with a wistful, pleading look in his eye. Those doughy eyes and familiar hands seemed to welcome me back to him, enticing me to forget everything and bury myself in him. But I couldn't. I had committed to the story. I had committed to believing it. I couldn't back out now. I had to be strong and face the facts. I couldn't give in to his charm. The truth of the situation hit me like a bus skidding into the back of a minivan. Tears started flowing down my cheeks despite my best effort to restrain them.

"I just don't understand why," I pleaded, looking into his eyes again. I maintained a bit of distance between us.

"Emma, what can I say to make you believe me? I love you," Corbin offered, a hint of pleading permeating his words. I paused, contemplating his words.

"But why would Jenn lie?" I asked, hoping he could come up with a satisfactory answer that could put this whole thing behind us. He couldn't.

"I don't know, Emma," he said, walking closer. He put his hands on my shoulders and locked eyes with me. I felt my stomach plummet even further, feeling what I was truly losing, what I had lost.

"All I know," he vowed, "is that I love you. I would *never* cheat on you. I don't want anyone but you," he said. I stood for a moment, tears still gushing down my face while looking into his eyes and seeing all that I was, all that I wanted, right there. And yet, something had changed. Something had come between us, floating in the small gap.

It was doubt.

"I don't know," I squeaked, a newfound sense of sorrow surfacing. "I don't know what to believe," I admitted. Corbin fixated on me with hurt in his eyes. He clenched his jaw, demonstrating how truly upset he was now becoming.

"You don't know what to believe? After all this time?" A hint of anger now boiled over in his tone. This only served to reignite the flame within me. "Emma, I can understand you questioning me about it. But for you to truly believe that I would do that to you? Do you not understand how much you mean to me? Has all of this time meant nothing to you? All of our memories, all of the things I've done for you?"

"Whoa, hold on," I bitterly protested, backing up from his grasp. "You mean to tell me that you're getting pissed at *me?* I'm not the one who was seen out with someone else," I said, raw emotion flooding my face.

"Like I said," he emphasized, "I have no freaking idea what you're talking about. If you choose to believe that shit, then maybe we don't have anything real between us. If, after all the time we've been together, you'll believe some lying, jealous girl who you barely talk to anymore, well then, I guess that says a hell of a lot about us, doesn't it?" Corbin's eyes were no longer inviting or warm. They were menacing and angry, rage flooding every part of him. I was shocked at his outburst. More than that, I was hurt. I hadn't seen him this angry...ever. I hated it.

"Why would she lie?"

"How the hell do I know? But why would I lie? If your theory is right and I'm into Bridget, why would I lie to you and keep this going? What purpose would that serve? Use your head."

I hated to admit it, but it seemed rational. Yet, the stubbornness that resonated in my blood refused to give in. Now, it was almost a matter of principle. His snappy attitude, no matter how righteous it was, had pushed me to the edge. Anger flooded my whole being, forbidding me from seeing his point of view. The bridge between us had been temporarily blocked off, preventing me from reaching out to him.

"I'm sick of your attitude. I'm sick of dealing with this. I'm done," I roared over my shoulder as I stormed off.

"Don't walk away from me," he threatened. "You'll regret it."

I stopped in my tracks, turning back to him. "What's that supposed to mean?"

"It means that if you walk away from me, then you're walking away from us. Period."

The coldness in his voice scared me enough to make me pause and think about what I was doing. However, it also made me even more upset with him. If I meant so much to him, how could he make threats like that? A part of me wanted to believe that he wouldn't let me walk away, that he would come after me. So the masochistic piece of me forced me to take that step, away from Corbin.

"Fine, then," he spit, storming off in the other direction. My anger drove my footsteps into the dirt hard and fast. As I felt the distance between us widen, however, my steps slowed. They became more dutiful, more sluggish. Would I regret this in the morning? Was it over? Was the story true? My mind was muddled with endless questions and possibilities but not a single answer. I carefully strode up to the house, brushing through the door and to my room. Thankfully, my parents had left to run some errands or something, which left me to brood in peace.

The last thing I needed was a pep talk, or, worse yet, an empathy talk from my mother. The day passed with uncharacteristic slowness, the clock's loud ticking reminding me of how dull my life was without Corbin. A part of me expected him to show up at the door or call. Conversely, the entire day passed and I did not hear from Corbin.

I didn't hear from him the next day, either. Or even the next week. Several times, I had picked up the phone to call him, but I gently slammed the receiver down before I could hit the last digit. I just couldn't do it. A large part of me had reconciled the story Jenn had told me as false. In my heart, I knew Corbin wouldn't do something like that. Yet, I couldn't bring myself to say those two words—I'm sorry. The week passed on in agony. I would see Corbin from a distance in the hallways at school. He would look at me but didn't come by to say hi. He simply walked on without even acknowledging my presence. This was perhaps what hurt the most.

At lunch, I opted to sit at a table by myself instead of with the girls. I couldn't bear to deal with their pity or, worse, their questions. I didn't want to hear any more about the story or their ideas. So my textbooks, as usual, substituted for companionship. I couldn't help but rejoice when I saw Corbin also sitting alone at a table across the cafeteria. Still, he didn't give in and come over to me. It was murderous being so close to him and yet so far away. He didn't seem happy about it either, though. At least he missed me, even if he wouldn't admit it.

Things went on like this for the longest two weeks of my life. Stubborn to the core, neither of us would give in and apologize. I was frightened by how meaningless everything seemed without Corbin. My school days were filled with academics. At night, I moped in my room, going to bed at eight p.m. just to avoid empty time. Weekends were worse. Without our ritualistic visits to our favorite spots, my life was void of happiness and fun. My mom tried to cheer me up by taking me shopping and out to lunch, but it was no use. In fact, it just exacerbated the situation. Although I didn't tell her many details, my mother seemed convinced that I should apologize for the fight. She seemed assured that Corbin couldn't have done anything wrong. So much for family loyalty.

Just like the dilemma flew in on a Friday, it was also lifted on a Friday two weeks later. I was sitting at my table, alone of course, when he walked up, a chicken patty on his tray and a bashful look on his face.

"Hey," he offered weakly. "Is this seat taken?"

"I suppose not," I added coldly. The formality of the exchange seemed so awkward.

He sat down and for a moment, we just stared at each other. He finally spoke.

"Look, Emma, I'm sorry for the things I said. This is so ridiculous. I miss you so much," he confessed calmly.

With these words, the tension dissipated and the words came flooding out.

"I've missed you, too. And I'm the one who's sorry. I know you didn't do it."

With that he walked around the table to sit beside me. He put his arms around me. Despite the rules and hovering teachers, I relented to his touch.

"I know I shouldn't have gotten so mad. It's just, it hurt when I realized you didn't trust me," he apologized.

"I don't blame you. I just...I didn't want to believe it. I was so confused, and Jenn was so convincing," I explained. At the mention of her name, I peered across the lunchroom. Jenn was glancing over at us, seemingly distraught by what she saw. I would deal with her later. For now, I had some catching up to do.

"This was so stupid. These last few weeks have been hell," he said.

"They were for me, too. And my mom misses you," I professed, smiling.

"Did you tell her about it?" he asked.

"No. But you'll be happy to know that she took your side anyway," I admitted with a characteristic eye roll.

"Of course she did. No woman can resist my charm," he scoffed, stroking my hair.

"Well, that little fact is what got us into this mess to begin with," I said smiling.

"Let's not even go there," Corbin added while pulling away to take a bite of his chicken patty.

"Seriously, Corbin. I love you so much. I just don't want to lose you. And you're so great. Any girl would want you. I guess I was just afraid that maybe you realized that," I added hesitantly.

"Emma, honestly I'm not as great as you think. Not every girl wants me the way you think they do. Besides, even if they do, there's only one person I want, and she's sitting right beside me. I love you. Forever," he added seriously.

"I know. I love you, too. Forever," I smiled, overjoyed that it was finally over.

After school, I stopped by his house for our study date, although I knew we probably wouldn't get much studying done. It was a few hours into our "session," which turned out to be more of a make-out session since his dad wasn't home, when I had to make a "pit stop." It was then I noticed that the once bright orange bathroom was now a misty blue.

The next day at school, I confronted Jenn about the whole story. I presented her with the evidence that I knew she was lying. She knew she was cornered.

With tears threatening to overflow from her eyes, she muttered, "I'm sorry."

"Why, Jenn?" I demanded, stunned at the finality of the fact that she had made up the story.

"I guess I was just sick of seeing you two so happy. I was jealous. I know, I'm a bitch," she confessed.

I paused. *Yeah, you are a bitch,* I thought. But the softer side of me shone through. "Why are you jealous of us? What about you and Rodger?"

"We broke up. He cheated on me with Sasha," she admitted.

"I thought things were going great?" I asked, stunned from this new revelation.

"Yeah, so did I," she said.

"But what does that have to do with me?" I questioned, anger rebuilding.

"I know, it was stupid. I just...I was so upset over Rodger. And then there was you and Corbin, all lovey-dovey, all perfectly happy. I was jealous. I hated that you two were so overjoyed. You know, the whole misery loves company thing. I'm sorry. It was dumb. I don't blame you if you hate me," she muttered, eyes glancing at the ground.

I paused for a few minutes. I wanted to hate her for what she almost did. I should have hated her. But I couldn't. Even though she had incited the worst two weeks of my life, she also helped Corbin and I in a strange sort of way. She helped us see what we truly had. She made me realize that our love was real, that we were meant for each other. She made us realize that we truly couldn't live without each other. So I found myself wanting to forgive her.

"It's okay. I understand. Let's just forget about it, okay?" I said.

"Really?" Jenn asked, shock on her face as she gaped at me.

"Yes, really," I said with a smile.

Just then, Bridget Hodges strutted right by. We both burst out laughing.

* * * *

Corbin and I had other tiffs, of course, but none as bad as that fight. It was that fight that made me believe we were meant to be together, regardless of the circumstances. I believed that no matter what came between us, the universe would toss us back together somehow. If only this had been the case.

I sigh, realizing that even the bad memories catapult me right back into the good ones. No matter how hard I try, I cannot force a dark cloud to loom over the past that we share. I can try to focus on the blackness of our days, but the light always shines through. I am blessed with vivid, beautiful, happy memories from our days together. Yet, this is also a curse.

I realize for the first time that my back and shoulders are aching, either from my tensed position on the couch, or perhaps from the mental strain of the day. I lazily trod up the stairs, making a sharp right into the bathroom. I can't help but notice the misty blue color in a way that I hadn't before. What a cruel coincidence. Or perhaps it wasn't a coincidence at all. Perhaps this was the universe's way of sticking its tongue out at me.

I light a few vanilla candles, pour oodles of pumpkin spice bubble bath into the tub as I turn on the hot water. The oversized bathtub is perhaps another perk of my current life, one I have never appreciated as much as today. As I take off my socks and step onto the white tile floor, a shiver runs through my body. I quickly strip off the "man pants" and sloppy shirt. I pull the ponytail out of my embarrassingly greasy hair. As I reach into the linen closet for a fluffy towel, a washcloth drops to the floor. I bend down to pick it up when my eyes inadvertently catch a glimpse of something on my hip. I am frozen in place at the sight. I can hear the water softly thudding into the tub and smell the pumpkin aroma filling the room, but I cannot move. I am standing on the achingly cold ceramic tiles naked and free, yet my mind and heart are not here. They have again been transported to another time, despite my heart's protest.

Chapter Eighteen
Painful Promises

~ Emma ~

Memories

"*Happy Birthday to you...*"
A horrible, screeching voice boomed an off-tune version of the familiar song. I groaned as I kept my face buried in my pillowcase.
"*Happy Birthday to you,*"
Was I having a bad dream? At least in my nightmares, though, the voice was a little more in tune.
"*Happy Birthday dear Emma,*"
The voice was getting closer. I pulled the covers over my head in a vague attempt to hide from whatever was facing me today. The covers were yanked back as the last line of the song rang through the room louder and more forceful than before.
"*Happy Birthday to youuuu!*"
With the grogginess of sleep finally breaking down, I recognized my mother's voice as she basked in the last note way too long.
"Mom, what are you doing?" I asked, glancing up to see a pink frosted cupcake with a candle in the middle of it.
"Singing happy birthday to my freshly eighteen-year-old daughter. What's it look like I'm doing?" she smirked, sitting on the edge of my bed. "Now make a wish!"
I blinked at her, then eyed the alarm clock on my nightstand.
"It's seven in the morning. And it's Saturday. Are you nuts?" I interrogated, shaking my head.

"Actually, it's 7:02. The exact time you were born. Sooooo, you know what that means, don't you?" she half-sang. The candle wax was starting to drip all over the sugary treat still sitting on the plate five inches from my face.

"That you're crazy?"

"No, idiot. It means you are officially eighteen! An adult! And I'm officially old," she sighed. This temporary instance of bad news didn't keep her down too long, though. In a millisecond, she was beaming again. "Anyway, blow out the damn candle so you can eat your cupcake without a half pound of wax!" she ordered.

Pushing air through my teeth in extreme frustration, I obeyed. The sooner I did as I was told, the sooner I could go back to bed. I huffed and puffed and blew out the candle. I'm sure my mother would have been disappointed to know that I didn't make a wish.

She clapped in mock celebration. "Now, Corbin will be here in, oh, an hour or so."

"What?!?" I yelled.

"Yeah, he's coming in an hour. So get your lazy butt out of bed, get dressed, and then we can eat breakfast together before he comes. I'm sure he's got quite the day planned," she winked.

"Doesn't anyone appreciate the idea of sleep around here?" I asked grumpily.

"Sleep is overrated, anyway," she added. How could the woman be so chipper this early? I sighed, knowing it was no use arguing.

"Well, birthdays are overrated, too," I insisted as I climbed out of bed and headed for the bathroom. "What's for breakfast?" I asked, pausing in the doorway to look back at her. She was still perched on the edge of my bed. She gave me a look like I was an idiot, and then held up the plate with the now-dripping cupcake.

"What, do you think I made these for show?" she asked incredulously.

"Cupcakes? For breakfast?" I asked.

"Why not?" she said, stealing a tad of icing from the plate.

I shook my head. "You *are* crazy. How did I turn out half normal?" I murmured, stumbling to the bathroom. She just laughed.

After completing my morning ritual, slothfully due to my lack of

Voice of Innocence

sufficient sleep, I might add, I joined my mother at the table. Dad was, of course, at the office. Lawyers don't understand the concept of weekends.

"Soo...Corbin has a day planned for you," my mom insisted. I was worried by how excited she was. "Then, tonight we're having birthday festivities here! Dad promised he'd be home in time," she added with a hint of suspicion in her voice. Lateness accompanied my dad as often as craziness accompanied my mother.

"I told you guys I didn't want to celebrate," I argued. Birthdays and surprises had never been my thing. I hated being the center of attention.

"Too bad. Do we ever listen to you?" she observed as she bit into a pink frosted cupcake. There were at least three dozen of them on the table.

"When did you bake these?" I asked, changing the subject.

"This morning."

"Are you kidding?" I asked. "Do you ever sleep?"

"Nope, not really. It's a writer thing," she said smiling.

"Remind me never to be writer then," I mentioned. "These are good, though. Thanks," I said, truly appreciating the efforts she had put into making this day special.

"I'll wait to give you your presents until Dad's here tonight," she exclaimed. "You'll love them, I promise," she added as an afterthought. Like everything else, Mom got overly enthused with birthdays. Anything that could possibly involve a party and food pretty much enthralled her.

I devoured my cupcake, resisting the urge to gorge on a second. Then I went back upstairs to finish getting ready. I had no idea what Corbin had planned. I didn't even know he was coming to pick me up this early. I hated the prospect that my mom was in on his plan—the two of them conniving together was never a comforting thought. Not having a clue what was in store for me, I opted for a pair of jeans and a plain, royal blue shirt. Comfy, casual, and versatile—everything I needed to get through the day. I threw my hair in a ponytail and found my jacket. As I was applying a few touches of blue eye shadow and freezing a few reluctant wisps of hair with spray, the doorbell beckoned me. Within a few seconds, my mother was popping open the door, as usual. I skipped down the stairs and was greeted with another "Happy Birthday" and a bouquet of wildflowers.

"I'll shove these in a vase," my overly helpful mother offered. "You two have fun!" she called over her shoulder on her way to scrounge up the perfect vessel for the flowers she was admiring. She was awfully excited for this day to get underway. I shrugged and walked out the door with Corbin. The cool, March air slammed me like a knife. I was glad I brought a jacket.

"How's it feel to be old?" he asked jokingly.

"If I'm old, so are you," I said matter-of-factly. Corbin had turned eighteen back in September. "Now where are we going?" I begged.

Corbin shook his head in an outright refusal. "You're mom's right. You're horrible with surprises." I sighed, feeling like a conspiracy between Corbin and my mom was undeniable at this point.

* * * *

Try as I might, I couldn't hide the pure disdain that covered my face as the pickup truck lurched to a stop in a less-than-glamorous part of town. We were about fifteen minutes from home, but it felt as if we were in another country. The buildings around us would undeniably clamor to the ground if I shut the truck door too hard. A few shady characters eyed us from across the street, resting on the curb. I tried to nonchalantly avert my eyes from them, afraid of what staring too long might do. A truck that was even more dilapidated than Corbin's sat beside us, barely in the parking space. In front of us was a red brick "building," dingy and in severe need of repair. A glowing, neon sign read Ted's Tats. I glanced over at Corbin slowly, with shock and horror on my face.

"What the hell are we doing here?" I asked.

"What's it look like we're doing?" he beamed, seeming oblivious to our surroundings.

"Um, well, if we don't get murdered, raped, shot, or all of the above in the next five seconds, then I don't have a clue."

"Stop being so dramatic. We're fine."

"Are we fine? Because I don't call this," I said, motioning at our surroundings, "fine. I thought you were planning an amazing birthday surprise?"

"I did," he said with a smug grin on his face.

"What's the surprise? It better not have anything to do with Ted," I said, pointing to the neon sign. I knew deep down that it did, but I was in denial.

"No, it doesn't have anything to do with Ted, not really. It has a lot more to do with us," he said, getting out of the truck. I stayed in my seat, my customary stance when I was angry, disappointed, nervous, or all of the above, which was true in this case. He came around and opened my door. I didn't move.

"What do you mean by *us?* Corbin, what's going on? I hate surprises. I especially hate surprises that have to do with Ted. And shady neighborhoods. And most of all, 'tats.' This place doesn't even look safe," I argued, panic overflowing in my voice.

"Just relax," Corbin reassured me. "I did my homework. This place is reputable. Now get out of the truck," he ordered, yanking at my seatbelt.

"Why?"

"Why do you think?"

"Well," I proclaimed smugly, "I don't know what you're doing. But I know what I'm *not* doing here."

"Yes you are. Now don't be a pain," he said, grabbing my arm closest to him. "Get out so I can talk to you," he said.

"Talk to me? You brought me to this glorious place to talk?" I asked, pouring extra sarcasm on the word *glorious*.

"Stop asking questions. Now just get out, shut up, and relax," he ordered.

"Stop being so bossy," I sassed.

"Stop being difficult," he argued. He had succeeded in pulling me out of the truck. I humphed, knowing I had been defeated.

"Okay, now, remember that first day we met?" he asked excitedly.

"Nope. No clue what you're talking about," I denied, looking away. A grin threatened to spread across my face. Being difficult was kind of fun. I should try this more often.

"Can you just humor me, okay?" he pleaded, true frustration building in his voice.

"Fine," I begrudged. "Of course I remember. What about it?"

"Well, remember when I asked you to tell me some deep, dark secret? Remember?" I searched my mind for a minute, thinking back to that day. I shoved memories of his sparkling eyes and flowing hair out of my mind in order to retrieve the other memories. I didn't have to dig far before it hit me.

"Corbin, no, you can't think I was serious," I said, horror starting to fill my mind.

"Of course you were serious," he said, realizing that what we were doing was finally sinking in. "And so, today, your secret desire comes true," he announced. "Isn't this great?"

"Um, no," I contradicted him, truly terrified now. If only I could go back and retract those stupid words. How could I have known that a few years down the road, those words would lead me to Ted and his tats?

"Oh, come on, it'll be fine. What's a little pain?" he said, tugging on my hand.

"Um, a lot of pain, first of all. And second, I'm not going in there. I'm sorry, but your surprise sucks. You're going to have to cancel," I ordered. The prospect of needles jabbing into my skin was horrifying. The thought of what Ted potentially looked like, judging by the side of his building, was also enough to scare away even the staunchest tattoo connoisseur.

"I'll go first. It won't be that bad, you'll see," Corbin grinned. "Don't be such a wimp. Besides, what better way to assert your newfound adult independence than getting a tattoo?"

"What do you mean, 'you'll go first?'" I inquired, truly surprised.

"I mean, we're getting matching tattoos," he said. Hesitation filled his face, "I mean, if, well…" he stammered, "If you're okay with it. I mean the matching part. I just thought that it could be a sign—that we are in it for the long haul. I mean, I don't have any reservations about it. But if you do…" he suddenly seemed worried for the first time all day, tripping over his words as they spilled from his lips. I grinned. He was charming when he was being humble and awkward.

"Of course I don't have reservations about us, you idiot," I said, laughing for the first time. "I think it's kind of cute. But I can't," I said. Suddenly, regret crept up in my voice. I started to think about how serious of a step it was for Corbin to set this up, and for a moment, I had second thoughts about turning down his offer.

"Why not?" he asked, feeling relieved that my wavering had nothing to do with him.

Voice of Innocence

"First of all, my dad would kill me. *Kill* me," I annunciated with gravity.

"No he won't," he assured.

"How do you know?"

"Because I already asked your mom before I set this entire thing up," he beamed.

"What?!"

"Yep. She was cool with it, of course. She thought it was sweet of me. Plus, she said you need to loosen up a bit and do something crazy. She said it will be fine."

Great. Even my own mother thought I was too stiff. Just wonderful.

"Okay, fine, so my loony mother thinks it's fine. But my dad will murder me," I noted, groaning at the prospect. Sure, my dad and I weren't all that close. His job consumed basically all of his time. But as long as I lived in his house, his words still ruled, even if he wasn't around to enforce them.

"Your mom said she'd take care of it," he said. "So what else is stopping you? Come on, throw out another excuse so I can slam it down."

"Pain."

"Pain? Oh please, Emma, it'll be over before you know it. Suck it up. I'm not even entertaining that one. Any other excuses?"

I racked my mind for a valid reason. My brain was running down lists and lists of why this was a bad idea. This wasn't something I did. Period. But for some reason, I felt my mental resolve wearing down. Maybe I was just tired or overwhelmed from the shock of the surprise. Regardless, I felt excuses and rationale leaking out of my body, replaced with adrenaline and thrill. The more I considered it, the closer to the truth I came. If I was being truly introspective, the truth was I wanted to get a tattoo. I wanted to "live a little," so to speak. I wanted to do something completely out of character, completely crazy, and completely with Corbin. So I relented.

"Okay, fine. I'll do it. But one more question," I said.

Corbin smiled. "I knew you'd give in. Okay, shoot."

"What are we getting?"

He winked at me, shaking his head. "Do you have to ask? After all, it was designed by you."

I goggled him with both shock and wonder that he had remembered.

So, that afternoon, all two-hundred and fifty pounds of Ted tattooed a tiny white dove on mine and Corbin's hip. Despite the shear, unbearable pain, I was all smiles…well, eventually I was all smiles. After the tears in my eyes stopped stinging and the throbbing on my hip became almost bearable if not forgettable, I was able to revel in what I had accomplished that afternoon. I, Emma Groves, the squarest rule-follower around, had done something crazy. I had thrown caution to the wind, had taken a risk, had trusted in Corbin, and Ted, too. Best of all, Corbin and I would be forever tied together by this tiny symbol and adventurous afternoon, I thought as the bells on Ted's Tat's tinkled to announce our exit.

I cautiously sauntered out of the dilapidated shop, letting the screeching screen door slam against its own hinge. Each step jammed a figurative knife into my intensely sensitive skin. With the adrenaline and excitement wearing off, I was again starting to realize the downside of tattoos—agony.

"I could kill you right now," I whined. "I feel like someone's stabbing me."

Corbin, pretending to be Mr. Tough Guy, said, "It's not that bad. I don't even feel it." The grimace on his face suggested otherwise. He was feeling it, too.

"Admit it, it was fun," he said.

"Oh, yes, being jabbed with needles for forty-five minutes was a blast," I said sarcastically.

"Well, you'll be happy to know, then, that the rest of your surprise doesn't involve a single sharp object," he said as he started the truck. He flashed those perfectly white teeth as he said it. I paused for a second, looking at him, confused.

"What do you mean by 'the rest of your surprise'? You mean there's more?" I asked in true disbelief. This couldn't be good.

"That's what I said. Don't get all huffy about it. Just go with it for once, okay? I don't feel like hearing you complaining the whole way there," he said. "And don't even try to figure it out. I promise you won't."

Voice of Innocence

"Great. I can hardly wait for what's next," I said, shaking my head. Inside, however, I had to admit that I was a little excited. This surprise thing wasn't so bad after all. Besides, what could be worse than getting a tattoo? Of course, if my mother was in on this part of the surprise, I was terrified to even think about that prospect.

I glanced out the front windshield in a feeble attempt to gauge where the truck was headed. When we finally ended up on a familiar rutty road, recognition clicked in—we were headed to our tree. Okay, this definitely couldn't be a bad surprise.

After he had parked the truck in its familiar spot, Corbin dug behind his seat. He reached under the blanket that he kept in his truck for such occasions and pulled out his backpack. It was filled with the picnic essentials. We still hadn't outgrown our adolescent eating habits.

I smiled at him, saying, "Okay, you're right. This is a nice surprise." He gave me a mischievous look, which suddenly made me feel uneasy. Maybe I was underestimating him after all.

Lunch went as usual. I wolfed down my bag of chips and chugged a soda. I finished it off with a chocolate bar. Corbin ate the same items, except double the quantity. Everything seemed normal, but Corbin barely uttered two words, which made me more than a little nervous.

After we had finished lunch and scooped up the remnants of our trash, I realized that the anxiety on his face was more than a little discernible. It was overpowering his whole being.

"Corbin, what's wrong?" I asked. "You've been quiet since we got here."

"Nothing's wrong," he said reassuringly. "Here, just sit down for a second, okay?" He grabbed my hands as I sat back down on the blanket. Flashbacks of that confession he made to me years ago started plaguing my mind. I was terrified of what he might tell me. It couldn't be bad, though, right? He wouldn't wait until my birthday to reveal something else tragic or awful...would he?

Corbin knelt down on both knees beside me. I noticed that his hands were shaking a little bit as he began to speak. "Look, Emma, there's something I've got to say," he said. I nodded, encouraging him to continue. Inside, my heart was starting to sink.

"I know that you've been worried about next year, with us being apart and all," he said slowly.

I, of course, had been accepted to the local university. Although my family had whooped and cheered at the acceptance letter last month, I thought it was a little ridiculous. The true cheers had come a few weeks later when Corbin had received his acceptance letter to the Art Institute in Pittsburgh. His sheer exuberance at his future proved that art school had been more than just a passing thought to him—it was his ultimate dream.

While I was thrilled at the prospect of our futures holding everything we wanted individually, I couldn't deny that I was nervous about how our individual dreams would affect our common future. How could things stay the same if we were several hours apart? Certainly, it wasn't an insurmountable distance. Corbin would be home almost every weekend. Still, I wouldn't be able to see him every day. How would the separation change us? Would our relationship be able to survive without our daily interactions? Would we grow apart? The questions and uncertainties of the future invaded my thoughts and threatened to banish my excitement for the future. I had told Corbin about my concerns. Of course, he didn't share them. He felt that we would be fine, that we would make it. His confidence only made me feel worse about my lack of it.

"Yeah, I'm a little worried. I'm sure it'll be fine, though," I said, insecurity hinting into my tone.

"We'll be fine, Emma. We *will*," he affirmed. "But I know that you could use a little reassurance...some sense of commitment," he insinuated.

"Yeah, and we have that now. Remember?" I said, pointing where my aching tattoo now marked me.

"Yeah, we do. But I think we could use something a little more public," he said. Recognition of what was happening started to dawn on me. A new sense of anxiety panged my stomach, my mind, my heart. Panic also set in. This was all happening *way* too fast.

"Corbin, what are you saying?" I asked, wanting to know the answer, yet not ready to know either. My eyes poured over him as he reached into his pocket. He pulled out a black velvet box.

"Wait, that's not a..." I said, but Corbin interrupted me.

Voice of Innocence

"It is...sort of," he said.

"Sort of? How is it sort of?" I asked, rushing the words. Alarm sped up and slurred my pronunciation.

"Just be quiet for two seconds, okay? God, you're a control freak," he said, a nervous laugh following his words.

"Look, I know we're young. And we're not ready to get married, not really. But I am ready to promise you that I will marry you some day. I love you. Forever. So..." He opened the tiny black box that was now in his hand. "I bought you this. It's a promise ring," he said. I was staring at the shiny gold band studded with several tiny diamond chips.

Everything around us started to whirl and blur into a big pile of mush in my brain. I could barely focus on the ring or Corbin. My head was absolutely spinning. I loved Corbin with all my heart and knew that someday we would get married. I just hadn't expected it all to happen so soon. Sure, it wasn't an engagement ring. But it was the closest thing to it. I felt tears welling in my eyes, but I held them back. I couldn't utter a single word. I just stared at him while he continued.

Nervousness caused his words to tumble out so fast that they almost whirred right by me.

"Emma, I'm giving you this ring as a sign of our future together, of my confidence in our future. No matter how far apart we may be, no matter what dreams we may chase after individually, I want you to know that you will always be my first priority. I will always, always love you. I promise that no matter what life throws at us, I won't let anything come between us. This ring is a promise that someday I will replace it with a real engagement ring and eventually a wedding ring. As long as that's what you want." He paused now, waiting for an answer. His fingers aimlessly smoothed over the ring, waiting to rip it out of the box and shove it onto my finger.

I was still frozen. Shock had dilapidated my ability to react. In the movies, the girl always knew exactly what to say. The words came out effortlessly, followed by a passionate kiss. This was not going so smoothly. The only word to truly describe my reaction was *graceless*.

Eventually, three words came to my lips, and I barely managed to stammer them. "Oh my God," I proclaimed.

Corbin scrutinized me, scrunching his eyebrows. "Is that a good oh my God, or a bad one?" he asked.

I just stared at him, glancing at the ring. I shook my head in disbelief. I still couldn't believe this was happening.

"Um, yeah," I said unintelligently.

"Emma, yeah what?" Corbin's impatience was starting to shine through. The wait was killing him.

"Yeah, I want to marry you, too. Someday." I smiled at my clumsy words. Thank God I would have another chance at all of this when he proposed for real.

A smile pervaded Corbin's entire face, flickering through his brown eyes. He ripped the ring out of the box, throwing delicacy and smoothness to the wind. He glided it on the ring finger of my left hand.

"Perfect fit," he said, wrapping his arms around me. In fact, it was, almost like a sign of good fortune to come. I squeezed him tightly, then pulled back just enough to kiss him.

"I love you," I muttered when I surfaced from our kiss for air.

"I kind of love you, too," Corbin said back, grinning.

My shock was quickly replaced by a new feeling—ecstasy. The one person who meant the world to me loved me back enough to promise his future to me. Suddenly, the fears I had about the next year seemed juvenile. Corbin was in this for the long haul, and so was I. Life was going to be hard and throw us some punches, but we would manage. I felt sure of it. If I ever forgot, that shiny ring on my finger would remind me of what we had. If that failed, the tattoo would serve as backup. What more could I ask for? What more proof did I need? It had been a monumental day, and a truly special birthday. As we rose to stand, a thought suddenly struck me.

"Corbin?" I said, brushing his arm. He pulled back enough to look at me.

"Yeah?"

"One question."

"What?"

"What if I had said no? To the ring? I mean, didn't you kind of do things backward? Shouldn't you have asked me if I wanted to be with you forever before we got the matching tattoos?"

He just laughed. "Do I ever do things rationally?"

"True," I said, smiling, too.

"And besides," he added, "I figured I could always have Ted turn it into a black crow or something, worst case scenario."

"A crow? Lovely," I said, poking at his ribs. After a few more kisses, we gathered up the blanket and headed for the truck.

"Come on, we can't be late," he said as he rushed me to the truck.

"For what?"

"Your mom's extravaganza. You didn't forget, did you?"

"How could I," I said.

Corbin grinned. "She'll be so excited to see that ring on your finger," he said.

"She knew about this, right?" I said, knowing the answer.

"Of course. I asked her if she'd be okay with it all," he said as he started driving home.

"And? As if I have to ask," I said, shaking my head.

"And she is thrilled at the prospect of having such an amazing son-in-law in the future," he added. "Plus, she said she would change your mind if you turned me down. It was good reassurance for my ego," he said.

I shook my head. "Isn't she supposed to be on *my* side?"

"Well, she is," he said, looking at me. "What kind of mother would let this," he said, motioning to himself, "get away?" A smug grin filled his face.

I shook my head again. "You're hopeless," I said.

"Better get used to it," he smirked.

I peered down at my left hand. The tiny diamonds caught a ray of sunlight and glimmered back at me. I liked the look of that ring on my finger, the shiny gold enveloping the tiny, iridescent chips. Looking over at Corbin, though, I realized I liked the look of the guy who had put it there even more.

Chapter Nineteen
The Coffee Angel

~ Emma ~

I glance down at my hand now, noticing the absence of that particular diamond chipped band on my hand. A diamond solitaire and a solid gold band now sit where it once had rested, but they are not Corbin's. They belong to another man and another time. Truth be told, they belong to a woman who is completely different than that naive girl who relished in the simplicity of love and its promises. Sitting in that truck on my eighteenth birthday, I had wondered what the engagement ring Corbin would give me would look like. I wondered how he would propose, where we would get married. I never thought for a second that his promises wouldn't come true.

I realize that I have somehow ended up in the tub in the midst of my memories. Mountains of suds and bubbles cover my body as the now-chilled water taunts my skin, goose-bumped and wrinkled. As I debate whether or not I truly have to wash my grotesque, greasy hair, the phone rings, pounding in its urgency. Ignoring the water splashing onto the floor, I leap out of the tub, grab my towel, and slide across the tile, bone chillingly icy on my slippery feet. Trickles of water cascade down my back in the hall as I traipse to my bedroom where a cordless phone rests on its receiver. I pick up the phone, hoping not to zap myself from getting water on the receiver.

"Hello?" I say, my voice gritty from not being used for hours.

"Hey, baby, how are you?" The familiar voice, warm and sinuous, clutches me with its familiarity, making me feel at home. The depth of his greeting, as simple as it is, soothes the edginess in my soul. It's amazing how just a few words from him can melt away the coarseness of my inner being.

"I'm good, John. What's up?" Despite the comfort I find in his voice, my words still sound spacey. I'm not fooling anyone with my "I'm fine" act.

John rarely calls me while he's at work. His hectic schedule leaves few minutes for eating, let alone phone calls just to chat. Thus, I know he is worried about me, worried about what today might do to me. Maybe he is worried about what it might do to us.

"I just wanted to make sure you're okay," he admitted. Great. Just as I suspected, he is concerned about me. Do I seem that fragile to everyone these days? Everyone seems to think I am going to crack into pieces today. I feel like my family has worked out a suicide watch schedule, ready to pounce in with a SWAT team the second I seem on edge.

"I'm fine. Just took a bath and read a magazine. Hank's sleeping already," I added, hoping to change the focus of the conversation. I try to sound confident, collected, like it's a regular day. It doesn't seem to be working because John just breathes loudly in the phone, a sign of his uneasiness.

"Listen, Emma, I feel bad about leaving you. Maybe I can call Steve and see if he can cover for me tonight. I don't want to leave you all alone," John adds sensitively. That's John for you, always thinking about someone else. Always considerate, even if I don't deserve it. What other man would be so delicate about this situation?

"John, please, I'm fine. I promise. I'm actually getting ready for bed," I lie. "It would be pointless for you to come home. Stay and get your work done. I'll see you in the morning."

John pauses for a few moments. He finally gives in, saying, "Okay, if you're sure. If you change your mind, just call. Oh, babe, the alarm's going off. Got to go. Love you. I'll be home sometime tomorrow morning." And with that, the phone clicks.

Most women would be upset over John's absence. Missed dinners, late nights, and infrequent calls often strain an ER doctor's relationship back at home. Many women struggle with coming in second place. Eventually, the attraction of Jacuzzis, lavish vacations, and pricy shoes that are stereotypically associated with a doctor's salary wear off.

Material goods seem worthless when time and attention are what is truly craved.

John's hectic work schedule has never bothered me, though. Part of it stems from my father. I was used to him being gone for his job. I saw how hard he worked to support the family, and I appreciated his determination. The other part of my acceptance comes from the fact that I spent the majority of my adult life alone. I guess I'm just used to crawling into an empty bed and waking up to one just the same. John may not be around much, but the little companionship and time we spend together is more than I ever thought I would have.

I put the phone back in the receiver as I trudge back to the bathroom. A tidal wave has apparently struck the room. Puddles of water are oozing through the cracks in the tile, while suds drip from the edge of the tub. I pull the drain on the chilly water, throw my towel on the ground, and shove it around with my foot in a lazy attempt to mop up the puddles. It sort of works. It's satisfactory at least. Realizing that I'll be alone until at least mid-morning, I toss the man-pants and shirt back on. Hank doesn't care if I am a little smelly tonight. I don't care, either.

I pause in the hallway, decisions hounding me. I feel like crawling into bed and going to sleep would be a good idea. A part of me just wants this horrible day to be over. The other part of me knows that sleep won't come. There will be no reprieve under my down comforter. So I march back down the stairs. Hank has managed to flop himself onto the couch again, his chainsaw-cutting impression the only sound resonating in the whole house. I turn on the lamp on the end table and plop down beside him. As I reposition myself cumbersomely on the fluffy cushions, I catch a glimpse of my wedding picture propped up by the lamp. The silver frame accentuates my knee-length dress, shimmering in its white simplicity. A few lilies bloom out of my hands. John is in tan pants and a teal shirt. White sand caresses our toes as blue waves careen the shore behind us. In short, paradise paints a wondrous backdrop to the blissful occasion. Our smiles stem from genuine joy as evidenced by the deep laugh lines and shimmering eyes.

* * * *

Our wedding in Jamaica had been a shock to me. Not that I had ever pictured myself as the white church wedding type. It was the wedding

Voice of Innocence

idea period that was truly wondrous and unexpected. As months had turned into years, I hadn't expected to find love again. Sure, I hadn't been a nun after the incident. I had dated guys here and there, but usually the dates ended in polite goodbyes. A few had led to simple, unsatisfying relationships that ended in our mutual parting after a few months. If I'm being honest, I can't blame those guys I dated over the years because, in actuality, I wasn't really available to them. I found that no matter how wonderful a man was, he never lived up to the unrealistic expectations I had formed. Certainly Corbin wasn't perfect by a long shot, but distance and circumstance can sometimes jade a picture. For me, Corbin became a saintly figure whose image resided somewhere with the stars. I don't think a single man could have possibly touched Corbin in my mind, especially in those early years. I always managed to find an excuse, despite my mother's encouragement. I didn't like his career choice, he didn't have enough drive, he didn't want kids, he wasn't funny enough, he was too funny.

My dating life simply became an endless rut of excuses and reasons why no one was good enough. So after agreeing to several dates, including blind dates, I decided that the single life was probably my reality. As my youth eventually faded and I stepped closer to middle-age, I knew that it was more like a certainty. I figured I would be the mousey office lady whose biggest excitement in life was going to the bookstore alone on Saturday nights to live vicariously through characters in romance novels while sipping on Chai tea. I would be the woman who was set up on twenty blind dates by her desperate mother who feared she would die without ever holding a grandchild. I was the girl who would climb into bed with a slobbering, snoring dog her only warmth and comfort. Nevertheless, the thought didn't bother me.

Sure, it would be nice to share my life with someone, to find the excitement that I had owned in my teenage years. A piece of me, though, a piece I kept hidden in my depths, feared that a relationship would never work because I could never be happy without him. Part of me also feared that he would see it as a betrayal, that if things ever did work out, he wouldn't keep his promise. I guess I felt that if I was single, I hadn't completely given up on us, as ridiculous as that prospect seemed. So I continued into a life of solitude, surrounding myself with my family, a few pets over the years, and thousands of empty nights.

That was pretty much my life for over two decades.

And then, out of the blue, came John. He snuck into my life and my heart in such a way that I barely noticed it was happening. Suddenly, I found someone who might not be Corbin, but he could fulfill me in a way that Corbin hadn't, in a different way. Not better, just different.

It was hardly love at first sight. By the time John walked into that small café in the bookstore, I had banished such an idea from my entire core. In many ways, I had banished love altogether from my vocabulary and belief system. Scoping for men wasn't even on the radar or in my mind, which is probably why he was able to smoothly sneak into my soul.

* * * *

Memories

I was sipping on my mocha frappuccino—I had decided to be "risky" that day and spice things up, choosing this treat over my usual tea—and reading *Crime and Punishment* for the third time. There was something about an ax and a prostitute that could deaden one's sensitivity. Slurping on my straw, I realized with angst that my cup was empty. I sighed, reaching for my purse and standing from my seat to get in line. An empty cup with the tantalizing coffee aroma floating through the air wouldn't do. I browsed the menu, and when it was my turn, I ordered "the usual" (yes, the café worker knew my order). I read the total on the cash register—$3.42—and reached into my purse. I pulled out my wallet, and then it hit me. *What an idiot,* I thought. Right between the pickax and the old lady's scream, I had forgotten that I had spent my last few bucks on the mocha. Great. This was going to make me look like an idiot.

"Um, I'll be right back," I stammered at the clerk. I prepared to dash out of line and run to my car to scrounge up some change. I didn't have my credit cards or an ATM card with me. Of course. As fate would have it, though, I wouldn't need to do any of the above. As I prepared for my dash, I heard a smooth voice reverberate over my frantic words. "I've got it. It's on me." I turned to see the face of my rescuer and was shocked at my own sense of awe.

Before me stood a man who I approximated at six feet one. His blonde hair was sort of disheveled, but in a hot surfer-guy and not dirty, creepy man kind of way. His blue eyes were truly as clear as a June day or ocean water lapping at your feet—Caribbean ocean water, not the disgustingly gray Atlantic waters. As he smiled at me and handed the clerk his cash, I noticed two perfect dimples on his cheeks. A few lines wore on his face, demonstrating age in a way that was pleasant and notable. He was probably about my age. Something stirred deep within me, and it wasn't my mocha frappuccino. This feeling, though, had been such a distant memory that I quickly discredited it, allowing my embarrassment at the situation to take center stage.

The "coffee angel" who had rescued me proceeded to order himself a coffee. I managed to mutter "thanks," as I mentally surveyed my own outfit. I was wearing my old, trustworthy jeans. They made my ass look pretty okay, I thought with relief. Nothing spectacular, but nothing terrifying, either. I had on a simple, turquoise sweater and my hair was in a ponytail. I probably looked like the ultimate, English-major nerd. Which I obviously wasn't. But still, he was here, too. He couldn't judge me for spending my Saturday evening here. I glanced quickly to his hand and was relieved that I didn't find a wedding ring.

And then panic struck me. Was I worrying about this guy's relationship status? Was I devouring his looks like a hungry tiger? *This was ridiculous*. I, Emma Groves, hadn't ogled a man since...

Thankfully, I didn't have time to consider the rest, because the café worker called my name to pick up the order. *His* order was ready, too, and as he walked over to pick it up, he began to talk to me. In my flustered state, I stupidly forgot to listen for his name as the server called out his order. Genius.

"So, do you come here a lot?" he questioned as he poured cream and sugar into his drink and I reached for a napkin. I mentally tried to avoid brushing against him, afraid of what electricity I might find. He seemed a little nervous and self-conscious as well, like talking to women wasn't something he was accustomed to. He grabbed his coffee after putting on the lid as I grabbed my tea, heading toward my claimed table. I shuddered at *Crime and Punishment* propped open on the table. He was going to think I was some kind of psycho.

"Every Saturday," I said. Why did I say this? Now he knew I was a freak. "How about you?"

"Nope. First time here in months," he said. Of course not. He probably had a real life, complete with numerous social gatherings, hobbies, and women. This wasn't looking too promising.

We neared my table, and he noticed the empty seat. "Anyone joining you?" he asked.

"Nope. Just me and Raskolnikov," I grinned. Hey, I might as well just dump all of it on the table.

"A classics kind of girl," he nodded in approval. "Dostoyevsky's all right. I always liked Melville, though, personally." Okay, so maybe he was a little nerdy, too. I smiled back at him as he asked, "May I?" He gestured to the chair.

"Of course," I said, feeling a little looser now. This guy was easy to talk to. His warmth radiated around him like a lighthouse signal beaming across the Atlantic. "Thanks for saving me back there," I grinned, holding up my cup in a mock toast. "Guess my addiction is wearing on my wallet more than I thought. I can go out to the car and scrounge up your money," I offered, my cheeks undoubtedly glowing with humiliation.

He smiled and said, "It's fine. I'll just take an IOU. I'm John, by the way." He yanked out the flimsy chair and sat down.

"Emma. Emma Groves," I said looking into those mesmerizing eyes. As nervous as I should have felt, I wasn't. Besides asking the produce man where the kiwis were or taking my car to the town's mechanic for new brakes, I barely ever had contact with men. John just put me right at ease. I realized that for the first time in a long, long time, I actually was interested in learning about him.

"Emma. Nice to meet you, officially," he said, offering his hand across the table. It was warm and strong.

"So," he continued, "did you major in English or do you just like books?" he asked.

"The second one," I said. "My mom's a writer, so I kind of got it from her."

"Really? What does she write?"

"Romance."

"Oh, that's great," he contrived with a little less enthusiasm.

Voice of Innocence

"Not a romance fan?" I prodded.

"The genre of fiction? Nope," he clarified as I sipped my tea. "Then again, I don't have much time for books at all." He seemed truly disheartened at this prospect.

"Why not?"

"Work," he added simply. So he was a workaholic. I could handle a workaholic.

"What do you do?" I asked.

"I work in the ER," he said, taking a break to sip his coffee.

"You're a doctor?" I asked casually, glancing down at my hands grasping my cup of tea.

"Yeah. It's great, and I love it. But sometimes it leaves little room for socializing or normal life. Hell, I haven't been in here forever."

"Wow, that's great. I don't think I could do it. The long hours, the stress. It's admirable."

"Yeah, it's not quite as glamorous as they make it out to be on television. I wish I had time for my love life to be half as amazing as the doctors on TV," he added grinning.

I laughed. Not a fake laugh, either. A true, soulful laugh, something my body wasn't accustomed to these days. I felt a beam of life radiating from me, resurrecting from the depths of despair and darkness that had clouded most of my adult life.

"So what do you do?" he interrupted my thoughts.

"I'm a secretary. It's boring. Not admirable either," I said jokingly.

"Do you like it?"

"Nope," I said. "But I've been there so long that it's hard to leave, you know. I don't know where I'd go," I added. Why was I revealing all of this? This guy probably didn't want to hear all my sob stories. He was just being polite.

"A beautiful, well-read woman like you? Anyone would be lucky to have you," he said, looking at me with a hint of curiosity.

"Well, thanks," I said, not believing him. "So do you have the day off or something?" I asked him.

"I'm on call," he answered glumly.

"So no, then, I'm assuming? I bet you get called in all the time."

"Try every time I'm on call," he said. "Goes with the territory, I guess."

As if the universe were answering his complaints, a beeper on his belt went off. Taking another sip of his coffee as if to give him strength to acknowledge the call, he groaned.

"And it beckons," he said, grimacing over at me. "I'm sorry, but I've got to go." He seemed truly distraught over the prospect.

"It's fine. I've got someone waiting for me," I grinned as I motioned to the novel on the table.

"You need to find some better company to keep."

"Any suggestions?" I asked jokingly.

"I've heard that Conrad has some pretty interesting friends, although I'm not sure if Kurtz fares much better than good old Raskolnikov. Or, you know, there's always a romance," he offered, eyeing the vast shelves behind us.

"I'll keep that in mind," I said. "It was nice talking to you. And thanks again," I added, motioning toward my now half-empty cup.

"Not a problem. It was great talking to you," he beamed. I watched him throw out his cup and start heading to the exit. A tiny piece of me sunk as I realized that the one man who had managed to interest me, even enthrall me, was walking away. I'd probably never see him again. Before I could ponder this any longer, though, he stopped and turned back at me.

"Oh, and about that IOU," he mentioned. "How's next Saturday? I'm on call, but I should be able to make it here to feed my caffeine addiction before this damn thing goes off," he said.

I couldn't detain the huge grin that filled my face. "You've got it," I mustered. "And hopefully you won't have to help me scavenge under the seat for change," I laughed.

He smiled back. "It's a date then," he announced.

A date, I thought, *a real date with a gorgeous man whom I couldn't help but like.* Okay, so it wasn't the "I'll pick you up at seven" kind of date, but beggars couldn't be choosers, right? I knew I was in trouble.

And from there on out, my Saturday nights were devoid of mysteries, romances, and thrillers, replaced by a real-life romance instead. After a few weeks, my weeknights were filled, too. John worked crazy hours, and it was often hard to find time for a date. Even if we weren't physically together, we were mentally.

Before I knew it, I was trading in my plain sweaters and jeans for flirty, feminine dresses. I visited the cosmetics counter at the mall for the first time in ages and asked for all the works. I got my hair cut and highlighted. Finally having a reason to care about the way my ass looked, I joined a Tuesday and Thursday night exercise class. Where once I had sat log-like on the couch in my tiny apartment and ate TV dinners, I now couldn't seem to sit still. Energy and exuberance radiated from every pore. I danced around the apartment, repainted the bathroom, and even cooked myself exotic dinners. I even found myself singing in the shower, but I was cursed with my mother's horrible lack of pitch, sad to say.

I don't know why, but suddenly I felt like I had the energy to let a man into my life. Maybe it was just that enough time had passed, enough distance had been linearly placed between Corbin and I, that someone else stood a chance. Maybe it was simply because John was such an easy man to be around that you couldn't help but light up around him, to feel a sense of simple joy at the idea of letting him into your life. Regardless, I found that things were different with John. Unlike my other sad dating attempts, I found that although Corbin was often buried somewhere in my consciousness at all times, he wasn't the forerunner. I wasn't always comparing John to Corbin's standards. John inhabited a completely different portion of my awareness altogether, standing on his own two feet instead of standing in the shadow of a man who had become a ghost in my life. Finally, against all odds, I had the strength, the ability, and even the desire to let someone else in, to see where my life could go. I had the desire to let love take over my destiny instead of the darkness of solitude.

I wasn't the only one to notice the change in myself. My mom couldn't help but be thrilled at the sudden shock of energy in me. She noticed my new and, unarguably, better appearance. She made underhanded but quite obvious remarks about how my hair suddenly didn't look so mousey and that *something* must have opened my eyes to the wonders of the beauty world. When I turned her down for dinner one Wednesday night since I had a date with John, she finally snapped.

"Okay, who is he?" she demanded on the phone.

"Who?"

"Emma Groves, don't lie to your mother. It's bad enough you've been keeping secrets from me," she complained.

"What makes you think there's a *he* in my life?" I asked smiling. I knew I was going to have to tell her soon. I was just putting it off, choosing to savor my newfound happiness alone for a few weeks. It was actually fun having a good secret.

"Well, you don't look like crap anymore. You take the time to put on some real clothes and do your makeup. And you actually have life in your eyes," she said seriously. "So who is it?"

I sighed, abandoning any prospect of keeping my secret hidden any longer. "You don't know him," I said. "His name is John Ranstein. Dr. John Ranstein, actually."

"A doctor! Sweet Jesus, my plain-Jane, dull daughter snags a doctor? Guess my prayers at church have gone straight to God's ears," she exclaimed with glee. "I bet he's gorgeous," she added.

"You could say that," I grinned, ignoring the insults.

"Bet he's amazing in other ways, too," she snuck in, thinking I wouldn't notice.

"Mother!"

"Sorry, I had to," she laughed. You would think that at her age, she would mellow out in the inappropriate comments department. In actuality, I think she only got worse with age.

"Enough," I yelled. Any guilt I had felt for keeping this secret dissipated.

"Well, bring him to dinner sometime soon, okay?" she added. *When hell freezes over*, I thought to myself.

"I have this great recipe for Tahitian pork chops. Oh, maybe I can make some triple chocolate cheesecake. And I'll have your father dig out that fondue fountain..." She hadn't changed an ounce. She was still the same, over-the-top woman she'd always been. After about five more minutes of her exploring the possibilities of this new relationship and what it could potentially mean for her Sunday night dinner, she finally agreed to hang up the phone. She promised she would be calling me soon to hear more details about John and to confirm our dinner plans. After a lot of secret eye rolling, I finally got off the phone. Sometimes secrets were okay, I decided all too late. I hoped John liked adventure because dinner with my mother was always a journey. I was worried it would end in calamitous disaster. I could always drown myself in the fondue fountain, I supposed, if things got too out of control. Or claim I was adopted.

I only had a week to ponder the possibilities because that was all my mother would allow me to keep John from her. When the incessant phone calls became too much, I begrudgingly agreed to dinner plans. I gave John a solid, one-hour conversation prepping him for the wacky woman who was about to engulf him. He smirked the entire time, telling me it would be fine. "You haven't met this woman yet. Trust me, she could be a deal breaker," I mumbled. He kissed me on the cheek, told me to stop worrying, and said that he couldn't wait for the Tahitian pork chops. I sighed in frustration, fearing the worst.

On the night of D-day, I was over-the-top nervous, but John was, as usual, relaxed and collected. He greeted my mother at the door with a bouquet of flowers, a truly winning choice. Naturally, my mother fell in love with him from the moment she took the flowers, shouting at my dad to find the vase because a handsome young man had finally appreciated her enough to get her flowers and didn't he get the hint. She rated John's looks as astoundingly gorgeous, meaning he had her approval. John seemed to be open to my mother's craziness as well. He and my dad actually had a lot to talk about, too, with both of them into classic cars. It couldn't have gone better, to my complete and utter relief.

Over the next few months, John and I spent as much time together as physically possible. We learned about each other, not able to take in enough information to quench our thirsts. It seemed secrets were just pointless between us. I knew there was nothing he could tell me that would make me like him any less, and I felt the need to be honest with him about everything. I felt the need to just be myself. Thus, I told him about Corbin two months after we met.

As with everything, John was overly understanding. He was even sympathetic. Not that John didn't come with his own baggage. He had been married right out of high school. She couldn't stand not being his priority, feeling as if his career came first, which, in many ways, it did. You don't marry an aspiring doctor thinking you're going to be first. I could tell there was still some pain from that situation, pain not unlike mine. Yet, with decades passing, we were both ready to start something new.

Physically, the chemistry was strong, especially in those first few months. I had been alone for some time. I suspected John had been, too. And so we were starved. Starved for love, starved for passion, and above all, starved for each other.

Four months after we first met, John got down on one knee at the bookstore's café. I was surprised but not shocked. Things between John and I were natural. It just seemed to fit, to make sense. I beamed and said yes without a second's hesitation. The servers who had become like family clapped in a circle around us while other regular customers cheered. As I leapt into his arms with a one carat diamond now perched on my ring finger, I couldn't help but think about how smooth the whole thing had been. I finally had gotten my movie star proposal, complete with a Chai tea and an audience. It just wasn't with the man I had originally hoped for.

* * * *

Hank flips and flops on the couch beside me, drawing me back to the present. I glance again at that wedding picture. Those smiles were as true as smiles could be. We had been thrilled to be joined at that tranquil ceremony, the sun grazing the horizon as we said our "I-dos." We were electrified that we had finally found companions, that our love lives hadn't remained empty through old age. I had found John at a time when I needed him most. He had reawakened me to life. I didn't just aim to exist with John in my world. I wanted to grab life and run. He had stirred my passions and my personality, roused it from the hollow inside of me. For that I would always be grateful.

Marriage with John is as easy as our dating life had been. Even though he works a lot, he always knows what I need and when. He is my best friend. I can't imagine not having him by my side, and I will always love him. Without him, who knows where my life would have gone, if anywhere at all.

Nonetheless, love is a funny thing. More specifically, second loves are a funny thing. For no matter how special that second or third or even fourth love is, no matter how much you can't live without him, the first

Voice of Innocence

one always creeps in. It's always when I least expect it. We'll be out to dinner and John will start talking about camping as a kid, and he'll creep in. I'll picture our tree in the woods and all of the moments that happened there. Or at Christmas time, I'll be sitting beside John at midnight Mass when the twinkling lights around the manger scene will catch my eye, and I'll go back to that barn where Corbin and I shared those special nights. No matter how much John fills my life and my heart, or how many years separate us as time marches on, Corbin always holds a place in my life. My relationship with John is always haunted by glimmers of Corbin. My heart is never completely my own.

    I reach for the remote on the coffee table, hoping to find mindless garbage to again clutter my mind. Big mistake. I should have known that he would be plastered on every channel, the star of countless news shows.

    I try to turn the channel but find that I physically can't. As the news anchor quickly divulges the basics about his release, I hear her refer to "the" date—the date that changed my life and Corbin's. The date that would haunt me every year as it passed by without him. The date that had sucked the life right out of me, turning me into a walking corpse, waiting, wishing, to die.

Chapter Twenty
Love Preserved

~ Corbin ~

The car screeches as it slows around the familiar bend. My dad eases up on the gas as we approach the house that stirs my youth within me. Has it been decades since I've been home?

As he parks in the driveway, I am tempted to jump out of the car and leap for joy at this familiar sight. Instead, I sit for a long minute, just staring at the structure that seems so recognizable yet so foreign at the same time.

When I first went into prison, I imagined what it would be like to run into this home, ransack the kitchen, and curl up in my own bed. I dreamt of this home so vividly that I ached for it to be true. I would have given anything to wake up in that bed, to walk down those familiar stairs in search of a pastry or a glass of milk. As the months turned into years and my hopes diminished to dust, this place seemed like a figment of my imagination. I thought I would never step foot on the plush carpet in the foyer or see those familiar baby photos hanging in the living room. Concrete and fluorescent lights had replaced the cozy décor of this home in my mind. Yet, here I was. Miracles do happen, I guess. Although, with miracles comes a lot of hell on earth.

I grab my bundle of prison belongings from the backseat to take into the house. I consider throwing the entire bag on the curb by the trash can in order to eliminate any remnants of that horrible time in my life, yet I cannot bring myself to do it. After all, no matter how atrocious that part of my life was, it was in fact my life. What other memories or belongings

Voice of Innocence

do I have left? I sling the bag over my shoulder, reminiscent of a broken-down Santa Claus. As my dad hobbles out of the car, he walks near me at the front. He shakily puts a hand on my shoulder.

"It's good to have you home, son."

I silently smile at him, truly believing he is thankful to have me back.

I follow my dad through the front door, oddly feeling like a stranger. How do I act in this alien world? How do I tread these waters? Simple things everyone takes for granted have become complex arrangements for me. I try to push my anxiety aside as I walk over that threshold into a new life that was once my own.

My dad has changed few things since I was last here. Those familiar lamps from my grandmother's house still flank both sides of the tan, reclining couch. I notice he has upgraded to a flat-screen television, complete with a DVD player. All of the photographs, the pictures, and the décor, which were always miniscule in amount due to the circumstances of our move, are in exactly the same places. I stand in the living room, glancing awkwardly at my father. Should I ask about it? How do I go about it? Will it seem too assuming?

My dad rambles nervously. "I didn't change a thing in your room, if you're wondering. It's the same as when you left. We can update it once you get settled in. Probably will need a few things, I'm assuming. We can go to the store tomorrow if you want. Why don't you go put your stuff down and I'll order a pizza. Sound okay?" As weird as this is for me, it must also be hard for him. He is used to living alone, not having to worry about another person's wants or opinions. It must also be troublesome for his own son to have become a practical stranger. It's not much different than inviting a person in off the street. We have a lot of catching up to do, yet we don't want to rush anything. The situation is overwhelming by itself. I thank him, though, say that pizza would be wonderful, and head up the familiar stairs to my room.

Most middle-aged men would cringe at the prospect of living at home with their parents, residing in the room of their teenage years. Certainly, living here is not my ultimate dream or plan. All things considered, though, as I open the door to my room, I am filled with a sense of peace. I feel at home, I feel free. To have your own room is something many take for granted, but I will not. If nothing else, my time in prison has put a lot into perspective as far as priorities and appreciation.

My dad told the truth—he hasn't changed anything. My deodorant still sits in the same position on my messy dresser beside a photograph of Henry, who died decades ago without ever knowing what happened to me. My stomach sinks at the thought. My books, movies, and clothes are all still strewn about the room. My bed has the same sheets, the same comforter, the same pillows. As I look at the mess from my teenage years, I'm filled with a deep sense of appreciation for my father's love. Growing up, I had never seen him as a loving, compassionate father. True, he never abused me and always made sure I had whatever I needed. But he wasn't the kind of dad who would tuck me into bed and read me a bedtime story. He didn't hug and kiss me or tell me he loved me. However, looking at the museum-like state of my room, I quickly realize how much I meant to him. This man stood beside me even when everyone else in my life quickly exited, discrediting my character and my story because of a single night. As the masses herded out of the picture, my dad faithfully stood by me. He was at every hearing, every motion, every sentencing, and every appeal. He fought for me when fighting seemed pointless. Most of all, as evidenced by this room, he never gave up on the hope that I would return. He loved me. He might not tell me these words directly, but he did something even greater—he showed me his love through his selfless, dedicated actions.

I take a seat on the bed, thinking about the last time I sat here, when I was still a free man. I had a life ahead of me. I had big dreams about the Art Institute and a successful career that I loved. I was getting ready for graduation and the next phase in my life, in *our* lives together.

Glancing at the nightstand, I see a note from a lifetime ago. I glance at it, although I still remember what it says.

1. Pick up flowers
2. Pick up tux
3. Music
4. Confirm reservations
5. Deliver dress

Voice of Innocence

6. Ring!

It was the list of tasks of a nervous boy about to do the task of a man. It was a list that would never be fulfilled and all but forgotten. It was a list that was cursed from the moment I put the pen to the paper, but I could only know that in hindsight. At the time, excitement pulsed through my veins into the pen as I wrote what I thought would be a momentous list for a night I would never forget. Instead, this list became a mockery of a future that would never happen, of a surprise that would never have the chance to unfold.

I slide the piece of paper through my fingers, thinking about the boy who wrote this list and how different he was from the man who sits here now. In reality, the boy who wrote the list and the boy he was a few hours later were two completely different entities. It was funny how the course of a few events could change one's entire life, could alter his entire being in such an irrevocable way that he would be almost unrecognizable. Yet here I am, a different being than the creature who thought this list would be accomplished and the world never hurt good people.

Chapter Twenty-One
The Red Dress

~ Emma ~

Memories

June 5, 1985

    Like two initials joined by a heart on the bark of a tree, the date was forever carved into my being.

    It was originally supposed to be a memorable day for positive reasons. It had been the last day of classes in my senior year. Our graduation ceremony was to be held the following evening at the football stadium. We would walk across that stage and say goodbye to our friends, our hometown, and our memories, in order to walk toward the new horizon.

    But the next day, while our peers donned the traditional graduation garb, we would don feelings of hopelessness, confusion, and betrayal.

* * * *

    Walking into my bedroom to put down my backpack for the final time, I noticed a note on my bed. I threw the backpack on the floor, rushing to read what it said.

> *Look in your closet. You'll find something special. I'll pick you up at 5:00. No barns tonight. It's about time we celebrate...in style.*

Voice of Innocence

Love, Me

I could tell who the "me" was immediately. Besides the *love* part, the handwriting was so horrific that I would know it was Corbin regardless. Even though I hated surprises, I felt a sudden pang of excitement and expectancy. Then I realized that my mom had to be involved…again. How else would Corbin have gotten all of this in my room while he was at school? Pushing back surfacing fears, I rushed to the closet and hurled the door open. Hanging dead-center on the rack of clothes, between my grungy T-shirts and sweatpants, was a fire-engine-red dress, sultry in every sense of the word.

This was not the kind of dress I would ever be caught buying.

The neckline plunged gracefully into a *V*, while the length was certainly shorter than I would ever deem appropriate. Its glossy satin fabric suggested that it would cling in all the right places, while seed-like beads grazed the bodice in intricate patterns. It was, in a word, fabulous. I couldn't even imagine what the night would hold for us. I rushed back downstairs to the kitchen to grab a drink, when I noticed another note on the table along with a camera.

Dad and I went out for dinner and a movie. Have a great time tonight, honnie! You deserve it. Lots of Love.
PS: take a million pictures, or else.

What was up with this note thing? I grabbed a soda off the refrigerator shelf, clicking it open with my fingernail. Slurping down the drink in a hurry, I decided that I should probably put a little extra effort into my hair and makeup. I didn't want to look like a child playing dress-up, after all. With that, I headed to the shower, feeling like I didn't have a moment to waste. I spent extra time lathering, smoothing, shaving, and moisturizing. By the looks of the dress, it seemed like the night would be magical.

For the next two hours, I primped, plucked, polished, dusted, twisted, curled, sprayed, and coated. It was more time than I had spent on my appearance in the past two weeks. Although I would never admit it, I silently wished that my mom was home to help me master the eye makeup that she was unarguably awesome at applying. Nonetheless, I maneuvered through more makeup than I ever used, doing my best to look sophisticated. All of the extra time was worth it, though. When I was finished, I truly felt beautiful and worthy of the slinky dress waiting for me to step into.

It was 4:45, so I decided to slither into the dress. I dug out my best push-up bra—I needed it so that the plunging neckline had something to plunge to—and squirmed into the satiny fabric, careful to avoid ripping the dress. After I gracelessly wrangled into the dress and somehow twisted and turned enough to zip it up, I glanced in the mirror at the final product. I had to admit that it highlighted my waist and my figure, although I had to constantly pull down on the hem that was creeping up my thigh like a vine.

And then I waited. I touched up my lip gloss, checked myself in the mirror a few times. I snapped a few candid, close-ups with the camera. I glanced at the clock. It was 5:01. I dug out my best diamond stud earrings and put them in. Then, I decided to wear my diamond bracelet, too. Two minutes passed. Then ten. Soon it was 5:30. Where the hell was he? I figured something must have gone awry with his plan or he was fixing some small detail. I sat like a statue on the couch, afraid to move and cause a bead of sweat to drip down my face.

By six o'clock, fear had wiped away any anger that was permeating my thoughts. During all of our years together, Corbin had never been late for a date, not once. Maybe his truck broke down or he got a flat tire. I picked up the phone in the kitchen and dialed the memorized digits.

"Hello?" a tired voice questioned.

"Mr. Jones? Hey, it's Emma. Is Corbin there?"

"No. I just got home, though. He must have left to pick you up? Didn't you two have plans for tonight?"

Panic seized my chest and clutched at my sanity.

"Yeah, he was supposed to pick me up at five. He never showed up," I stated simply, cutting to the point.

Mr. Jones paused for what seemed like an eternity. "Maybe he broke down. I'll get in my car and go look for him. You stay put in case he shows up." For the first time in years, I heard genuine concern in Mr. Jones' voice. After all that he lost, I knew he was fearful of yet another family member disappearing.

The phone clicked to signal the end of the phone call. I walked out onto the porch, scanning the horizon for the sight of that familiar truck. No luck. I paced back and forth, back and forth, praying silently for Corbin's safe arrival. Suddenly the red dress and the fancy dinner seemed completely irrelevant. All I wanted was to be standing in Corbin's arms and for him to be in one piece, even if that meant eating peanut butter sandwiches and watching television together.

Suddenly, the phone stabbed the silence with its echoing ring. I bolted straight for the phone, reaching it without incident, despite my dangerously high heels.

"Hello?" I screamed into the phone.

"Emma, Emma it's me. Listen, I only have a minute." Corbin's voice was shaking. However, he was talking so that had to be a good sign.

"Corbin! Where are you? I've been worried sick. Do you know what time it is?" Glancing at the clock, I realized that it was almost seven.

"Emma, I know, I'm sorry, but you need to listen. I need you to call my dad. I need him to come to the police station."

"Why? What happened?" I shrieked. I'm not sure what I expected Corbin to say. Maybe I was thinking that he'd been in a fender-bender and had to go to the station to report it. Maybe he had been a victim of a hit-and-run and was reporting it. Whatever the case, I wasn't expecting anything as horrible as the true reason for his visit.

"I don't have time to explain. Just call my dad and tell him to get down here immediately. I'll have him call you later to talk to you about everything. I love you, Emma," I could hear his voice cracking with emotion.

"Corbin, wait, what's going on? Just tell me!" I spewed, begging for answers.

"Time's up!" I heard a voice bellow in the background. The phone clicked, leaving me with silence and questions.

Dazed by confusion, emotion, and fear, I force my hand to hang up the phone, pick it up, and dial the number again. His dad didn't answer; he was probably still searching for Corbin, checking with neighbors to see if they knew anything. I left an urgent message to call me immediately. Mr. Jones obeyed the message about ten minutes later.

"Emma, I couldn't find him. Do you know something?" Mr. Jones rambled.

"Not much. I know he's okay, at least physically. He called me and told me to get hold of you. He needs you to go to the police station. He didn't have time to explain. He just said it was urgent."

"The police station? God, what for?"

"I have no idea. I just know that he specifically asked for you to hurry down there," I said.

"All right, I'll head over right now," Mr. Jones muttered.

"Can I come, too?" I begged.

"You better stay home for now. I'll call you later and let you know what's going on, okay?" Mr. Jones stated coolly, denying my plea.

"Call me the second you know anything, please," I beseeched desperately.

"Will do," Mr. Jones promised and then clicked the phone.

After I hung up, I returned to the couch. I must have sat there in a daze for quite some time, because before I knew it, my mom and dad returned. Everything seemed like a whirlwind of sights and sounds, but nothing was clear to me. My mom asked me what was wrong, but I just shook my head and stared ahead in a comatose state. I remember my mom helping me out of the dress and into pajamas as I stared blankly ahead, tears gliding down my face. I remember her saying she was going to storm right over there and find out what was going on. I remember feeling worried and not knowing why. I remember finally falling asleep after making Mom promise to wake me up when the phone rang.

When she woke me up, the first thing I noticed was that the sun was beaming into my windows, casting an ethereal light over everything. The red dress draped over my chair reflected the light with such intensity that I shielded my eyes.

"Honey, Mr. Jones just called," Mom noted seriously, which was uncharacteristic of her. I knew something was terribly wrong.

"What happened? What time is it?" I sat up quickly, rubbing the grogginess out of my eyes with the backs of my hands.

"You need to get dressed. Corbin wants to see you."

"Where is he?"

"He's at the county jail. Visiting hours are coming up, and you won't have much time." Tears welled up in my mother's face. Usually the one to see the glass as half full, it seemed like only gloom and doom were emanating from her.

"Jail? What?" I shrieked in disbelief. My head was spinning as was the room.

"He's a prime suspect. First degree murder," she said matter-of-factly. My mother wasn't one to hide the truth or try to shield me. She told it like it was. As my jaw fell and the tears started streaming, she turned away to pick an outfit for me. I could tell that the clutching pain in my chest, my heart, and my head were being experienced by her as well. This couldn't be happening. I just froze, trying to stutter my confusion, but only silence befell my lips.

I snapped out of my daze and got out of bed, grabbed the red dress, and threw it into the trash can. I stomped around the room, grabbed the outfit my mother handed me, threw it on, and headed for the car. My mom dashed behind me, keys in her hand.

"I'll drive you," she offered. For once, I was thankful for her hovering nature. I didn't think I could manage to see straight, let alone drive myself to the jail.

And so began the longest few months of my life, months that would plague and destroy and disintegrate any shred of hope for the future that I possessed. Those months murdered my faith, my love, and the dove that grazed my hip. They wrung our family out and left it dry and cracking.

They severed the rope that held me and Corbin together, not leaving even one thread for us to weave back together.

Chapter Twenty-Two
Unfinished Promises

~ Corbin ~

The night that had changed my life, destroyed it, the night that had chewed me up and spit me out like a piece of leathery meat, began as one of the happiest nights of my life. It was a night of hope and of dreams, of feathery clouds gently guiding me toward a solid future of satisfaction. It was a night that I impatiently waited for. When it finally arrived, I was filled with joy for what would soon unfold. Now, looking back, I feel sorry for that guy getting ready in this room. I look at this list with pity for what would never be. I wonder how things could have been different. I wonder what Emma felt that night, what she must have experienced. I wonder, above all, why.

* * * *

Memories

With the scent of summer in the air, the seniors seemed to skip gleefully through the hallways on that last day of classes. The next day, they would be walking across the stage, handed that final degree declaring them competent for the real world, and be moving on with their lives. That night, many of my fellow classmates would be partying their way into adulthood.

But not us.

When I had put that promise ring on her finger, I had told her that someday I would replace it with the real thing. At the time, the promise

Voice of Innocence

ring seemed like a big enough step. We had committed ourselves to each other fully. Even I hadn't predicted how soon that commitment would wane away. With our senior year closing and the real world pounding on our doors, I felt the need to upgrade my commitment to her. It was time.

Yes, many would call it foolish. The world would mock us, two teenagers barely out of school, ready to be loyal to each other. How could we possibly know what we wanted, the world would ask. But I was ready to answer because in Emma, I saw my entire future laid out. With Emma, things felt right. Our love had blossomed and matured beyond question. With her, I saw a steadfast connection that would not be broken. I saw us walking into the impending future, heads held high, hands clenched together, ready to face the world, no matter what it would throw at us. I saw weddings, houses, children, pets, and love. I saw us waking up to each other every morning and falling asleep in each other's arms every night. I knew she saw it, too. So why wait?

When I had made my decision back at the beginning of May, I was sure of it. Yet I wasn't so sure of one thing—how her parents would react. I thought about taking the easy road and letting Emma deal with telling them after the fact, but I knew that wasn't fair. So I had made a decision to confront the Groves about it before I popped the question.

I was shocked at their lack of surprise when I cornered them one afternoon while Emma was playing her clarinet scales at practice. I was, in fact, greeted with two different but similarly positive responses from Mr. and Mrs. Groves.

Response One: *"Just so you know how you're going to support her. This is a big step, kid. Just be sure that you're sure. I don't want her to get hurt. If she gets hurt, you get hurt."* Followed with a handshake.

Response Two: *"Oh my God, I knew this was coming! I'm so excited! We're going to have the best wedding this town has ever seen! I can't wait to tell everyone what a handsome son-in-law I'm getting! Where's the ring?"*

I'll let you be the judge of who responded in what way.

So with parental approval, I was ready to move forward. I spent weeks planning, doubting my plans, enhancing my plans, and worrying. I had wanted everything to be immaculate and undoubtedly perfect for this big moment. I saved as much money as I could, even resorting to selling some of my favorite things and mowing lawns for extra cash. I took on some extra hours at the local pizza shop (the amusement park wasn't open yet). I bought the biggest, nicest ring that I could afford, which despite my best efforts and heartfelt intentions, was barely a diamond chip. It only overshadowed the promise ring by a few diamond chips. But I knew that Emma wouldn't care. I knew she would love it, even if it had come from a quarter machine, which it didn't, but it wasn't *much* of an upgrade. It was what the ring meant that mattered, and I knew Emma well enough to know she would feel the same way.

Finally, after many sleepless nights and cumbersome conversations with Emma where she sensed I was a bit "off," the day had arrived. I had pre-arranged for Emma's mom to come by my house and get the dress after I picked Emma up for school. She was more than pleased to be my "accomplice" as she liked to call herself. *"It sounds so exciting!"* she added.

While that last day of school flew by for the excited and tearful seniors, my day ticked by with infuriating sluggishness. Finally, the end of the day mercifully sounded with the school's bell, and I met Emma at her locker as usual.

"Can you believe it? Last day! It's sort of sad, isn't it?" Emma beckoned at her locker, a bit despondent about the prospect of it all being over.

"No, it's not sad. It's awesome. Our lives are just beginning," I said, then silently cursed myself for being so obvious. Emma didn't notice, though, thankfully.

"I guess you're right. It just seems depressing, like a big part of our lives, a good part, is over."

We gathered our things and headed toward my truck. As we walked, her hand cradled in mine, she turned to me.

"So what do you want to do tonight?" she asked. "Katie's having a pre-graduation party if you want to go. It might be fun."

"No, I can't."

Emma paused, squinting at me inquisitively. "Why not?"

"I have to work."

"Tonight? Can't you take one day off? We're graduating tomorrow."

Voice of Innocence

"I know, I'm sorry, it sucks. But they wanted me to come in tonight. Plus, you know that I could use the money with the fall semester coming up."

"I know. It's okay. We'll hang out tomorrow." She glumly walked with me to my truck, trying to mask her disappointment by chattering away about the day's occurrences.

When we got to her house, I felt my stomach drop a little bit. The next time I saw her, there would be no covering what was going on. It would be happening. A vital shift in our relationship was about to take place. Although I was a bit fretful and hoping that things would go smoothly, mostly I was just excited.

Emma leaned over to kiss me goodbye.

"See you tomorrow, I love you!" she said cheerfully.

"I love you, too." I replied.

"Forever?"

"Forever."

And with that, Emma headed into her house. And my plan began.

* * * *

As soon as Emma was safely inside the door, my truck leaped toward the road. I had plenty of time, but my heart was nervously jumping as adrenaline plunged my actions into super drive. I accelerated home, mentally preparing a list of all of the things I needed to accomplish in the next two hours. I started with a quick snack because I felt like I was going to pass out.

The next hour and a half zoomed by me as circles of showers, cologne, tuxes, cameras, rings, flowers, music, and worries nauseated my mind. When I finally felt like I looked the part of a man ready to promise his heart away, I headed toward my truck. *Let the future begin*, I thought to myself. I jumped into the driver's seat and didn't look back.

Little did I know that it would be an entire day until I saw Emma again, and she would hardly be jumping into my arms saying, "Yes." I was on the precipice of disaster, on the brink of life- altering change, but not the sort of change I had anticipated. The universe was awaiting the moment to throw me a curveball that I couldn't possibly be prepared to swing at.

Lindsay Detwiler

* * * *

"Corbin, pizza's here!" a voice yells up the steps. I am brought back to the present, seated on the bed where I had sprayed on that last bout of cologne before heading for what was to be a special night. My mind is temporarily offered reprieve from the hauntings of the past. I trade in my memories for a few slices of pepperoni and a beer with my dad, leaving those torturous memories undisturbed amidst those piles of dust.

Chapter Twenty-Three
Disarray

~ Corbin ~

My dad and I talk about whatever trivial subject we can muster up. We talk about the weather, job prospects for me, and some minor house repairs that I can help him with. Conversation is easy yet superficial. We try to act like this is a normal dinner, but it's not. How do you pretend you haven't just left a six by eight foot barred room for a life of freedom?

I wash my plate, finish my beer, and follow my dad into the living room. I sink down on the ancient recliner as my dad flips on the evening news. I'm already molding into his daily routine, like it or not. As he clicks the remote, my dad mutters *"Stupid media"* as he scrambles to flip through the stations quickly. All we can see on every channel is me.

"Innocent man stripped of his life," says one reporter, while a reporter on another channel defines my situation as a *"tragic shame."* *"Fingernail scrapings overturn ruling"* another proclaims. With my release, I have become a hero. But this angers me instead of filling me with peace. These reporters are so interested in my story, yet where were they when that young boy needed an outlet to share the truth? Where were these investigators and delvers when the truth needed to be uncovered? They were on the other side of the fence, leading the angry mob to my slaughter. Now they want to play fair redeemers of my character? I scoff at their money-hungry souls. They would take any side of the story just so it led to profit. They didn't give a shit about whose

life was being defiled in the process.

I decide to wander out to the deck, finding comfort in the patio chair by the railing. My dad stays put in the living room, sensing that I need a few minutes to digest everything that is happening. In his old age, he has become sensitive to the needs and emotions of others, a trait that has certainly suited him well.

Glancing at the sky, I can't help but think about the night that started it all. In truth, I have replayed that night in my mind hundreds if not thousands of times. The "what ifs" pop up every few seconds as I wonder why things unfolded as they did. Was it just sheer bad luck that those events happened the way they did, or was it something more? Was fate haunting me, lurking in the distance, selecting its prey from hundreds of the weak? Why did it set its fangs into me?

When I drove away that night with excitement and anxiety churning in my stomach, I didn't bother to look back. Yet within only a few hours, I was failing to look forward either.

* * * *

Memories

"Shit!" I yelled, fist jarring against the steering wheel. The flashing gas light taunted my stupidity. I had thought of everything for tonight—except that we would need gas in my truck.

Calm down, I told myself. I still had plenty of time until I had to pick up Emma, and she was only a few minutes away. It was only 4:55. I would just have to swing by the gas station and dump some gas into the truck. No problem.

My rusty, faithful truck squeaked its way into the gas pump lane. I jumped out, jammed the nozzle into the tank, and began pumping. At exactly ten dollars and one cent, I stopped the pump and jogged inside to pay the cashier. I would only lose a few minutes for this entire escapade. As the familiar chime on the door announced my appearance, I beelined for the counter. Out of the corner of my eye, though, I saw a troubling sight—Randy. Jerking and swaying, he headed up the candy bar aisle. The clerk eyed him uneasily, as she was the only worker in the store. It was just the three of us.

The incident at prom had occurred a long time ago, so long ago that

Voice of Innocence

I would have completely pushed it out of my mind. Except Randy couldn't. Angered by the situation and aggravated by his home circumstances, Randy had let the fight swamp his entire being. When he passed me in the hallway, he often threw insults and an attempted punch my way. Emma became a focal point for his pervasive attitude, which only intensified my hatred for the asshole. Our relationship was violently unstable, to say the least. We had a few close calls at school and even a day at the principal's office for a round in the cafeteria. I wasn't afraid of him. But on today of all days, the last thing I wanted was a confrontation. I headed toward the clerk, money in hand, hoping to get out of the store without Randy even detecting me. He seemed less than aware of the environment around him. Just my luck, though, he spotted me like a zombie spots its next meal. With the same clumsy yet focused energy of the undead, he lunged straight toward me.

"Hey dick, are you following me?" His eyes couldn't focus on me and his words melted together like a box of crayons in a car in July. I tried ignoring him as I slid a ten to the clerk, voice wavering with fear of a brawl in her store. She glanced at the situation tenuously before sliding a penny out of the "leave a penny" bin by the register; she wasn't about to point out the one cent missing from my money with a scene like this unfolding.

"Hey asshole, I'm talking to you," Randy prodded, now physically poking at me. I instantaneously and unconsciously pushed him away, his back slamming into the newspaper rack beside the register.

"Watch your back. Don't touch me," he yelled, recovering into an attack stance. My heart sank as I realized that a confrontation was going to be unavoidable. I tried one more time to resist the incitation for a fight.

"Randy, look, I don't want any problems. Not now," I reasoned as I gathered my receipt from the clerk's hand. I was turning to head out the door when Randy took a weakly powered and poorly aimed swing at me. This was too much. I turned and punched him square in the jaw, sending him to the floor as bones crackled from the force of my blow. The clerk, verging on the label of elderly, screamed and backed away from the counter, trying to retreat into a safe haven between the cigarette displays. Randy didn't even attempt to get up, probably the result of his liquor. I headed straight for the door, stopping only to utter one more sentence. "If you touch me or Emma again, I'll kill you." These were not words to be taken lightly, for I wasn't the type of guy who sought out trouble. But I had it with Randy. With a guy like him, you had to show dominance.

I threw the door open, cuing the chiming again. I made a decision. I was done thinking about Randy. He would get up from being knocked on his ass, be pissed, but probably forget what happened the next day when he woke up from his inebriation stint. Panting from the exchange, I climbed in my truck, assessed my face for potential damage, and headed toward Emma's.

I tried to mentally prepare myself and turn my thoughts to Emma. I didn't want Randy swaying another second of our night. At the red light near the gas station, I reached in my pocket to feel for that familiar ring box, only to find my heart clutching with panic for the second time—it wasn't there. My chest felt heavy as I realized the intense possibility that this would ruin my night with Emma. I mentally retraced my steps until I remembered that life-changing detail. I hadn't put it in my pocket. On top of forgetting gas, I had made a much larger mistake. I had forgotten the ring.

Now, all pretenses of calm, collected Corbin were kicked into the dust that I left behind my truck as I ran that red light, turning my truck around to head back home. The clock on my dash now read 5:02. I was going to be late. I stamped on the gas, truck hovering near illegal speeds as I made my way back to the house. I squealed to a stop, leaped out of the truck like I was in an action movie, and dashed up the stairs to my room. I rustled through the calamity that was my room, tossing dirty clothing and misplaced belongings in sheer terror; the most important item of the night was nowhere in sight and I was already late. I kicked over a stack of textbooks, rummaged through my laundry basket, and threw myself to the floor to peer under the bed in desperation. Finally, I found the ring box resting between two candy bar wrappers near my dresser and made a crazy run for it back to the truck. It was 5:14. I was officially late. But at least I wasn't ring-less on the night of the proposal.

I took a second to catch my breath, pull myself together, and mentally assess the situation. I now had everything I needed. I was a few minutes late, some sweat beaded on my forehead, and I had somewhat of an altercation with Randy. It wasn't perfect, but it also wasn't enough to destroy the night. At least, I wasn't about to let it. I would be at Emma's in a few minutes. Maybe a little bit of anticipation would add to her excitement. All of this would be a distant memory in an hour or so, the optimism of a wedding blotting out these minor imperfections in the day.

"It's fine," I reassured myself again, out loud this time, as I aimed my truck down the driveway and the pathway to Emma.

As I maneuvered the treacherous curves in the back road and approached the straightaway on the way to Emma's, I glanced over toward the side of the road. Something was lying in the ditch about twenty yards ahead, something big. I slowed the truck instinctively. At first, my mind thought it was probably a deer that had been hit and crawled to the ditch to die. As I was driving past, I slowed a bit more and realized that this "deer" was clothed. I slammed on my brakes, not even considering that danger might be lurking around. This was not a well-traveled road, so if someone was in need, I was probably their only shot for the next few hours.

Slamming my truck's heavy door, I scurried toward the ditch. A sudden recognition sank into me. This was a familiar face. The name that belonged to the face—Randy Clark.

I skidded into the ditch, shouting Randy's name. Gravel loosening my step, I slid down to the ground, taken back by puddles of blood pooling around him. Although he was clearly intoxicated at the gas station, he still didn't even begin to compare to the rough, unhealthy appearance he was sporting now. His face was a sickly gray that warned of looming death. *What the hell had happened?* I wondered. My chest still tight from panic, I quickly surveyed the scene to rationalize the surroundings. Mind blurring and whirling, trepidation and shock paralyzed my physical and mental reactions. I couldn't seem to think, to breathe, to do anything but stare. As the shock slowly waned, my eyes were able to catch the glimmer of something besides just the cesspools of blood. There was a knife sticking out of his stomach.

Instinct kicked in as I straddled Randy, still calling out his name. I checked for a pulse, ignoring the blood spatters that were drenching my clothes and my skin. Suddenly, the proposal seemed like a distant event. Right now my only concern was why Randy was covered in blood and how I was going to help him. Although I had just shouted out a death threat to him a few minutes ago, I hadn't meant it.

Randy stirred slightly, almost undetectably, his hands clutching the knife protruding from his stomach as an animalistic groan trembled in his throat. I irrationally screamed for help, hoping against all odds that someone at the gas station would hear me. It was about four blocks from where we were, but the way the roads were situated, we were behind it, surrounded by wilderness and barren fields. It was unlikely that with the roar of the road in front, anyone would hear us. Randy was fading fast, blood slowly trickling from his lips as the sticky, hot liquid pooled around his gut.

"Stay with me, Randy, it's going to be okay," I uttered, giving up on attracting help and needing to hear the reassurance myself. Things were bad, and there was no help in sight. I couldn't get him to the truck myself. I thought about dashing to my truck and driving the four blocks to get help, but I was afraid to leave him. Out of an instinctual, knee-jerk reaction, I did the only thing I thought I could do. I tried to free the knife so I could stop the bleeding. I yanked the weapon free, tossing it into the brush nearby, and immediately applied pressure. The blood continued surging, and so did my panic. My idea wasn't working, not by a long shot.

I started seriously considering that the best chance Randy had was for me to go and flag down help. I delicately attempted to place his hand over the wound to stop the bleeding, scrambled up out of the ditch, and stumbled toward my truck. As I slammed my body, which was frail from sheer terror, against the truck door and reached for the handle, I realized a car was approaching from the distance. *Thank God!* I thought as I leaped back out, preparing to wave the car down, not wanting to chance that it would pass us.

I didn't have to beg for it to stop, though, because it was a police car. My mind didn't panic or worry what the scene would look like. I was just so thankful to have backup. It was truly a miracle that this cop had been traveling the road back here, probably a mere matter of coincidence, or maybe a result of the fearful clerk after our altercation. Regardless, I waved my blood-soaked hands in the air as the car slowed.

The cop pulled behind my truck, dashing out of the door with his

Voice of Innocence

weapon drawn. I threw my hands in the air in automatic response.

"Help! Please! He's been stabbed!" I uttered almost incoherently. The cop evaluated the scene without moving an eye from me.

"Get on the ground," he demanded, weapon drawn and aimed. Horrified, I slowly bent down on my knees, hands behind my head as I had seen in so many movies. The officer approached, searched me for weapons, and then jammed handcuffs on me.

"What are you doing?" I asked, tears now forming and blurring my vision.

The officer reached into his car without moving his weapon from me. He called for backup.

The next twenty minutes offered more chaos than a movie or television show could ever hope to capture. An ambulance slammed onto the scene, setting off an explosion of Emergency Medical Technicians and stretchers. Five more policemen showed up, searched the area, bagged up evidence, and evaluated the scene. I was quickly stuffed into the back of the car, read my rights, and driven to the station. *This must be a mistake,* I thought. How did I end up here? I was just trying to help.

I was taken to the station where I sat for several hours before I was finally awarded my phone call. Clearly, this had all been a huge misunderstanding. Looking back as I sat in that metal chair, I realized the police were probably confused. It certainly looked bad. The two of us on a back road, Randy stabbed, me covered in blood jumping into my truck. It was only a matter of time until things were straightened out. As I sat waiting for my dad to come and help sort out the mess, I felt the ring box bulging in my pocket and realized that night would be memorable, but not for the right reasons.

Chapter Twenty-Four
The Meeting

~ Emma ~

Memories

    The dark, damp smell in the waiting area reminded me of the putrid smell of death. Mom and I had been poked, prodded, interrogated, inspected, and practically violated by prison officials to make sure that we weren't smuggling anything into the jail. Like I would be capable of pulling that off. I didn't even know what would be considered contraband. Then, we were led to a room, if you could call it that, to wait our turn. A churning in the pit of my stomach reminded me of how nervous I truly was.

    When the guard finally turned to us and told us to go ahead, I sprang out of my seat, nerves increasing the intensity of all my actions. Mom stayed seated as I looked at her inquisitively.

    "You go on. I'll wait here. I can visit him later."

    I gave her a faint smile, appreciating her respect of our privacy. She knew we would want to talk alone.

    "I'll fill you in," I called over my shoulder as the guard led me through a series of locked doors. We passed through a ridiculous maze until we came to the visitor's room. It was a tiny room, dank and depressing, accessorized with only a stiff metal table and two lonely chairs.

    "You have ten minutes," the guard gruffly muttered. As I turned to say thank you, another guard led Corbin into the room.

What a difference a few hours could make. Gone was the smiling, carefree Corbin of my memories who had hidden a red dress in my closet for a wonderful surprise. In front of me stood a broken, hopeless man. He was wearing the traditional orange prison garb. Tears instantaneously streamed down my face. I rose to go to him when the guard crassly reminded me that there was no physical contact with prisoners. I lowered myself back to my seat.

Countless thoughts swirled through my mind and attempted to overthrow my sanity. I had so many questions I wanted to ask, so many worries to cover, so many fears to divulge. However, at this moment and with only ten minutes to talk, it seemed like Corbin's physical and mental well- being were of more importance.

"Corbin, how are you? Are you okay? When are you getting out of here? What happened?" Once the questions started, they leaped out rapid-fire.

Corbin gazed at me, a sense of blankness permeating his face. I could still see the same old Corbin hidden deep within the stare. However, I also sensed the distance between us. The drawbridge had opened smoothly, but neither of us had noticed the flashing sign warning us to stay away. It was too late—we were crashing into the depths of the river below.

Corbin began. "Emma, listen to me. We don't have much time. I'm sorry. I'm so sorry for all of this. For ruining your night. I'm so sorry..." His voice trailed off as it began to crack.

"Don't worry about me or last night. It's you that I'm worried about. What's going on? It can't be that bad. Just some mistake, right?"

"Yeah, it's a mistake. But good luck explaining that. It's bad, Em. Really bad." His eyes darted from mine as he uttered those cursed claims.

"Corbin, whatever it is, it'll be fine. We'll clear it all up and then no big deal, right?" I pleaded for reassurance. He sat in silence as the seconds ticked into minutes. He finally glanced up at me, tears welling in his eyes.

"I don't think this is getting cleared up. Randy died last night, *died*, Em. They think I did it. They think I killed him. The whole situation looks really bad, and I don't know how to prove them wrong. Dad got me a lawyer, and he's good and all. But even he thinks it doesn't look good. It's just a mess, a huge mess. If only I had gone for help right away, or if I hadn't said those things. Baby, I'm sorry. I'm so sorry," Corbin's words pleaded for understanding, understanding that I was certain he had. He was wringing his hands through his hair, true despair coursing through his words. It looked like a dramatic scene from a movie, but it wasn't. This had become real life.

"Look, it's going to be fine, okay? Just tell me what happened."

Corbin nodded, although he glanced at the nearby guard suspiciously. He weighed his options and then began to speak.

"I wanted to surprise you, to do something truly memorable to celebrate graduation. I just wanted to do something classy. So, I worked with your mom. I had her sneak the dress into your room, the notes, everything. I wanted it to be perfect. I was getting everything ready to go for five o'clock. I had spent so much time on all of the details that I forgot about getting gas for my truck. I decided to stop and get some on my way to pick you up. While I was paying, that's when I saw him."

Corbin's eyes got a hazy look to them. I could feel his pain, his sorrow, and his regrets. Tears continued to run down my face. I was getting ready to reach for his hand. Although it was illegal, I didn't care. Suddenly, the dreaded words burst from the guard's mouth like a cattle bell.

"Time's up! Let's go, Jones."

I leaped to my feet, "Sir, wait, just a few more minutes." I might as well have been a piece of lint on the floor, for they completely disregarded my appeals and led Corbin away before I could even say goodbye. He squinted back at me with a tearful look. Then, he was gone. The guard led me back through a series of complicated gates and locks. I aimlessly put one foot in front of the other until my mom was in view. Without a word, I crumpled into her arms and began sobbing.

It was a long ride home. It would seem that the rides to and from the jail would get longer and longer as the weeks turned into months.

Chapter Twenty-Five
Separation

~ Emma ~

Memories

At first, I had thought this was just a short nightmare stemming from miscommunication and confusion. Once Corbin's lawyer cleared everything up, he would be released and we would move on with our lives. It never occurred to me that he wouldn't be released. Those doubts would vine their way through me in the months to come, but one thing would stay constant even when things looked worse than bad—I knew Corbin didn't do it. The Corbin I had spent countless days and nights with, the guy who cried over his sister, who brought me flowers just because he wanted to, the guy who shared dinners with my family and holidays, was not a guy who could stab another guy, even if that guy was Randy Clark.

The rest of the town, though, didn't know the Corbin that I knew. They saw this kid who'd been through hellish ordeals, who had somewhat of a temper, who had threatened to kill Randy just moments before, and they stamped him as guilty. They peered at me, even in those early days, as a victim of love and naivety. Their eyes beckoned me to see the light, to save myself and my pride while I still could. But I didn't listen. I became alienated from the world around us because of my commitment to Corbin, to the truth. The real world and its inhabitants became a distant place from my world of jail cell visits and prayers for the truth.

Days passed. Weekends passed. June passed. The absence of Corbin from my daily life beleaguered me like a lingering illness. Everything lost its luster, even in the summer sun's gorgeous rays. Letters about college visiting days and orientations piled up on my desk, but all I could think about was Corbin. I had already forfeited my job at the mall because I had called off so many days to visit the jail. Suddenly, folding sweaters for superficial teenagers to peruse didn't seem to matter as much as the ordeal we were going through. In actuality, nothing mattered. When I wasn't visiting him, I was sitting by the phone hoping he would earn a phone call, or on my knees praying for a swift reveal of the truth. I hardly recognized myself in photographs from just a few months before. Where was that illustrious, smiling girl who had everything ahead of her? What had happened to our lives?

If I had changed for the worst, Corbin had changed for the horrendous. At first, he tried to stay strong and keep his optimism. We would talk about our favorite memories and plan for the future. We planned a return to the barn on the first day he was let out. Steadily, however, the harsh climate a jail inflicts began to degrade his spirit. My heart sank every time I saw a new bruise or slash. He always tried to reassure me that it was nothing, just an accident. Even naïve me knew better. As the weeks passed, I saw him sinking into a melancholy state that never dissipated. No matter how hard I tried to help him stay positive, I couldn't succeed.

After the initial visit with Corbin that was cut short, I quickly went to his father to hear the rest of the story. Between visiting with his dad and the phone calls I would receive from Corbin over the next few days, I was able to piece together Corbin's side of the story. Unfortunately, the law was only choosing to see one side of the story, and it wasn't in favor of Corbin.

Between the blood on Corbin and the clerk's witnessing of the incident between the two, the evidence against Corbin was pretty damning. There was a clear, contentious history between the two boys. Corbin had openly threatened Randy. Then there was the blood. There were Corbin's fingerprints on the knife. There seemed to be a target on Corbin's back. With every detail about that night that surfaced, the bull's-eye seemed to grow. Even though the Clarks certainly weren't respected in town, the Joneses were basically an unknown entity. The family everyone in town had been curious about a few years earlier suddenly became the villainous, monstrous family that had fostered and harbored a criminal.

In addition to the growing evidence against Corbin, the fact that the truth remained such a mystery didn't help. It gave Corbin's lawyer little to found his defense on. There didn't seem to be an explanation that placed the murderous knife in any hand but Corbin's. Corbin had no idea how to explain why Randy ended up in the ditch. Corbin's theory was that Randy had wandered off from the gas station and started walking toward an unknown destination. The distance between the gas station and where he was found was only a few blocks. He suspected that perhaps it was a drug deal gone awry. Word had it that Randy had owed some people some money. Having a theory, though, is one thing, and proving it is a completely different story. Regardless, there wasn't any solid evidence supporting Corbin's theory. After the incident at the gas station, no one had seen Randy again until he was found in the ditch. No one saw anyone pick him up. No security cameras from local businesses showed anything suspicious. The elapsed time from Corbin's threat to Randy's death was short, short enough for an enraged Corbin to lose his temper, the prosecutors suggested, and seek revenge.

Word about the incident spread rampantly, as does anything in a small town. People would whisper in the grocery store when I would pass them. I would catch pieces of *"Yes, that's her,"* or *"Poor thing,"* or *"conspirator?"* I learned that the best place to be was at home. People started speculating about why or how Corbin did it. *"I always knew he had a temper. One time, I saw him..."* they would say. Or, *"Well, that's probably why the family moved. Probably an incident in another state."* Speculations and theories were thrown around like discussions about the weather. No one seemed to realize that all of this was impacting the future of a life. Everyone seemed to know everything about Corbin, and no one was saying anything good.

Despite the evidence, despite the stares, despite the theories, I kept my faith in Corbin in the beginning. I kept my faith that things would work out, that he would be proven innocent, and that all of those grocery store gossipers would be proven wrong. I also kept my faith that if I could just stay close, stay supportive, Corbin would make it through the horrors of prison life. So when classes began in August, I wasn't on any of the class rosters. For the first time in my life, I ignored my parents' warnings and threats and pleas. I skipped college. I told myself it would just be for a semester until everything was straightened out. My parents knew better.

I focused my attention on Corbin. I worked on making him feel confident, on trying to piece together anything that could help his case, on gathering supporters. I was his biggest cheerleader, his staunchest support system. My parents jumped onboard, too, after their anger over my choice proved to be pointless. They helped carry Corbin's torch. Collectively, with Corbin's dad, we were his voices of innocence. We searched for answers about what happened that night. We rallied as much support behind Corbin as we could. We visited him, sent him books, wrote to him, and talked to him. We kept him as connected with the outside world as possible. Despite our efforts and our optimism, however, the flame would die. The voices would be silenced once the trial began.

Chapter Twenty-Six
The Trial

~ Emma ~

Memories

    The summer began to fade into autumn, and the bitter wind whipped us into winter. Soon, it was time for the trial to begin. To my sheer disappointment and disbelief, the mistake had not been cleared up. There wasn't a miraculous discovery of evidence, a confession from the true perpetrator, a last-minute dismissal of the case. Corbin would face the courtroom; Corbin would have to plead for his life. For *our* life.

    I had been visiting Corbin nearly every day. Every day that passed, a glimmer of confidence also passed. Corbin's lawyer, one of the best choices Corbin's dad could afford, had worked hard and believed Corbin had a solid defense. I had already been prepared to testify, if needed, although I had little to contribute. Corbin's lawyer prepared us for what he knew would be a battle. He did not prepare us, however, for defeat.

    The courtroom trial was brutal. I was forced to sit behind Corbin as his life was decided by a handful of men and women who did not know him. They didn't see the way he held a door for a frantic mother in the grocery store, or how he tenderly kissed me when I was worried about something miniscule. They didn't see his heart, his strength, his humor like I did. All they saw was the picture painted by a few minor incidents and an unfortunate day.

    I sat listlessly as witness after witness testified. I flinched as one of our former teachers recalled the prom incident for the jury, and the principal noted Corbin's marred record from incidents with Randy. My heart fell as the gas station clerk also recalled the harsh words Corbin had yelled less than twenty minutes before Randy would be found dead in a ditch. Testimony whirled in and out of my mind as fear began to creep into my whole being. Up until this point, I had convinced myself the truth would come out. I had convinced myself that our justice system wouldn't let the unthinkable happen. Perhaps I was just afraid of what the unthinkable would mean for me. How could I face a life without him? How could I face week after week of visiting Corbin behind glass? Where would our dreams fall? I tried my best to silence these fears. I glanced to the jury box. All jurors were intently listening to the testimony, but their faces were unreadable. I mouthed a prayer that they would see the Corbin that I knew.

I was never called to the stand. I had been anxious about the prospect of having Corbin's life in my hands, or more specifically, my words. However, when I realized I would not be able to testify for him, I wished in a way that I had been given the chance. I wished I could paint the true picture of Corbin, that I could show the jurors the kind of man he was—the kind of man I was madly in love with, the man whom I would marry someday if I had the chance.

Corbin had also decided not to take the stand. His lawyer had urged that it would be too risky. Corbin had a hard time with this decision. He felt the need to defend himself and thought he could make the jury understand the true situation. However, after careful consideration, he heeded his lawyer's advice. The possibility of tricky cross-examination questions making him look guilty was too much of a risk. Corbin let his destiny lie in his lawyer's ability to argue.

I had expected the trial to drag laboriously. In actuality, it felt like a blur. Before I knew it, the jury was being led away to deliberate. Corbin was being led away to await his fate.

Then, before long, we were reconvening in the courtroom to hear the final decree.

Corbin gaped back at me with trepidation, hesitancy, and anguish all rolled into a single expression, before peering at the judge. My eyes never left the back of his head, even as he shifted his weight under the glowering eyes of the jury. I only looked away when I heard that single

Voice of Innocence

word, the word that forever would break him, the word that would torch my soul and my belief in humanity.

    My mom, who had been sitting beside me for the entire trial, grabbed hold of me as I wailed in searing pain. That single dreaded word still rings through my nightmares, day and night.

Chapter Twenty-Seven
Shattered

~ Corbin ~

Memories

Guilty.
A simple word that turned my world, Emma's world, the town's world, on its end.

It had been a strenuous, unbearable trial. As if a murder trial can be anything less.

Over the months, I had repeated my story to my lawyer too many times to count. It eventually became like a narrative I had memorized for a school project. I had uttered those words so many times that I had lost all emotional attachment to the story. I felt like the players in the tale were just characters in a story. I also felt like the last page was already written.

Unlike many in prison, I seemed to have the most authentic support system one could ask for. Between my dad, Emma, and Emma's parents, I was never alone during visiting hours. They tried their best to keep my spirits up and to keep the assurance burning for me, even when I felt like the conflagration had been drenched in a soaking rain. They knew that the truth would surface. I, on the other hand, had my doubts the entire time. Things looked bad, and I had no way of proving that it was any different.

Voice of Innocence

As the intricacies of the trial dragged on, I felt like I was in a horrible movie that needed to stop playing. Take my seat by the table. Glance back at Emma's sullen face. Stand for the judge. Sit back down. Listen to testimony damning me to a life within the inner circle of hell. Return to the handcuffs, to the jail cell. Face the tough realities of prison life. Stare into the darkness with a sense of emotional blankness, numb from the prospects of facing a life devoid of choice, devoid of Emma. Repeat the cycle.

My lawyer put up a seemingly good fight. He had prepped me for the worst, helped me to keep my eyes on the best case scenario, and gathered as much evidence as he could to make sure the latter happened. Character witnesses, diagrams of what happened and why my story was plausible, rebuttals to turn down the prosecution's side of the story—he covered our bases. The only base he couldn't cover, of course, was the alibi part.

From the time I fought with Randy to the time I was found with his blood on my hands, I had no witnesses. As my cursed fate would have it, my dad of course had been working late and hadn't been home to see my mad dash for the ring. No neighbors had witnessed me going back in the house. No cars had even passed me on the road to place me anywhere but at the scene of the crime. The blood on the knife had been tested and found to be Randy's, and the fingerprints on the handle, of course, matched mine. I had literally been caught with blood on my hands, the blood of a guy I had threatened to kill on more than one occasion.

And so, the prosecution succeeded in painting me out to be a troubled soul that finally snapped on a troublesome opponent. They showed no mercy in describing the story of my difficult youth, from the death of Chloe to the suicide of my mother. In short, they demonstrated that I was unstable, had motive, and had been at the scene of the crime.

And it all worked. The jury bought tickets to their show instead of mine.

Guilty. Final verdict. It was a word I thought I had been prepared to hear, but when it finally slipped through the mouth of that juror, it struck me with such force I thought I would fall to my knees.

Yet when that word jolted the air with its frankness, I did not instantly see my life slipping away as so many of the convicted do. I was not weeping for all of the family dinners, holidays, and vacations I would miss. I didn't take time to think about how my art career had been shattered before it even began. I didn't think about how the past nineteen years had led to this one, horrific moment, that everything before it seemed like such a waste. I didn't consider the years of the lifeless cell, debilitating in its literal and figurative blackness that faced me day in and day out.

No, when those words shambled across the room, there was only one thing on my mind— Emma.

I woefully turned to peer into those eyes, to see the agony that would be stabbing them. It was in her eyes that I found the true intensity of the loss I was about to bereave. It was in her eyes that I saw my whole life disappear like a grain of sand tossed into a violent gale.

As I was being led away, I wanted so badly to break free, to grab Emma in my arms, to tell her it would be okay. But I knew it wouldn't.

"We'll appeal, don't worry," my lawyer desperately threw at me as the guard shoved me across the floor. But I didn't hear him.

All I could hear were the shrieks from a girl whose life had just been flattened out by a bus, mowing down any remnants of hope. With her cries, my heart split into a thousand razor-sharp fragments, never to be fully reclaimed again.

Chapter Twenty-Eight
Shackled

~ Corbin ~

Memories

    Some say that the first night in prison is the worst. That first night I spent locked up after my arrest was certainly no picnic. I had been a frightened young man, clueless to the harsh obstacles that prison life presented. Naivety had convinced my young self that this was just a test, that the real story would come out, and I would return to normal life. The innocent didn't face jail time, and I certainly wasn't guilty. Being denied bail due to the nature of the crime, I had many nights after that to get accustomed to life behind a cage. I learned which men to avoid, which men to befriend. My taste buds acclimated to the stale prison food, and my mind learned to tolerate the incessant monotony. What I hadn't prepared for, though, was how the first night after the verdict would feel. I hadn't realized it, but before the trial I had somewhere deep inside lodged a single cell of hope that there was a light waiting for me, that I would one day set foot in the free world again. I felt that prison was just a temporary stop on the way to my real life, that it wasn't permanent. Even on the darkest days, I felt like I would survive this and return to Emma unscathed. With one word, though, the last glimmer succumbed to its final demise, leaving me with nothing but debilitating remnants of a powerless, pointless future. I looked ahead and saw nothing but blackness. The only brightness in my future was the color orange.
    The night after the verdict was the hardest night of my life. I would be lying if I said I didn't think about suicide. Looking into the years to

come, I saw hollowness so vast, it threatened to swallow me. I saw a life of meaningless days and a desire for something more squashed by the reality of the bars. The only thing that kept me from taking my life that night was the thought of what it would do to Emma. Even that became a weak deterrent as the hours ticked by. I thought maybe it would actually make things easier for her if I could disappear. At least then she could move on without any question.

I knew Emma would stand by me. She had stood by me this long, despite the naysayers and evil glares. She had believed in me even when the justice system had pointed its weighty finger at me, proving to the world I was guilty and useless to society. Emma, however, had not been poisoned by the lies. Her love for me and belief in the man that I was allowed her to prevail confidently beside me. She had already sacrificed so much for me. Even if the appeal failed, she was prepared to wait until the truth came out, no matter how long it took. We had talked about it countless times during visitation, with me always telling her to be realistic. No matter how hard I tried, though, I couldn't convince her it was better for her to move on. She felt a responsibility to be my rock through this, to be the voice shouting from the rooftop that I was innocent.

Not that I wanted to think about the prospect of her moving on in life while I stood still. I wanted nothing more than to be the man holding her hand through life, helping her grow, having children with her, marching steadily toward life in our rocking chairs reflecting over our photo albums of memories. But it seemed that this was not to be. The only thing worse than me being in prison was the prospect of her being imprisoned by a love for the man who couldn't live a life with her. When the trial began, there was still the potential that our dreams could work out. Now, though, we had to face the awful truth that life wasn't fair and that justice didn't always prevail. We had prepared for a lifetime together. What, then, should we do now that my life had been stripped from me? Did that mean Emma's life should stop, too?

As much as I wanted to be with Emma, I also wanted her to have a life full of excitement. I wanted her to reach her dreams, to have someone who could be physically beside her and emotionally available to her. I wanted her life to consist of more than just timed visits with a man in a hideous jumpsuit. I wanted her life to be more than security checks and buzzers. As much as I wanted Emma to myself, as easy as it would be to let her stand beside me during this hellacious time in my life, I knew it wasn't fair. We were so young, and I couldn't help but think of how much time Emma had already wasted beside me. As much as I didn't want it to be true, my life was most likely ruined by a lie and a tragic attack from the universe. But Emma's didn't have to be. Emma had a life of choice ahead of her. She was not shackled by the chains of my verdict, if she could just look up long enough to see into the horizon.

I had already told myself over the course of the trial that if things didn't turn out the way I had hoped, I would do what it took to make sure she wasn't held captive by her love for me. As hard as it was, I would force her to say goodbye, to move on, to forget about what could have been, and find herself a life in what could be.

Now it was time to face it. It was time to start preparing for goodbye.

Chapter Twenty-Nine
Reality Transformed

~ Emma ~

Memories

Back at home on that life-changing night, words of comfort swirled around me. "Appeal" was the term of the night. My parents thought this word would be enough to keep my head up and my heart open. To me, the word was synonymous with false hope.

When Corbin was led out of the courtroom, he turned to glance at me. The look was not for reassurance or comfort. It was a look of pure sorrow. His almost apologetic glance seemed to hint at goodbye. This alone was enough to send me into an inescapable depression.

That night, when I was finally able to shrug off my mother's hovering tendencies and find some alone time, I sat on the ledge by the window glancing out at the perfectly clear sky and the countless blinking stars. My eyes leaped from constellation to constellation, craving to be drowned in the empty, infinitive expanse that is space. My mind was on overdrive, making an exhausting day even more numbing. I thought of Corbin and how he couldn't even see this sky. I thought about how in the course of the trial, our worlds had become like different planets. No matter how much we wanted to stay connected, it was so hard with our vastly different worlds. We were drifting apart at the speed of light, unable to hold onto each other as we whirled further and further into the cold emptiness of the unknown.

At times, a determination surfaced within me. I felt like I couldn't give up, that I just needed to be strong and believe. The innocent were not persecuted and if they were, the truth always floated to the top of the murky waters called the justice system. I just had to be patient and know that the facts would bubble up.

Other times, I became angry. Angry at the court system, angry at the world, angry at Corbin for taking the wrong road that night, angry at Randy for being at the gas station. I became determined to actively find the evidence to get Corbin out of jail. I would uncover every stone in the town, interview every person in the area, and search far and wide for the true killer. I would carry the torch through the town, hunting for the one piece that would set Corbin free. If life wanted to attack us, I was ready to attack back. I would do what it took to reclaim our lives.

In the next moment, however, the futility of this project would hit me. If the professionals couldn't find anything, how would I? What if the evidence was never found? What if the truth didn't conquer? What if Corbin was forced to spend the rest of his life locked up? What if the man of my dreams, my foundation in life that everything was built on, was behind bars? What if our life together never got a chance to begin? How would I face a life without Corbin, with whom I had built all of my life plans, goals, and dreams?

I didn't sleep more than an hour that first night. My mind simply ping-ponged between various emotions, feelings, thoughts, and fears. By morning, my mind had blown a fuse and seemed incapable of processing any more information. When my mother came in at eight o'clock with a tray of food, I pushed it aside. I sat staring mindlessly, aimlessly, into the corner of the room. The corner of the room would rarely leave my sight for the next year.

****

The sentencing quickly followed the trial. I was forced to sit in my best dress and uncomfortable nylons, acting like the perfect lady, when inside I wanted to claw the judge's eyes out. I wanted to scream and shriek and punch. I wanted to grab Corbin and run off into the sunset. I wanted to disappear.

If the trial was excruciating, the sentencing was even worse. Corbin could face the death penalty, although his lawyers felt it wasn't likely due to the mitigating circumstances surrounding Randy's death and Corbin's clean record. After more deliberations, Corbin's life was again decided by a third party. Either way, though, things couldn't turn out well. I felt like both of our lives were over.

This time, instead of screaming, I simply choked back a sob against my mother when the sentence was read.

The sentence was life behind bars.

Corbin would live. He just wouldn't live the life we had imagined. I knew I should be relieved, that it could be much worse. I just couldn't find the elation in words that stripped Corbin's life away as much as a death sentence could have. A new reality officially slammed into our faces, not waiting for us to adjust or to question.

* * * *

I was able to visit Corbin the day after sentencing. I found out that when things seemed horrible, they could always get worse. Now that Corbin was sentenced, he would be transferred to the state penitentiary, which was three hours away.

While visiting Corbin, I halfheartedly reassured him that his lawyer was working hard on the appeal. It wasn't that I didn't want to believe in it; I was just afraid to. It's hard to reassure someone when you aren't reassured yourself.

"Emma, the appeal is going to take months if not longer. And if they convicted me the first time on the evidence, they'll do it again." Corbin looked at me seriously. There wasn't any hint of buoyancy left. Tears jetted down my face as his words and hopelessness sank in.

"But Corbin, we have to keep trying. We can't give up. I can't lose you." By now, I was sobbing, choking on my words, desperate for him to make things better. Desperate for the words he couldn't promise me.

Corbin's eyes pierced the table for an impenetrable pause. Slowly, he looked up at me, his mouth a tight line.

"Emma, there can't be a 'we' anymore. You have to let go. You can't keep hanging on." His words were icy, sharp. They jutted at me with precision, not even pausing to let the blood flow from the wound.

After everything we had been through the past few months, my stomach clenched tighter than it had all along.

"Don't talk like that," I spewed.

Voice of Innocence

Corbin looked at me gently this time, his mouth softening. "Emma, I love you. I always will. You have been my best friend. You are my entire world, and without you, I don't know…I don't know what I'll do. But that's something I have to face. I can't drag you down any longer. This isn't your fight anymore. Hell, it's not even my fight. I lost, Emma. I lost. My life is over. But yours isn't. You still have your freedom, you still have choices, and you still have so much ahead of you. It just can't have me in it anymore." Corbin was verging on tears now, too, but it was a calm wave of tears. He had made peace with this. He had let himself consider this possibility for months now. But I hadn't. I had clung so blindly to the fact that things would be okay that I hadn't entertained this possibility.

I violently shook my head, rage burning in my chest. "No, I won't let you do this. You're not getting rid of me. I'm going to stand by you and we're going to fight this." The doubts that had infiltrated my mind over the last few days were vehemently stopped at the prospect of Corbin pushing me away.

"Emma, c'mon. You have to be real. I don't want to face this either. Do you think this is what I wanted? Hell, I wanted to be marrying you in a year or two, having children, buying a house. You think this is easy for me? But do you know what makes it harder? Seeing you, week after week, put off your life to stand by me. Putting off college, putting off fun and friends to come here. Emma, I'm a dead end now. There's nothing here for you. You have to walk away. You have to move on. We've had a great run, Emma, and great memories. But I guess our future together just wasn't meant to be. All that's left for you to do now is walk out those doors and not look back. That's what you can do to help me, Emma. Go out there and live your life."

"Corbin, I won't do it. I won't leave you. I love you. I love you, and I can't do this without you. I won't. It's not fair." Desperation hurried my words.

"Emma, shhh, calm down. Look at me. This is what I want. I hate being in here, but I hate that being in here means you are practically in here, too. Learn from me. Go out and enjoy your life. Maybe you're right. Maybe someday the truth will come out. Maybe it will work out for us. But you can't sit around waiting for that to happen. You can't put your life on hold hoping for a miracle. So I am telling you that you need to walk out those doors and not come back."

"Corbin, I won't." My vision was blurry from the soggy tears filling my eyes. I couldn't believe he was doing this.

"Emma, I love you. If someday the truth comes out, I will come straight to you. I will come meet you at wherever you are in your life. Maybe there will be room for us then, maybe not. But I will not let you waste your life. You walk out that door and you don't look back. I won't accept your letters anymore. I won't accept your visits. This is it, Emma. This is the last time I'm going to see you. I love you, forever. I will never love anyone else. That's why I am doing this. That's why, don't ever think otherwise, okay? Now go, go live your life."

I shook my head aggressively, not believing what was happening. The collar of my shirt was damp from sopping up the tears that were darting down my face. I pawed away the moisture from my cheeks with a shaky hand.

"Corbin, I'm not giving up on us, I'm not. I won't."

Corbin cried softly for a few minutes. Ignoring the guard's scowl, he reached across the table and grabbed my hand. He kissed it quickly, softly. "I am, Emma. I am. I love you." With that, he stoically rose from his chair and called for the guard. He didn't glance back at me as he walked through the gate and out of my life. I crumpled into the dirty prison chair for several minutes, sobbing inconsolably, tears and snot soaking my face and the cold, steel table. When I refused to leave, the guard pulled me to my feet and led me back to the entrance. I managed to find my car and crawl in. I sat for an hour in the warm car, weeping for my sorrows, my lost life, and for Corbin. I had never felt so low in my life and didn't think things would ever look any better.

Chapter Thirty
Broken

~ Corbin ~

"Emma, I love you. If someday the truth comes out, I will come straight to you. I will come meet you at wherever you are in your life. Maybe there will be room for us then, maybe not."

At the time, *if* had overwhelmed any possibility of *when*. When I uttered those words to Emma as a sense of reassurance, I hadn't believed them to be true at all. I had hoped to simply set her free steadily, not giving her too much space to take off, just enough to liberate her from this hell we were living. I wanted her to walk out into the world without looking back, without worrying about a prospect that might never come. So I promised her that if things worked out, we would work out. In the pit of my stomach that day, though, I felt that those words would never come to fruition.

Here I sit, a patio chair ramming its cold, weathered metal into my spine, a night sky welcoming with its promises of tomorrow. Here I sit, in exactly the position I never thought I would be granted. And yet, now another question remains. Should I keep my promise? Should I set out on the mission to meet her, wherever her life may be? And will there be room for us?

Dizzied by the questions, I feel a subtle hint of doubt creeping through my blood. Emma has done what I asked, she has moved on with her life. In a small town, keeping up with someone's life is as easy as spotting a red rose in a sea of snow. Dad had heard whispers, first of a new man in Emma's life, then of a torrid romance, and finally of the wedding. She is married to a great man, has a career, and has a beautiful house, a symbol of success. Do I want to risk rocking the waters on the serene lake that was now her life? Why stir up the ragged feelings and regrets? Certainly my presence would incite nothing but raw hurt. Maybe some promises were better broken.

The selfless part of me wants to give in to this way of thinking, to steer clear of Emma and her new life, to drop off into a world of oblivion where the past doesn't exist, where we don't exist. I want to blot my freedom out of the town, out of her awareness, out of her life. It is foolish to think a romance sparked almost three decades ago could still have any sense of warmth left. Our fire isn't even embers anymore and, in fact, we are lucky if there's even a pile of ashes to commemorate our loss.

But another part of me smolders deep inside, threatening to ignite my secret desires. For if I am being honest, selfless isn't the word I would use to describe the way I am feeling. For me, the inferno is still ignited. Certainly there had been rains that threatened to suffocate the flames, yet somehow they still glower. Now, with new potential a real possibility, the fire leaps out of the depths, rising to meet a new day. I want, no, I *need*, to see her. I don't care that she is married, that she has moved on. I am glad she is happy, but I won't be able to fully appreciate this happiness until I can see it, judge it for myself. This side of me isn't about being the noble man or doing the right thing. This side is about heeding to my passion, heeding to my undying thirst for her. I had been an honorable man when I let her go, not knowing what the future held. Yet, now I do know what the future holds, to an extent. And I want to hold a part of her in that future, no matter how small it has to be. I want her back in my life, no matter what that looks like.

Life, as I've learned, fails to be a concrete, concise package that can easily be wrapped up and contained. Life is full of messy, unpredictable circumstances that test not only our characters, but the people around us as well. Our choices are not always about choosing between right and wrong, good or bad. They are sometimes about following the path that you simply have to follow, for one reason or another. Our choices are not always a matter of the present, either. Sometimes they are dictated by irrevocable forces from the past and untrainable longings for the future.

Voice of Innocence

In a word, our choices are not always rational. So I make the decision that I have to see her. Just like that, I slide the chair's legs across the deck, plant my feet on a fortress of determination, and head inside to take a shower.

Chapter Thirty-One
Aftermath

~ Emma ~

In the midst of the memories, I have mindlessly flicked off the television, mercifully relieving myself from the torturous images and words. Not that I can escape them even if I try. These memories are engrained in my core, and as a primary source to the tragedy, I cannot emotionally detach myself from them no matter how much I want to.

I drag my body from the depths of the couch, leaning back to crack my back that is sore from being hunched in the hollows of the cushion. Sighing with frustration, anxiety, confusion, and guilt, I drag my feet across the plush carpet and onto the cold ceramic tile of the kitchen. As I am pouring some water, the doorbell rings. I look at the clock. It's not too late, but late enough to cause a wary sensation in my blood. Could be an ax murderer. Although I don't think they are in the particular habit of ringing the doorbell to announce their presence. *What's the worst that could happen?* I think. Suddenly, though, a thought crosses my mind and my blood runs cold with anticipation. My heart leaps and adrenaline courses through my veins, more adrenaline than any psychopath serial killer could stir. *Stop it*, I tell myself. *It isn't.*

Nonetheless, I run my fingers through the ratty ends of my ponytail, tug at my wrinkled shirt, and head to the door. *This is not the reunion I was hoping for,* I think, looking down at my man-pants. I guess Mom was right that you should always look your best because you never know who you might run into. Scratching at an unidentifiable stain on the thigh of my sweatpants, I decide maybe I'll just throw them out. A new start.

As I approach the door and Hank lazily rolls off the couch to greet

Voice of Innocence

his company—some guard dog—the doorbell rings again. And again. Someone is quite impatient. As my heart leaps, I realize that deep down, this is what I have been waiting for all day. This is what has kept me suspended in time, waiting for the unthinkable to reach out and pull me simultaneously into the past and the future.

Here goes nothing, I think, wailing open the door. When it flies open on its hinge, it reveals a sight I couldn't have anticipated. I gasp in shock before muttering a simple, "Oh, it's you."

"Well, hello to you, too, darling. God, you are the worst hostess ever. Didn't I teach you anything?" My "guest" barges through the door, sunglasses plastered on top of her head, even though it's night, and a bottle of wine in her hand. She hasn't even bothered concealing it in any type of bag. She makes her way past me and straight toward the kitchen to grab some glasses.

"Mom, it's late, what are you doing?" I ask, shutting the door as a few pesky moths make their grand entrance through the door. Hank has dutifully followed his grandmother in, knowing that at least five dog treats are in his near future from the doting woman.

"What does it look like I'm doing?"

"Going on a wine binge."

"Oh, lighten up. I could tell from the phone call earlier that you needed *something* to cheer you up. No wonder though, judging by your outfit. God, even I would feel depressed wearing that outfit. Why don't you go put something better on? Huh?"

I roll my eyes, as is usual during a visit from my mother...nonetheless an impromptu one. "Mom, I'm home alone. Who cares what I'm wearing?"

Mom shrivels up her face into the typical *are you crazy* look. "Well, let's just put it this way. Thank God it was just your mother at the door and not someone else. How *does* John deal with you? Trust me, baby, you're a wonderful catch. But no man wants to come home to a unisex-looking wife. Do something with that hair, please!"

She has poured two gigantic glasses of wine. Not in wine glasses though...those would be too small. She has scavenged through our cupboards to find the perfect vessel for her ounces and ounces of fun—a beer mug.

"Wow, so glad you came to make me feel better, Mom. Trust me, you shouldn't have." Despite my sarcasm, I am glad to at least have some friendly banter. All of this silence on a night like tonight was quite possibly driving me toward insanity. Although a visit from my mother was almost guaranteed to do the same, at least I wouldn't be heading toward the white padded room in solitude.

"Who says I'm here to make you feel better?" she asks, taking a long pull on her glass of wine. "Mmm, delicious!" she adds as an afterthought.

"Well, you did say that I needed something to cheer me up," I say matter-of-factly.

"Okay, Miss smarty pants, but you need to check your facts. I said you needed something to cheer you up. I didn't say that was me," she adds, looking at me like I'm the insane one.

"Well then, why are you here?" I take a seat at the kitchen table. I'll probably need to for her response.

"I'm here because I want to witness it," she says, pulling up a chair as well.

"Witness what? My mental breakdown? Hank snoring? What?"

With the mention of Hank, she puts a finger in the air as an a-ha kind of moment. She reaches into her pants pocket, wiggles until she can pull the targeted item free. "Here you go, baby," she says as her entire hand is engulfed by Hank's slobbering mouth.

"Hello? Mom? What are you here to witness?"

"Oh, geesh. I thought you were the smart one of the family. You clearly lack some type of common sense. What would I be here to witness?"

I look at her inquisitively until reality starts to settle in. Certainly she couldn't mean…even she wouldn't go there…but the sparkle in her eye tells me that oh yes, she certainly would.

"Mom, please tell me you are not suggesting what I think you are," I say through gritted teeth.

"And what would that be, dear? That the love of your life has just been released from prison? That he's been exonerated from a crime he didn't commit, a crime that we knew he didn't commit? That he has been locked up for decades, that he hasn't stopped thinking about you, and that he will probably be making a beeline straight for here as soon as the opportunity arises? That my daughter who has spent most of her life pining away for this man, wishing against all odds that things could be different, finally has the chance for that to happen? And why wouldn't I want to witness that? Emma, it's a miracle! It's happening, all your hopes are happening. I want to be here to witness it all fabricate." Her words are accompanied by an uncharacteristic sense of seriousness. They take me aback at first, sinking in.

"Mom, really? You think he's just going to come waltzing up on my porch, say 'hey, I've missed you,' and we'll fall into each other's arms? Really?"

"Why not?"

"A lot of reasons. Things have changed. It's not that simple. We're much older now. Things don't just work like that at our age."

"When is life simple? Ask Corbin if he thinks it's simple. Hell, ask yourself," she says, looking intently at me. Tears have started to form in my eyes, but I wipe them away and mask them with a cover of anger.

"Mom, what's up with you? Have you forgotten that I'm married? Things have changed. I'm not pining away for Corbin like you think I am. Yeah, I loved him. I loved him a lot. But I'm with John now, and I love him, too. My life is with him."

I huff, teeth clenched, hand swiping at my tears, waiting for her to fire back. But for once, my mother has nothing to say. She sits for a long time, staring into her glass, lost in thought.

After a long silence filled with nothing but our breathing, she finally speaks up.

"I was nineteen when I gave birth to you. Nineteen years old. When I first got pregnant, I was scared out of my mind. Your father and I loved each other, don't get me wrong. I was lucky in that respect. But I was still terrified. We were so young, we didn't have good jobs, and we basically had nothing. I thought to myself, what are you doing? How are you going to raise this baby, how are you going to give her what she needs? How will you make sure that her life is as full as it can be?" She takes a sip of her wine, leaving me in complete suspense. I had no idea where this was going or why she was talking about it now. But I humored her.

"And then there you were. All nine pounds, six ounces of you. When I held you for the first time, all of those fears slipped away. Oh sure, I knew that it wasn't going to be easy. Life was going to throw us a lot of obstacles and threaten to tear us down. But yet, it seemed like nothing could tear apart that love and hope I had for you and for our family. You gave my life a sense of purpose because in you, I saw the future. I saw that my purpose in life was to lead you toward your purpose, toward fulfillment. And that became my mission."

She reaches across the table for my hand. She is grave in her approach, a true stillness quieting her usually wild statements.

"And so the years passed. You outgrew your pigtails and your dolls and before I knew it, you were off to school. My little bookworm, always so rational and serious. I worried about you, you know. I worried that life was going to pass right through your fingers as you had your nose in those books. Sure, I was proud of your academic achievements. But I wanted to shake you, to tell you that the real world wasn't experienced in pages of a book. It was experienced through living. But I didn't have to do that, because right around the time I started to consider it, there he came strolling into your life. Most moms are terrified at the prospect of their daughters dating. Not me, though, because I trusted you, I trusted your instinct. And as soon as I met him, I knew I was right to. Corbin. What can we say about Corbin that you don't already know? He was charming, humorous, absolutely stunning as far as guys go. But more importantly, he made you live. You went sled riding and to movies. You didn't forget about your academics, but you would close those books from time to time to go be in nature, to go have a water balloon fight, to just make memories. I saw the smile growing on your face every day as you two grew together. And I knew. I knew from that first time I met him that he was it. He was what would make your life full, would carry on my job of bringing you joy. I knew he was the one that I would trust to carry you through this crazy life."

By this time, tears have begun streaming down my face. I can't even look at my mom. I know that she hasn't started this tale to make me weep for the past, but I can't help it. To think about these thoughts is one thing; to hear them affirmed from another soul only agitates the pain even more.

Voice of Innocence

"But before I could send you off into the sunset with him, hell struck our family. I'm not going to rehash the details because I'm sure you haven't forgotten. None of us have. When Corbin lost that battle, it was like we all did. I tried to be strong for you, to not show you that on the inside, my whole world was falling apart, too. Sure, I was sad for Corbin and for what he was going through. But I was sad for my little girl, too. With the words of that jury, I saw your future being crunched into the ground like a rotten, soggy leaf in the dead of winter. I mourned for the loss of Corbin's future but also for the loss of yours. The years went by, and I kept worrying about you. Would you ever be happy again? Would you even come close? These are not easy prospects for a mother to face about her baby. No mother ever gives birth to a child thinking, 'My child is going to be miserable,' or 'My child is going to have a life of agony.' No, every mother thinks that nothing but happiness will surround her child, success and happiness. Every mother thinks her child's life will turn out better than her own. So when that doesn't happen, when things start to fall apart for the child, it's a special kind of hell. Misery pounding against my heart, I watched you, day in and day out, praying for a change to the hand I felt you'd been dealt. I prayed for a miracle. It took a long, long time to surface, but it came. It came in the form of another handsome man at, of all places, the bookstore. So yet again your studious slash nerdy behavior leads you to another man." She's smiling now. I return the expression.

"John is a wonderful man. He brought you back to the land of the living, just like Corbin did. In him, I saw so many good qualities and so much potential to bring you back to joy. Not the joy that I had mapped out for you, not the happiness that was overflowing. But happiness nonetheless. As a mother, I rejoiced in the fact that all was not lost for you, that your life could still turn out to have purpose and peace. And that it has. In him, you have found a piece of yourself again, Emma. And I know you will always love John for that. So will I."

I wipe at my tears and nod. There is another moment of silence that I finally interrupt. "I feel a *but* coming on," I offer.

She nods, still sullen in her atypical aura of momentousness. "I know you will always love John, but he's not Corbin. He's not the man who was meant for you, the man who connects you to your youth and the dreams and optimism that accompany it. He's not the man who can fully deliver you to your full purpose, your full state of being. He's not it, Emma. And it would have been okay to settle for him if that was your only choice. If the true target of your desire wasn't available. But that's not the case now. It's just not. And as confusing and complicated as it is, you have a second chance now. You have a chance to fulfill your deepest, self-defining wants. You have a chance to find the girl again who had her heart and mind focused on a successful future. You have the chance to right the wrongs, to conquer your biggest dreams, and to live them. Not everyone gets a second chance. I know it's scary and complicated. I know that it seems late in the game, or like too many years have gone by. I even know that maybe it won't work. But I think you owe it to him, to yourself, to give it a try. To just see what is left of the pieces of your dream. Because, honnie, life goes fast and you don't want to be sitting on the couch someday asking yourself what if. There have been too many of those already. It's not too late to silence them and to ask what could be. It's not too late."

She sips on her wine again, her eyes degraded to the floor.

I look at her, appreciating the courage it must have taken to spew out these words of wisdom. I know that it was out of love and a feeling that I needed to hear them.

"But what about John, Mom? What am I supposed to do with that? Even if, against all odds, Corbin comes back, even if too much time hasn't passed, what am I supposed to do with John? I love him, I do. How can I hurt him the way that I was hurt?" I beg, my mouth finally admitting the fears my mind wouldn't recognize.

Mom clutches my fingers in hers, squeezing gently. "I don't know, Emma. I don't have all of the answers, at least not about this. But you have to start thinking about yourself. You've suffered, you've had a life full of emptiness. It's time to grab what is yours, to take back your life. That might mean some people get hurt, that might mean making hard decisions, but you have to. You don't have time to waste thinking about what is most rational or what will hurt the least. You have to think about what it is that will make you happy in the long run. I've said my piece, but I can't tell you what to do. I can just tell you that no matter what happens, I'll be here."

"Thanks, Mom. I mean it." I rise and hug her, but the moment for heart-to-hearts has passed. After a few seconds of our embrace, my mom jerks away.

"Oh, my God, Emma, have you washed that nasty hair in the past week? I feel like a cake of butter just slapped me in the face. I'll tell you, you'd think you grew up with a cavewoman for a mother. I don't know where you got your lack of womanly qualities, but it wasn't from me." She shakes her head in disgust, heads to the sink to rinse her glass, and sighs.

"Well, it's getting late. I better head home before your father burns the house down trying to cook himself a snack or something. Here you go, honnie, one more from your grammy-wammy," she rambles as she leans down to give Hank another treat.

"Mom, no wonder he's getting fat," I scold.

"Oh really? And you don't enjoy a few treats from time to time? Please. Tell Mommy, when she starts eating lettuce and carrots for her meals, you'll stop eating treats," she says, scrunching Hank's face up into a horrid contortion.

"I hate it when you talk dog," I say, truly annoyed.

"And I hate those man-pants. Seriously, a grown woman, and you dress like you're a college frat girl." She shakes her head in disgust yet again. "So we'll call it even. I love you, I'll talk to you tomorrow."

"What about the reunion you were hell-bent on witnessing?" I poke.

"Oh, it's still going to happen," she smirks. "I just figure you might need a little…privacy for it."

"Mom…" I sigh, true frustration returning. Why did she have to ruin any potentially tender moment?

"Okay, Okay, I'm leaving. Keep me posted," she demands as she scurries toward the door.

"Do I have a choice?" I add, ready to shut and lock the door as soon as she is through.

"Oh, you'll miss me someday. Someday you'll wish you had your awesome mother to fill in with details. Not everyone's so lucky, you know. Now toodles!" and with that, she whooshes to her car.

"Are you sure you're okay to drive?" I shout out the door as an afterthought.

"Are you serious? One glass? Pu-leaze." She hops in the car, flips on the lights, honks her characteristic two toots, and is gone.

Although I haven't done much except slug around the house, I am suddenly exhausted. I find the couch again, where Hank has already laid claim to about seventy-five percent of it. I melt into the cushion, exhale, and find myself again transported to another time, a time when my mother was truly my saving grace, whether I wanted to admit it or not.

Chapter Thirty-Two
Tough Love

~ Emma ~

Memories

    For the next few weeks, I refused to believe that things were actually done. I kept trying to visit Corbin. Every time I went, he refused to see me and asked to be taken back to his cell. I gave up on the visits and started writing letters instead. I wrote every week, begging him to let me back into his life. I pleaded that I wouldn't move on, that I refused to, and that he might as well let me back in because I wasn't going anywhere. I never received any responses. As the weeks floated into months, reality slowly sank in—he was done. Corbin wasn't getting out of jail, and he wasn't letting me sit by him. I was alone.
    I heard from his dad that Corbin's lawyer was working on an appeal, but it wasn't expected to go well. The evidence was too damning. So I had no choice but to try to carry on. I wasn't ready to face that.
    Everyone else around me had moved on long ago, making me realize that the world truly doesn't stop turning. My classmates had gone on to college and to the workforce. They were building the foundations for their lives while I was wallowing in pity over the loss of mine before it had even started. In the early days after the sentencing, some old friends offered support. Although they were away at college, Jenn and Hannah sent letters of encouragement and sympathy. They were short and superficial, though. What did you say to someone in my situation? Katie had gone above and beyond the others, stopping by to visit me on a

weekend home from college.

"I'm so sorry!" she exclaimed as she hugged me at my door. She didn't seem to notice the disarray of my hair or my lack of hygiene. I didn't notice either because both had become constants in my life of sadness.

"Thanks, Katie. I appreciate it."

She stayed for an hour, saying how shocked she was and how she knew Corbin couldn't possibly do it. She asked what we were going to do.

"We aren't doing anything," I mumbled, tears free-flowing. "He's pushed me away. He wants me to move on, a symbol of his selflessness. I hate him for it," I admitted, shocked that the words flowed so easily. In reality, I did hate him for what he had done. I hated him for making me step away, for making me essentially give up on us.

Katie hugged me again. "Emma, I know it hurts. I know. But maybe it's for the best. I know you love him, but I think Corbin knows that. He loves you so much that he wants to see you happy. I think maybe it's easiest for him to think that you're happy, even if it's without him. I think you owe it to him to try." She spoke the words so gently that they didn't offend me like they did when they tumbled out of my mom's mouth. For a second, I even considered them. Katie continued talking about moving on and "eventually getting back out there," but by that time, I had retreated back into myself. We parted ways, Katie promising she would be there if I ever needed her. I think she would have been if I had let her back into my life. With my depressive state, though, friendly pleasantries and staying in touch didn't rank high on my list. I would receive several letters from her over the next few years, but that was it. I couldn't blame her or anyone else for that matter. Sure, they felt sorry for me and for the situation, but it didn't mean that they should harp on it. Their lives were still moving forward. They had to live them.

Despite my detachment toward Katie during her visit, it did strike a chord with me. I realized maybe everyone was right. Maybe Corbin needed me to move on with my life to validate what he did. Maybe I needed to show Corbin that I loved him by letting him do this one final act of selfless love. Everything had been stripped from him. This was all he had left to offer me, the only way he could show that he cared. Maybe

I should appreciate his efforts and do something with my life. I wasn't ready to think about love, but maybe I could at least try appreciating my days. I vowed to try to start living again.

I didn't try very hard. Sure, I got out of bed in the morning. I brushed my teeth and ate pretty regularly. Once in a while, I would take a walk around the block to clear my head. Other than that, though, I became a recluse, never leaving the house except when my mother forced me. Once a cosmetic addict, I rarely even looked in the mirror anymore. My daily uniform became a pair of ratty old sweatpants and a T-shirt from my high school. Mom and Dad tried to get me to rediscover my desire to attend college, to give me something to keep me busy and to keep my eyes on what lie ahead.

"You've only missed one year, Emma. It's not too late to enroll now. You'll only be graduating a year later than expected. Corbin would want you to go," Mom reasoned with me about three months after the sentencing.

"Please don't say his name," I responded while mindlessly stirring the cream in my coffee at the table.

"Emma, I know it's hard. I do. But you can't just stop your life. You have to pick it up and find something to do. You can't mope around this house forever. I love you, but you need to get your own life. Dad and I can't baby you forever. You can't keep lying around doing nothing."

I paused from my stirring and looked up at her. "Are you saying that you're throwing me out?" I defiantly implored. Just what I needed.

"Emma, don't be ridiculous. I'm not throwing you out. I'm just saying I'm sick of watching you throw your life away."

"Mom, what am I supposed to do? Just pretend he didn't exist? Pretend my life is awesome?" I protested with anger slipping into my voice.

"Well, yeah, Emma, if that's what it takes. Corbin would want you to do something. I don't think he broke up with you so you could sit around here looking like that!" she noted forcefully, shriveling her nose up at my outfit.

"What the hell, Mom? Now you're bashing my outfit? If you haven't noticed, my life freaking sucks right now. Everything was ripped away from me. Everything. I'm not just going to carry on like it doesn't matter. I don't even want to go to college. What's the point?" I contended, leaping from my chair. I was getting ready to storm upstairs to my room like an insolent teenager when my mother grabbed my arm.

"Emma, stop. I'm on your side. I'm not going to deal with this flippant attitude, though. Yes, what happened sucked. It still sucks. I'm just as mad and sad and pissed and confused as you. But you are my concern now. I can't do anything for Corbin, but I can make sure that your life starts to pull back together. I love you. I don't want you to look back with regrets, okay? I'm not throwing you out. You don't have to go to college if you don't want to, that's your choice. But I am making a new rule. You have thirty days to find yourself a job. I don't care if it's making sandwiches at Big Bob's Deli or working as a tattoo artist, but you have to find it in thirty days. Within thirty days, I want you to have somewhere you have to be and somewhere you have to look decent to go to. No more sitting in your room weeping in your saggy sweatpants. Let's get you back out into the world."

"Mom, really? You're giving me an ultimatum now?" I groaned.

"Well, Miss Intelligent, an ultimatum requires some sort of consequence if you don't follow through. Have I given you a consequence?"

"Well, not yet, but I'm afraid to ask."

"Well, you should be afraid. For now, the consequence is my little secret. But I don't think you want to find out what it is."

I rolled my eyes but leaned in to give my mom a hug. Although a part of me hated her for her hovering nature, I also loved that she was trying to get me motivated again. In a way, a piece of me knew she was right. I couldn't curl up in my room and wait to die. I had to do something with my life. I didn't have to love it. Hell, I didn't even have to smile. But I had to do something.

That night, I perused the classifieds in the newspaper. It was then that I saw an ad for a local trucking company. They were hiring an office assistant. The pay was half decent, the job seemed easy, and I was qualified with my high school degree. I knew one of Mom's friends even worked there, so it would probably be an easy in. It wasn't a life-changing revelation, but it was at least a step in the right direction, and it would get Mom off of my back.

Voice of Innocence

So that night, I took a major step toward my new life. I sent in an application.

That was also the night I took a few steps away from Corbin Jones, whether I liked it or not.

Chapter Thirty-Three
Wings and Words

~ Corbin ~

Undressing, I bask in a luxury that hasn't been all my own for a decade—a hot shower. As the water ricochets off my body against the shower door and the steam cleanses my lungs, I revel in the simple pleasures that would have been overlooked by my teenage self. What once seemed like a chore is now a piece of paradise.

The gravity of what I'm preparing for hasn't slipped away from my mind. A part of me thinks I must be crazy, the air of the free world intoxicating me and cracking my rationale. No sane man, let alone one let out of prison, would think to do this. There are so many reasons why this is a bad idea.

Yet there is one reason I can't get the prospect of seeing her tonight out of my mind.

I still love her.

I had never stopped loving her, not for a second. Some would assume it was just the emotional ramblings of a broken man, beaten down by the dismal days of prison. True, I had little to fill my life except the memories of what had once been. But despite all of that, I feel like it was something more. Emma and I had something special, something I believed was a once-in-a-lifetime occurrence. We would have been so happy if that night hadn't happened. The feelings that still linger, decade after decade, aren't just the residue of a love lost. They are as real as the first day I told her I loved her. That love hadn't died when I chopped her out of my life, when that cell door swung shut. I had never stopped loving her. Not when I uttered that final goodbye or got up from the prison table that final day we saw each other. Not that night as I agonized over whether or not I had done the right thing. Not for the next several months as letter upon letter poured in from her, all of which still lie in that wooden box, my prized possessions in prison. For the next twenty-eight years, those letters would be my sole link to a girl I had let go. They had been reminders of what I did to her and of how much pain I had caused. They were daggers in my shield of resolve to let her go. Tonight, they are questions of whether or not I had done the right thing.

I had labeled those letters as they came to my cell, keeping a rigid time line for myself, allowing me to retrace our relationship as it fell to shambles. Meanwhile, I sat back in silence, hoping the girl I wanted nothing more than to hold would get over me. Yet, I silently hoped she never would.

* * * *

Letter 1:

Corbin,

I can't stop crying over what you said last night. I can't stop thinking of the way you walked away from me, claiming that it was for my own good. I can't bear the thought of it being true.

I know that things are hard—hopeless, even. I sit awake at night, fretting over the possibility that this nightmare might never end. I wonder how I am going to live a life loving you so much yet being forced apart from you. More than that, though, I wonder how I am going to live knowing that you can't. Knowing that your world consists of those four walls. I wish that I could trade places with you. Better yet, I wish that they could lock me up with you, too. I've spent a lot of time enraged over the past few months, pissed at the situation and how unfair life is. Things were great for us, perfect even. We had so much to look forward to, but it was all shattered by one stupid night that wasn't even our fault. I can't stop asking myself why. Why us? Why this? I'm sure that this is just redundant rambling to you, because I know that as hard as this is for me, it is worse for you. I can't imagine what it's like to be in your shoes. But I want to try. I want to be there for you. Please Corbin, let me do this.

I love you. I love you so much that I can't, no I won't, face a life without you. I know you are trying to do the right thing, the noble thing. I love you for that. I appreciate that. That's the kind of guy you are. But I won't let you. I won't let you try to push me away for your own good. Here's the thing, Corbin: It won't be good for me. Having to be physically apart from you is awful. But being emotionally away from you would be even worse. I can tolerate the physical distance because I know that someday this nightmare will end. It just has to. And when it does, we will be together again. I know it.

So please, Corbin, don't do this. I know you're hurting and confused. I know that you think this is best. It's not. Please don't give up on us. Don't give up on yourself. It's going to be okay. Just let me stand by you, let me be there for you. If the tables were turned, what would you want?

I love you. Forever. I'm not giving up. I'll be by to see you next visiting hours.

Love always,
Emma

* * * *

Letter 4:

Corbin,

It's been two weeks now. I tried to visit you again yesterday, but you wouldn't see me. I try not to be mad at you, to remind myself that you're hurting. But Corbin, you're hurting me by refusing to see me. I need to see you, even if it's just in that dismal room with guards watching. I need to hear your voice, to see with my own eyes that you're hanging in there. It's not ideal, I know that. I would rather be in your arms than sitting arms-length

Voice of Innocence

away from you. I would rather be taking a walk or sitting at my mom's table eating breakfast. I would do anything to just go back to the way things used to be.

But we can't, Corbin. Not yet. I don't know where this is all going, I don't know how it's going to turn out. But I do know one thing. I can't just walk away from this. No matter how much you want me to, no matter how much easier it would be, I can't. I can't bear the thought of leaving you alone in this.

I know you still love me. I know that you don't really want this.

Corbin, I miss you. Yes, it's not the same with you behind bars. We can't hug and kiss. We can't walk to our tree or spend time in the barn. I would give anything to have that time back. I would give anything just to hold hands with you. I miss you.

But what's even worse is not even being able to talk to you. I haven't even heard back from you in a letter. Corbin, I need you. I need to hear from you, to talk to you. This is the hardest thing I've ever gone through, and I need my best friend beside me. Please don't shut me out like this.

I'm still not giving up. I love you. Stay strong.
I love you. Forever.
Emma

* * * *

Letter 48:

Corbin,

This is probably the hardest thing I've ever done. Even harder than watching you walk away from me that day in the prison cell.

I know this is what you want. I don't claim to understand it. I don't agree with it. I'm not even sure if I've accepted it. But I know that you think it's best. For a while, I hated you for it. I hated you for the way you've shut me out, how you've forced silence onto me to push me away. I denied it, writing to you even though I knew I'd be met with silence. I guess that even if I didn't hear from you, just knowing that I was still connected to you, even if just by writing to you, comforted me. It made me feel like it wasn't over. I still don't know if it is.

But I know this can't go on. I find myself foolishly checking the mailbox every day, hoping against all odds that you've responded. I still run every time the phone rings, thinking that maybe you've changed your mind. But your silence these past months has convinced me otherwise.

Mom and I had a talk a few weeks ago. She convinced me that I can't keep this up, that I have to rejoin the land of the living. She said it's what you want, so I should honor that. For the past few months, I didn't know if I was ready to agree with her. I halfheartedly committed to the notion, putting one foot into the land of the living and keeping one foot behind. I've kept writing to you as I slowly rejoined the world, not ready to completely let go. I still don't think I am completely ready. I know this isn't what I want. But I also know that I have to do something. I can't just wait to die. I have to do something.

So I've decided that this is it. This will be my last letter. Even as I write this, I don't know if I can bring myself to believe it, but I know that I have to. I have to step back, for both of us. I have to let go.

I still love you, Corbin. I still haven't lost faith. The truth will come out. You will get your life back. I just don't know when.

I want you to know that I'll keep praying for you. I'll keep hoping against hope that the truth prevails. Corbin, you're a good man. I know that it will work out.

But I also know you're right, that we can't know when that will be. I know now that my sitting around waiting for you is hurting you more. I realize that now.

Voice of Innocence

This doesn't mean that I don't still love you. It doesn't mean that I've given up on the idea or hope of us. I still have visions of our reunion, the idea of us being together in some distant place, in some distant time.

Corbin, despite the hell that we've been through, you are the best thing that ever happened to me. You brought me joy when I had all but forgotten. You woke me up to the beauties of life and the ecstasy of love. You opened my heart. The truth is, you stole it. I know that as long as I live, I will never look at another man the way I looked at you—the way I still look at you in my heart.

I don't know why all of this happened. I don't know if I ever will. But I do know that I am thankful for the time we had. In those few years, we had more love and memories than some people ever have. We found each other when youth and optimism helped propel our relationship to dizzying heights and to strong connections. I know that I am better for having known you. I will never forget the way that my hand felt in yours, the way that your lips awoke a sense of vibrancy in the depths of my soul. I will never forget the joys in the simplicity of our moments together. I will never settle for anything less than what we had.

I don't think that love is in my cards for the future other than the love I feel for you. I know that even though I'm young, I could never find someone who completes me the way you do. I know you don't want to hear that, I know you want me to try to move on. But Corbin, in some respects I can't. I can try to find a career, try to experience life. But that is one line I don't think I'll ever cross. No one can soothe my inner being like you. No one can make me look to the future with such excitement like you did. No one can understand me, fulfill me, fit me like you did. I know that.

So I suppose we've come to goodbye again. It's such a harsh word, as harsh as the word that was proclaimed at your sentencing. It has such power, such control. It has the ability to take our lives and twist them in a new direction that we never wanted or expected.

Corbin, I love you. I always will. If you ever need me, if you ever change your mind, don't hesitate to contact me. Don't hesitate to break your resolve, to reach out to me. Because no matter where I am in my life, no matter what I am doing, I will never be far from you in my heart. I may be moving on, but I'm not moving away from you. You will always be in my soul, a part of my present, and a fleeting dream for my future.

I love you. Forever.
Emma

* * * *

Water dripping onto the comforter, I sit cradled in my towel as I fold the last letter, putting it back in the box. I can't help but feel tightness in my chest at her words. Reading the letters in order as I have so many times, it's easy to see the despair that builds in her. I remember the despair I felt with each letter. I hadn't wanted to read them, yet I felt the need to know. So many times I almost broke down and wrote back. So many times, I almost let her words get through to me, I almost let her pull me back in. But I couldn't. It was this last letter that had convinced me I had done the right thing. She was moving on, she was doing what I had asked. I knew, when I received this letter, that I had done the right thing for Emma. I had given her the wings she needed to fly to a new life. She had done that.

But now I wonder if she had flown so far away that I couldn't reach her. I wonder if that last part of her letter still rings true.

Could forever truly exist? Could time and circumstances tarnish even the most resolute love?

I was about to find out, despite my wavering hesitancy. I rummage through my old dressers, hoping to find something that would still fit.

Chapter Thirty-Four
Hauntings

~ Emma ~

I shift on the couch, stretching out my legs as my knees crack. Pretty soon, I will develop bed sores, yet I don't have the energy to even move. I feel like I'm nineteen again, sitting in my parents' house waiting for something to happen. Waiting to wake up and have a normal life again, a thought foreign to me even at this age.

The clock ticks, reminding me of the remaining monotony of the night to come. John probably won't be home for hours, not that I would be effective or enthralling company at this point anyway. It's too late to go anywhere. Television is clearly not an option, and the magazine has already lost my attention. With few other options, I shake Hank awake and head upstairs. Maybe luck will be on my side and I will drown in a puddle of sleep, waking up to a new day. I am not sure how helpful a new day of these boggling thoughts will be.

I climb into our bed under the quilt, fluffing the pillows to trick my brain into being tired. Sleep does not come to my rescue, though. Instead, the memories that have been whirling around me continue to usurp my thoughts. Images and pictures swirl together like a depressing home movie. I see his face right in front of me and my stomach still plummets. I hear his laugh, his jokes, feel his kisses on my lips. I see him in his prison jumpsuit, despondent and hardened. I imagine him sitting in that cell, day after day, all alone, cut off from the outside world. I imagine the pain he must have gone through, having lost everything and everyone that mattered to him. Certainly, my life without him hadn't been a picnic. I had suffered in my own prison, of sorts, cut off emotionally from the world around me by the pain and hauntings of the past. In a way, I had given myself a prison sentence, not allowing myself to enjoy too much or to live too fully out of subconscious sorrow for Corbin. It was not fair that I could continue living while his life had stopped so abruptly. I had chosen, though, to live my life like this. Corbin hadn't. Corbin had no choice but to face a ceaseless train of similar days with no true purpose or value to society. His talents, his warmth were all harnessed in the coldness of those thick walls, a hidden secret in a world that valued nothing.

But then another type of guilt creeps in, derailing me once more.

What about John? That sweet man who had pulled me out from the hermit-like life I had been leading up until I met him. What about all of our sweet memories—the midnight walks by the lake, the Saturday night trips to the club for some crazy dancing, the family barbecues in Maine with his sister and her family. We had been together for five years, and in those years we had shared laughs, embraces, and tender moments. John had reintroduced me to life, taking me out to experience what it had to offer. He was the warmth that had been missing, the glow stick in a sea of blackness. He was a hero in the ER, but he was also a hero in my life, saving me from a meaningless, emotionless existence. Why weren't all of the beautiful moments we had shared pervading my thoughts? Why couldn't I just be happy with what I had? What was wrong with me?

My mom seemed to think this was my chance to get what I wanted, but didn't I have what I wanted? Didn't John fulfill me? Certainly it wasn't the same as that fulfillment I had found as a teenager with Corbin. It wasn't the life I had mapped out for myself. But did that matter? Life doesn't always work out the way we individualistic humans think it should. Sometimes life evolves in ways we couldn't imagine, but does that make the new life less valuable? Should my relationship with John be degraded, demeaned simply because he wasn't my first love? Maybe first loves were meant to simply be prequels to the main acts in our lives. They set the stage for reality. John, not Corbin, was now my reality. Could I throw that away for a man I had only known once but didn't really know now? Maybe I was getting ahead of myself. Maybe Corbin wasn't even a remote possibility at this point. But even if he was, I had to consider what it could mean for John and me and whether or not I was truly ready to throw all of that away for a man from my past.

In the depths of the night, though, I am forced to be honest with myself. Corbin isn't just a fling from the past, a symbol of who I was in a distant history. Corbin is me. Corbin has shaped me into the woman I have become. Everything I am, everything I had been, is related to our relationship. Some of those elements are positive, and many are certainly negative, stemming from the tragedy we had endured. Regardless, though, Corbin is as integral a part of myself as my own soul. If I am being candid, he is still an ever-present part of my heart, shaping my emotions even though he isn't around. Time has not stretched our love thin to the point of cracking. Time has simply solidified the fact that our love was real. And now I am faced with the question of what all of this means for us, for our future that we never thought was a possibility. Where do we go from here?

My mind wasn't always this reminiscent. Up until a few months ago, my life had seemed to move on. Certainly, Corbin still owned a piece of my heart, but he had not flooded my everyday life to this extreme. I was not, on a daily basis, incapacitated by memories of us. Sure, he infiltrated my mind from time to time. Red barns, sled rides, almost anything could bring his memories swirling to the forefront of my mind. Nonetheless, I had learned to assuage thoughts of him by focusing on John. Yes, life had not turned out exactly as I had planned. I never got the true, fairy-tale ending. Yes, I worried about Corbin and wondered how he was doing. I wondered how life could be so unfair and how he could possibly have survived all these years. However, I had resigned Corbin as a distant memory, a part of life that no longer existed and could never exist again. He was a relic from a part of my life that could not be reclaimed. He was a symbol of the injustice in life and the requirement to move on. I felt our relationship had become one-sided, with me simply basking in its glory from time to time in a pointless reverie of what had been and never could be. I had learned in the past few years to let Corbin be a part of my heart without owning it. I had learned that the heart is elastic, that it isn't always a one-or-the-other type of thing. I still loved Corbin, but I was in love with John. And I was happy.

That all changed, however, two months ago, when I received that mind-blowing letter in the mail. Suddenly, the "if-onlys" of the past became real possibilities. The past was coming to slam into my present, whether I liked it or not.

Chapter Thirty-Five
Innocence

Corbin Jones
Prisoner# 1825
SCI-Fayette
Dear Emma,
*   I know this letter must come as a shock to you. It has been so many years, decades, since we last saw each other. I know that is my fault. I'm still sorry for the way I pushed you away that fateful day. However, in many ways, I'm not sorry at all. I did what I thought was right, what I thought was best for you. I didn't want you to waste your life on a doomed man. I hope you can appreciate that now. I hope you did in fact go out and find that life to live. I've heard that you have. I hope you've found the happiness that you deserve, the happiness that just wasn't meant to be with me.*
*   Those first few months in jail were the hardest. I felt so trapped, so alone, and so hopeless. I missed you and thought about you every day. I wondered what you were doing. I longed to be at that kitchen table eating pancakes with your crazy mom or to take a walk to our tree. I longed to hold you, to tell you it would all be okay. Prison is funny that way—it makes you realize what's important.*
*   I got every letter you sent those first few months. It was so hard to read them and not write back or pick up the phone and call you. I longed to hear your voice, to*

answer your pleas. I wanted nothing more than to write to you and say I was sorry, to come back. But I couldn't do it. I couldn't be that selfish. I kept every letter you sent. I read them over and over for the next two decades. Even today, I still pull them out and read them from time to time. It's hard to read those final relics of us, but it's harder to imagine what your life would have been like if I hadn't done what I did. It hurt to let you go. It would have killed me, though, to watch you waste your life sitting on the sidelines of that jail, imprisoned by my verdict. I couldn't let that happen.

Emma, I think about our time together often. In fact, that's all I do. I remember those stolen kisses on our first sled ride, those days at the lunch table together, even our first fight. I remember confiding in you about Chloe. I remember what it felt like to hold you in the barn that night. I remember what it felt like to slide that cool, silver ring on your finger. I remember what it felt like to look into the horizon and see forever with you.

Despite everything that has happened, I wouldn't change a thing. You showed me so much in the years we spent together. You showed me how to have fun at a time when I only knew sorrow. You showed me what a real family could be like by sharing your mom with me. You showed me what it meant to be a real man, a man who loved and was loved. You showed me what it was to dream. I will always love you for that.

And so, I come to the point of this letter. It is not to make you sad for what once was or what should have been. It is not to beg you to come back to me and visit, to cheer up a pitiful inmate. It is simply to tell you that you were right. You were right all along, Emma.

The truth has finally shone through.

Even though I gave up on getting out, my dad and my lawyer never did. All of this time, my dad has been researching and investigating. With the help of my lawyer, he has been rustling for the truth. With the help of a foundation, he has finally found it. More importantly, he has found a way to prove it.

If you remember, the night I found Randy, there was a knife. At the time, all the police knew was that there was blood on the knife, there was blood on me, and there was a grudge. Case closed.

Luckily, however, the knife and other evidence were sealed in a plastic evidence bag, thrown in a case box, and jammed into storage where it has remained all these years. It was just six months ago that my dad finally found out that the evidence miraculously still existed. More importantly, he was able to convince an angelic team of amazing lawyers of my innocence. Once they got involved, things started to fall into place. With some serious digging, they were able to have DNA tests performed on some skin scrapings that were apparently taken from under Randy's nails. The DNA, of course, didn't match mine. The perpetrator wasn't me, and the prosecution finally had no choice but to believe it.

Although the state hasn't had a problem locking me up for decades for a crime I didn't commit, it sure is taking its time to get me out of here. There is legal tape we have to break through, more trials and meetings and examinations. But then, as my lawyer assures me, it will all be over. I will finally be a free man. Randy's killer is still out there. They haven't figured out who it is yet. But they know it isn't this man who is the killer, and that is good enough for me.

In many ways, it seems surreal. I expected to spend the rest of my days locked up in here and now reality is setting in. You would think I would be overjoyed. In some ways I am, but I am also just drowning in countless emotions. A part of me is thankful, thankful to the group of angels who toiled for a man they didn't even know just so that innocence could prevail. I'm angry that it took this many years for the truth to be revealed. I'm enraged that the evidence was sitting there in a box when I was locked up. How could this evidence be overlooked all these years? If I'm being honest, though, I'm also terrified. I never had to think about establishing a life beyond meal time, lifting weights, and avoiding the other inmates who were dangerous. Now I am faced with the ever-present question in the human lifespan: Now what? What place is there in a world for an ex-innocent-shouldn't-have-been-convict who has spent his entire adult life in prison? I don't even know what the world is like anymore. I only know the prison world. How do I adjust to freedom? Where do I go? How will people treat me? To be honest, Em, I am more afraid to face the outside world than to stay in here.

When I heard the official news, the first person I thought of was you. I hesitated to write this letter. I didn't want to intrude in a life that I know has been built without me. But I felt I owed it to you. I remember that last meeting we had, the one with the painful goodbye. I remember promising you if I ever got out, if I ever was freed, I would hope we could meet again. I promised I would keep my heart open for you. I thought you should know the truth has prevailed, just like you said it would. It just took a bit longer than expected.

I am not writing this to turn your world upside down or to beg for you back. I love you, Em, as much as I did when we were crazy, love-drunk teenagers. I truly believe that we could have been amazing together, that our lives would have been a tumult of memories and beautiful moments. I wish we had had the chance to find out.

I know, however, that time has passed. A lot of it. Our ship has sailed into the distance and it wasn't a round-trip fare. Life has marched on, and with it, I know that things have changed. I am sure you have built a beautiful life for yourself with beautiful people—that is what I wanted you to do. That is what I hope you did. I mean it, Em. I hope you got everything you ever wanted. I hope you are surrounded by success, love, and, most importantly, happiness.

I am writing this simply to tell you the truth, a truth that has finally been substantiated. I am writing this to say thank you for believing in me.

If I shall have the blessing to come across you in this crazy, free world, I will meet you with nothing but a smile and well wishes.

I am writing to tell you that you were the love of my life and always will be. There never comes a day when your face doesn't plaster itself in my mind, our memories don't dance in my daydreams.

I hope that you are not upset by this letter. I hope that, if anything, you will simply smile because the world, after all, does have a sense of fairness to it. I hope that through the years, you have seen nothing but evidence of this.

I love you, forever. Take care. Don't worry about me, I'll be fine. Farewell again.
    Love,
    Me

Chapter Thirty-Six
Pasta and Promises

~ Emma ~

I must have read that letter seventy times. I would sneak it out of its hiding place in my jewelry box when John was at work. I would read it in the middle of the night when he was at the ER. I would slip it into my purse and read it in the car when I was grocery shopping. I read it and read it until I didn't have to read it anymore. Every word was burned into my memory, carved on my soul.

When I first received that envelope in the mailbox, I had stopped in disbelief at the return address. My hands started sweating, my brain turned to mush, and I felt like my legs weren't even part of my body. I stood in the driveway, pausing for an eternity. I was debating with myself whether I should read it at all, though I don't think it was ever a question. Slowly, deliberately, I had ripped the envelope open.

The words flowed off the page, yet they didn't seem to make sense. I had to read it twice just to understand it. Even then, only a few phrases stood out. *"The truth...,"* *"DNA,"* *"Free,"* *"Love..."* So it was finally happening. After all this time, the evidence proved without a doubt that he didn't do it.

Not that I had ever doubted that fact. I had known from the beginning it wasn't true. Yet, I had walked away. I had chosen a life without Corbin rather than a life with him, even if that meant a life with him behind bars. I had made a choice, and now I was living with it. The question was could I live with that choice now, even when I didn't have to?

Voice of Innocence

For weeks, months, I was plagued by what the letter could mean. Corbin said he hadn't wanted to interrupt my life, and I believed him. But the simple truth was that this letter, in many ways, changed everything. The truth had surfaced. Everything I had hoped for had been substantiated. But was it too late? As Corbin said, *what now?*

If I could go back and tell my nineteen-year-old self that this would happen, would I have done things the same? Would I have still vowed to move on from Corbin, still turned my back on him, still obeyed his command to make a life for myself?

Would I still have said yes to John?

I was so happy to find out that Corbin was getting out, that his life could begin. Yet I was also devastated. For with this change of events came new pangs of guilt, new what ifs that rotated constantly through my mind.

Then came the questions. Would he be okay? Where would he go now? What would he do with his life? Did he have anyone to support him?

One question, though, rose above the rest, painting a clear picture of where my heart was, even after all these years: Would he keep his promise to find me, even after all of this time? And more importantly, did I want him to?

For weeks, I tossed the letter around in my mind, not sure what to do about it. A part of me raced for a tablet to write a reply. A part of me held back, not sure if I wanted to commit to that open bridge just yet.

To make matters more complicated, John started to notice my suddenly erratic behavior. One night at dinner, he finally confronted me.

"Em, is everything okay?" he asked, setting his fork down and reaching across the bistro table in the café to grasp my hand.

"It's fine, why would you ask?" I offered, casting my eyes toward my plate of pasta.

"Emma, it's me you're talking to. I know you. Something's off lately. What's going on?" John didn't move his eyes from mine, demanding the truth with his body language. I knew I couldn't keep this from him. Soon it would probably make headlines.

I sighed, putting down my fork as well and finally meeting his eyes. My heart palpitated as I brought myself to say the words. "There's been a development."

John just stared at me blankly, waiting for a more substantial explanation. "Okay…" he encouraged.

"With Corbin. He's been proven innocent."

John's eyebrows raised, demonstrating that this was far from what he had expected. "Oh my God, Em. That's crazy. I don't know what to say." His words were soft, melodious even. Comfort resonated from his voice, but turmoil softened his face. He wasn't sure what this meant, and his eyes seemed to search mine in hopes of finding an answer, an answer that he wanted.

"Yeah, it's crazy. It's just been on my mind lately. I mean, after all this time, to find the truth now. I just feel horrible that it took this long. Imagine, twenty-eight years…" My eyes instinctively averted down again as I found myself lost in the tidal wave of guilt and memories.

We sat in silence for a long moment before John finally spoke.

"Em, I don't want to sound insensitive or insecure. I know why this bothers you, and I understand. It's a lot to take in. It's such a heavy situation. But I have to ask. What does this mean for you? For us?" John ambled over the words cautiously, afraid to offend me or make me feel bad.

I quickly darted my eyes to him, "It doesn't mean anything. Not as far as we're concerned. John, if you're even insinuating that…" I pounced on him rapidly, without intending to. This is why I had kept the letter a secret, not mentioning it. I knew John would wonder. How couldn't he? I had told him the entire story, including the fact that we hadn't talked in decades because we knew there wasn't a chance for his release. With his release imminent, though, who could blame John for wondering if things were about to change?

"I'm sorry, I shouldn't have asked. I just had to know if this, you know, changed anything." John gazed at me intently, lovingly. John wasn't the kind of guy to be insecure or protective. He was always open with me, giving me a sense of easy freedom. He wasn't quick to judge or to grow jealous. He seemed secure in our relationship and in the fact that my past was the past.

"John, I'm serious. I love you. This is certainly a shock, and I'll admit it has been on my mind these past few weeks. But nothing has changed. What Corbin and I had was special, yes, but it was decades ago. We haven't even talked. There's nothing left of us except memories. I'm with you, and I'm happy. You came into my life at a time when I had given up on love, and you reminded me what it was all about. You showed me what it felt like to truly share your life with someone. How could you even question if anything would change? I love you, John, and only you." I grasped his hands firmly to solidify my words. He nodded, leaned across our plates of spaghetti with caution, and planted a kiss on my cheek.

"Do you think he'll come to see you?" John further inquired. I paused, not sure what to say.

"I don't know. I don't think so. It's been so long. We're different now. He's different. I think he'll want to respect that my life has moved on. But it doesn't matter, even if he did try to see me. I love you," I delicately said, putting great emphasis on the final phrase.

"I love you, too. Please don't be afraid to talk to me about this, okay? I'm here for you." And with that, the case was closed. We went back to shoveling in our pasta, sipping on our wine, and talking about the latest to be sent home on our favorite reality show.

But that night, after John had fallen asleep in our bed—a rare occasion, since it was one of his few days off during the month—I lie awake thinking about John's question. I had been honest with him at dinner. I did love him. I hadn't talked to Corbin in decades. But had I been completely truthful? Was our love truly a figment of the past? Was our love reduced to just memories?

A few months ago, I would have assuredly said yes. But now, questions bubbled in the back of my mind. Less than a year ago, our love was impossible, cut off by prison walls and time. Now, though, things were about to change. How would I fare knowing that Corbin Jones was again in the land of the living? Would things with John change knowing that Corbin was just a few minutes away? Did I *want* things to change?

And so began months of pondering, of torturous memories, and of falling back in love with the way things used to be.

Chapter Thirty-Seven
March On

~ Corbin ~

I step into a pair of pants and a T-shirt that seem to still be in style, slap on some of the deodorant that is still on my dresser, and head back to the bathroom to find some grooming tools. It was happening. After all of the sorrows and doubts, it was happening. I was going to see Emma again, face to face, the only bars between us the bars of time.

What would she look like? Would she be happy to see me? Had she read my letter? Question after question unsteady my shaky mind and heart. Was I making a mistake? What if she refused to talk to me? Then again, what did I have to lose?

I run a comb through my rugged hair, collect the remaining water droplets from my warm skin with the towel, and peer through the fuzzy reflection of the vapor-coated mirror, deciding that it's "go time."

On my way down the stairs, I glance at the clock. It's late. Really late. I almost talk myself out of the trip. Only a crazy man would haul himself onto the steps of his ex-girlfriend's house at this hour after so many years. Plus, what if her husband is home? Wouldn't that be a story for the media: *Ex-convict proven innocent shot dead on steps of ex-girlfriend's house the day of his release?* Okay, so they would have to improve the title, but still, it would be a hell of a tragic ending to a tragic story.

Despite my fears, the prospect of simply going to bed and forgetting about my plan seems out of the question. I have waited long enough to see her. No matter what the meeting brings, whether it be the wrath of an angry husband or the tears of a broken woman, I have to find out. Tonight. The heart wants what it wants, no matter how irrational or harebrained the scheme is. So I head into the living room to tell my dad where I'm off to, feeling a bit like an irrational adolescent asking permission to be out past curfew. The old man is snoring in his chair, mouth open, ready to catch any bugs or dust that float by his sopping-wet mouth. I head to the kitchen, rummage for some paper, and leave a note. Then it's out the front door to her house.

It's about an eight-minute walk to my destination. Dad had mentioned in passing a few months ago that Emma now lives in the old Holderbrook's place. The Holderbrook's place was quite famous in town because at Halloween every year, the elderly couple gave out whole candy bars *and* dollar bills to all of the town's trick-or-treaters. It was a trick-or-treater's paradise and remembered as a fond childhood memory by all. Now it was where Emma lived, adult Emma, achieving-the-American-dream Emma. I tried to picture her swinging lazily on the front porch, sipping lemonade in the summer. Did he sit with her? Did they joke like we once had, sharing secrets and dreams? Did he bare his soul to her on the back deck as they glanced at the stars? Did they have a tree that was all their own? Did he appreciate her for both the woman she had been and the woman she now was? Or was her past a mystery to this new man, a cloud which he didn't wish to float through? It was hard to imagine facing this "new" Emma, an Emma separated from the girl I once knew by twenty-eight years. Would time change her so much that I wouldn't recognize her? Was she still the girl I had once known and loved? How much of the old Emma had been shattered by this cruel game called life? I ache to know the answers to all of these questions, but fear I might not like what I find out.

After all, for the past twenty-eight years, I have preserved an image of Emma. To me, she is still that brown-haired girl who is hesitant around nature or anything involving coordination. She loves books and learning but loves to laugh even more. She is the girl who is rational and levelheaded but can be prodded into a looser character. She is the girl who only eats grape jelly on her pancakes, who orders rainbow sprinkles on her ice cream, who reads *Wuthering Heights* at least once a year. She is the girl who typically wears jeans and an old T-shirt, but looks better than any other girl I knew. She is the girl who I had shared everything with, from the deaths of my sister and mom, to my first kiss. She is the girl who captured my true self, who made me want to be better. She is the girl I saw myself walking hand in hand with through life.

For me, that image had stagnated because of my circumstance. While most relationships weather the difficulty of change, I hadn't been given that chance. Instead, I had preserved Emma like an Egyptian queen, carefully constructing the details so that everything was perfectly mummified in my mind. It had gotten me through the rough times in prison and helped me appreciate our relationship. I knew it wasn't realistic, that people change. But at the time it didn't matter, because I would never see the day we reconnected. I would never have to endure the shock of seeing the "real" Emma, transformed by time and life's realities.

But that was about to change.

Now, my carefully constructed picture of Emma is about to be put to the test. Certainly, she will be different. But what if she is so different that she isn't even the same girl? What if the Emma I have preserved in my mind is a distant shadow of the woman she is now? And on the flip side, what if I'm not the man she remembers me to be? Prison, no matter how hard I fought against it, has certainly morphed me into a different being as well. What if Emma can't find enough shards of the old Corbin within me? What if she doesn't recognize me?

And then more practical questions surface.

Will Emma think I am stalking her? Will she be creeped out that I have kept such a close eye on her? Will she hate me for re-entering her life, first through that letter and now in person?

Pull it together, I think to myself. I doubt that wondering how I found her address would be the forerunning thought in her mind. I bet other thoughts will surface before I have to explain myself.

In some ways, I wish I could snap my fingers and be on her porch, waiting only for the door to open. In other ways, though, I'm glad it will take me some time to reach her house. I need this time to relish in the anticipation, to collect my thoughts, and to revisit the person I was when Emma was mine.

Voice of Innocence

The years had dealt us some hard blows, to say the least. This was not your typical "go to college, break up, and reunite a few years later as grown-ups." No, it was much more complicated. The universe had seemingly spun us together in a web of commonalities, tightened the knots between us through memories and unconditional love. Too quickly, though, those threads had been forever snipped by the harsh realities of life and unfair stabs by fate. The love that was so perfect was intercepted by the harsh world. Our life never got to lift off the ground before it was shredded into a million unrecognizable pieces.

And so we went on, fighting against the tailwinds, struggling to find a way to reconcile this new outlook. Both of us faced different realities and struggles. Both of us found different ways of moving on. Yet, in my heart, I truly believe neither of us has completely forgotten the pattern of intricately woven strings that had tied us together before. The remnants of the strings may have been lost in the wind, but the intricate delicacies and interconnections of them would never be forgotten. They had woven us into the people that we were, whether we were together or not. Maybe now, against all odds, we could discover new threads, new patterns to bring us back together. Maybe the story wasn't erased. Maybe it just took us a lot longer than normal to fill the pages.

Then again, maybe the pages would just be different than what we expected. Maybe the days for our romantic encounters were gone, replaced by a mature version of friendship. Maybe I wasn't meant to re-enter Emma's life as a lover but as the best friend I had once been. Although this was less than ideal, I would certainly relish in any role I could play in her life, no matter what that role might be.

True, we were different now. No matter how much I tried to avoid the reality, prison had hardened me. It had taken me in as a young boy, chewed me up, and now spit me out for the world to see. I am stronger. I am more levelheaded. But I am also a lot different from that free-spirited boy who thought the worst thing in life that could happen was that your girlfriend could turn down your proposal. I see that naïve boy in my memories and wish like hell I could be him again. But I can't. I can't undo the past decades or the lessons I've learned. But maybe, in some strange way, I'm better for it. And Emma's different, too. Maybe she has weathered this storm a little bit better than I. Maybe she has managed to hang onto some semblance of optimism. At least I hope so. I hope life has been kind to her in ways it hasn't been kind to me. I hope that with my destruction of our final chain, she has been able to find some sense of peace that has eluded me. I hope she has found true joy.

I saunter on, into the darkness, hoping that somewhere in the near future the sun is about to dawn on a new life. Maybe it's not the life my teenage self-envisioned. But who knows, maybe it's better than I could have ever dreamed. No matter the case, I march into the blackness, stolid and steadfast, ready to meet fate's newest set of tricks.

Chapter Thirty-Eight
Time for Miracles

~ Emma ~

Glancing at the clock, I am shocked by the hour. Have I truly spent this much time doing nothing but reflecting? How could I get that lost in a world that has long since become extinct?

However, I am not truly upset at the prospect of a night that touts a low-calorie burn or plain lack of productivity. It is the prospect that the promise wasn't kept, that my hopes have died for the reunion I was inwardly awaiting.

I shake my head at my own stupidity. *Did you think he would come?* I mock myself. *It was decades ago, we were kids when he made that promise. He wanted you to move on, and you did. So why would he come? Besides, doesn't he have better things to do on his first night home than relive some childish memories?*

The cynic in me scorns the romantic. Yet, I also know the cynic can't see something the romantic can—the love we had was real. Yes, we were young, blind to the unfairness and destruction of the world. Our love hadn't yet weathered the day-in, day-out wear and tear that often tatters a relationship. We hadn't undergone financial issues and loyalty problems. We hadn't seen a lot of the world or completely figured ourselves out, let alone our relationship. Nonetheless, though, even now, I can't help but believe it truly was real.

Sure, there were many memories that confirmed it. I had just spent the better part of a night remembering the first meeting, the first kiss, sled rides, proms, picnics, I love you's, passion, promises, and tender moments. We had the framework of the traditional romance, even if it was cut short. We had all the elements that categorize a love affair, even if the players were mere adolescents.

Yet, despite all the beautiful moments we shared, despite all of the moments I find myself basking in, there is one that proves to me without a shadow of a doubt that it was love. Was it the promise ring? Was it the first kiss? Was it any of the traditional "signs" that people note? No. In fact, at first glance, the moment that affirms for me the power of our connection is a simple moment shared by two young kids who barely knew what love was. Yet, that single memory, that single moment, has stayed with me through it all, has cast confidence on the power of us, has reminded me every time I think about it that what I lost was a tragedy.

It is the memory that makes me think that someday, somehow, maybe it will all work out because what we had is unmatchable. What we had is a once-in-a-lifetime, knock your socks off, true connection kind of love.

As I finally decide to turn out the lights, I unabashedly grieve for what hasn't happened tonight as I revisit one more memory from the past, from a time before the tragedy began.

* * * *

Memories

Scarf and mittens securely in place, we shouted a faint goodbye to Mom and Dad as we braved the blustery wind that met us at the front door. Mom, usually up for almost anything, had opted to stay behind, relishing in the warmth of the living room's fireplace instead of facing the biting numbness of the December air.

Some Decembers in Pennsylvania were worse than others, offering mind-numbing temperatures and blustery snowfall. This happened to be one of those winters. Corbin grabbed my hand as we headed down the block. Despite his gloves and my mittens, I could still feel the electricity that characterized our physical touches. Snowdrifts dampened my sweatpants, but my feet stayed relatively dry in my boots. With every blow of the wind, I questioned our sanity.

"Are you sure you want to go? We could always go back to my place," I offered, praying he would give in to my idea.

Voice of Innocence

"Seriously?" Corbin said, stopping in his tracks. "And miss this? The annual event of the town? C'mon," he mocked, grinning.

"We're going to freeze to death before they even light the thing," I complained, already shivering from the core.

"We'll be fine. What's a little hypothermia? Think of the memories we're making," he added, tugging me along over the snow-covered roadways and sidewalks. We still had about ten blocks to go.

"Yes, fine memories they'll be when we're found dead in a snowbank, frozen," I added dryly.

"It's not *that* cold."

"Well, I'm freezing. Even my mother, my crazy mother, thought it was too cold. You seriously have to evaluate that."

"You'll be fine. Besides, you have a thick, handsome guy to wrap you up in his warmth if it gets too bad," Corbin smirked.

I rolled my eyes, although as I did so, I worried they might just stick that way, frozen in place by the icicles that were certainly hanging from my eyelashes.

"Well, we could have at least taken your truck," I whined, jumping over an especially high drift.

"Nope, that would nullify the experience. You have to breathe in the winter air, feel the snow under your feet. C'mon, admit it, it's putting you in the spirit," he beamed. Corbin had never gotten over his fascination with the white stuff since witnessing his first snow last year. To me, it was just an unnecessary source of cold and a pain in the ass. I had to admit, though, that seeing his joy over it had lightened my mood toward the Pennsylvania winters just a bit. But I was still cold.

We dragged on, hand in hand, until my legs felt like blocks of ice. I knew this was just the beginning, as the event would offer little reprieve from the cold other than some hot chocolate which would probably freeze in a matter of minutes. Okay, maybe not, but I doubted it would do much to warm me.

Despite my outward complaints, despite the frosty temperatures, I was happy on the inside. Walking hand in hand with Corbin on a Friday night, our second Christmas together just around the corner—everything seemed perfect in my life. It had been over a year since Corbin and I met, and what a year it had been. We had grown from acquaintances at the art table to best friends almost overnight. We had become inseparable, a package deal, relishing in the warmth of each other. A day without him was a wasted day, in my opinion, but I rarely had to deal with that. We did everything together.

Corbin had brought me out of my shell. Two years ago, I would have laughed at the prospect of attending this event, opting to catch up on some reading or some studying instead of braving the cold. Two years ago, a lot was different. I basked in solitude, opting to read about life instead of living it. Sure, I spent time with my friends, but I realized now that I hadn't taken time to appreciate the depth of life or the small things around me. It all changed when that crazy guy walked into the art room and asked me what my biggest secret was.

It had been almost a year since the magical Christmas when Corbin had admitted he "kind of" loved me, and ever since then, our relationship had only intensified. When people think of teenage love, they think of sparks and fizzles. Usually, they end almost as quickly and intensely as they began. But not us. Since that confession, our relationship had simply strengthened, matured. We weren't just lovesick teenagers who held hands and made out in the back of Corbin's truck. We were best friends, committed to each other and to us. We were a team, navigating the waters of life together, no matter how smooth or rough those waters were.

Yes, a year had changed us. The "I love you's" became more frequent and confident. In fact, they became common knowledge. It was no longer a question but an admission to something bigger happening than just two kids looking into each other's eyes. We had both felt it in the past year. This relationship that had begun at an art table over a simple project had gradually grown into a greater force, dictating where our lives were headed and who we were. Suddenly, my life seemed broader, more worthwhile simply because Corbin was in it. It had gained meaning I didn't think could be found so early in life.

So we trudged on into the winter evening, heading toward one of the few festivities our dinky town had to offer. The annual tree lighting in the town's square was perhaps the highlight of the year, offering small festivities that drew out most of the town's residents. Corbin had heard about this celebration of the season and begged me to go with him. I, of course, retorted with sarcasm about the "social event of the year" being a lame Christmas tree lighting. But I saw how much the child within Corbin wanted to go, so I relented.

As we neared the town, the sounds of the season echoed through the streets. The local alumni band tooted out carols, haloing the area in holiday reverie. People were everywhere, crawling the streets like a flock of birds heading south for the winter, waiting around until the final call by the leader. I didn't even know so many people lived in our town, let alone wanted to come to such a minute event. But come they did, as the streets buzzed with laughter and yelling as children and adults alike guffawed.

"Wow, look at this place! This is awesome," Corbin unabashedly reckoned, lighting up from the essence of the streets. "Let's check that out," he ordered, pulling me toward a tiny petting zoo set up for the kids.

"Really, Corbin? How old are you?" I smiled, watching him lunge toward the gate with a line of five-year-olds. I humored him and joined in his sense of awe at a bleating goat and a tiny calf as we watched children jam hay in their faces.

Neighbors, friends, teachers, they all crowded the area. I felt like "Hi" and "How are you" were flying out of my mouth at least five times a minute. Despite the superficial small talk, it felt nice to be surrounded by a community of familiar faces, of people I had known all my life. There was something magical in a gathered group of people in the midst of the snow, all awaiting an even more magical time of year. With Christmas so close, I couldn't help but appreciate the beauty of the scene, the warmth of the sounds coming from those streets. This was the definition of elation, experienced by an entire crowd of people.

Corbin and I traveled the booths of activities at the event. In reality, the tree-lighting festivities were somewhat lame. With the size of the crowd, you would think that an entire carnival or Barnum & Bailey's had just pulled up to town. In the streets were a hot dog vendor, a hot chocolate cart, the petting zoo, a few ice sculptures, and a tent peddling kettle corn. At the other end of the street sat the alumni band on a slipshod stage, caressing us with seasonal music. A carnival tent also sat in the middle, giving out soup samples from local vendors for the soup-tasting contest that happened every year. And that was it. Simple, boring even, but nonetheless, everyone gathered around these tents, basking in the glory of the town and of the surroundings. Despite its minimalism, you couldn't help but feel that Christmas was coming. You couldn't help but smile at the genuine excitement of the crowd and the close-knit feeling of this community.

So we continued to stroll the streets, buying hot chocolate, stopping to talk to a few friends from school. Corbin was simply beaming the entire time, stopping only to take a bite of the hot dog he had purchased. I had scrunched my nose at his offer to buy me one, too, proclaiming I would rather eat snow than a gristly hot dog from the little cart.

"This is great, we should come every year," Corbin observed.

"It's kind of lame, but it's also sort of festive in a strange way," I noted.

Corbin leaned over to kiss my cheek, rubbing his nose on me afterward.

"It is pretty cold, though, I'll admit," he slyly remarked, shivering at his own admission.

"Do you want to head back?" I asked, cupping the hot chocolate between my mittens and relishing in the bits of steam that were hitting my face.

Corbin squinted at me like I was crazy. "Really? You think that after all of this, we're going to just leave before the main event? Pu-lease."

I sighed before finally muttering an "Okay, okay." Corbin looked at his watch.

"We only have about fifteen more minutes. Let's head toward the tree," he ordered as I followed him through the crowd, weaving to avoid spilling my cocoa.

Many others in the crowd had the same idea, ushering screaming toddlers and even dogs to the other end of the square. The big moment was about to happen, marking the start of the holiday season. It was a simple tradition, started fifty years ago. I tried to imagine what this square would have looked like then, what life would have been like. I smiled at the idea of our busy, self-centered generation stopping to observe such a humble tradition as a tree lighting. It was a nice prospect, and I was glad, after all, that we had decided to participate. It was nice to stop for a minute and appreciate the simple joys of the season.

Voice of Innocence

As we edged closer to the tree and found a satisfactory view, Corbin reached into his pocket.

"I almost forgot," he beamed, pulling out his camera.

"Really?"

"Yeah, really. Stop pretending to be such a downer. I know you're having fun, even if you won't admit it. Your eyes are giving you away. Now smile," Corbin demanded, holding the camera out with one arm while pulling my face into his with the other.

"Say 'Christmas Tree'," he commanded.

I pulled away to look at him with skeptical eyes, but he just looked right back.

It was no use. So on the count of three, I yelled "Christmas Tree" with Corbin as those around us grinned. As he leaned out of the picture and I looked away, he snapped another picture of me from the side.

"Really?" I glowered. He gave me a shoulder shrug and then grinned. I gave him an intense glare until he agreed to put the camera away, pulling me into his arms and against his chest.

"I love you, Emma," he whispered into my hair as he pulled closer to me from behind. "I can't imagine my life without you."

I smiled, both inside and out, leaning back to look up into his face. "I love you, too, Corbin. I'm still freezing, but this is nice. I like being here with you."

We stood then, in silent reflection of the past year and of the year to come. I glanced around us at the sights and sounds of the hyper crowd, appreciating all the love that was standing with us. All around, girlfriends and boyfriends stood embracing, husbands and wives stood in each other's arms, children flailing about at their feet. I looked around at the town, our town, and appreciated for once the simple, genuine feel of it and its people. It was a place to embrace a family life, maybe not a life of thrills and excitement, but a life of purity and truth. For the first time since Corbin had uttered *I love you* a year ago, I realized that this would be our town, the place where we would settle with a family. I could picture myself at this dinky festival year after year, first with Corbin as my fiancé and then eventually as my husband. We would come here, years down the road, with my belly bulging underneath my winter coat, awaiting our first child. Eventually, we would be in the petting zoo with our own brood, watching them run at our feet in excitement of the season. Looking back at Corbin, I realized that he was my future, that a life with him would bring a life full of the serenity and comfort I was feeling at this gathering. His were the only arms I could ever picture myself in.

As the crowd began to count down to the lighting of the tree, I basked in the warm feeling of his arms around me, realizing that despite the bitter cold chilling my nose and my toes even through the winter gear, I was content. There was nowhere else I would rather be. Corbin joined in the countdown, and when we got to zero, we froze in anticipation. We awaited the mystical, fuzzy vision of hundreds of lights announcing the grand entrance of the time of year. But instead, the crowd stood silent in a sea of disappointment. Nothing had happened. The announcer on the tiny stage fretted as the electrical crew began arguing over cords and lights. So much for a magical moment.

Corbin just laughed, turning to me. "Well, so much for the tree lighting," he said, not disappointed.

"Yeah, some festival," I sighed.

"It doesn't matter. We still had fun, right?"

This time, I abandoned my sarcasm, looking up into his eyes. "Yeah, we did."

And with that, the crowd chorused in glee as the tree's lighting malfunction was fixed. The glow of the season finally lit up the town, and the band began honking out "Oh, Christmas Tree."

We took in the sight for a moment, Corbin's arms still around me. I smiled, realizing that all was not lost. Sometimes it took a little bit of work, but the lights would eventually fill the darkness.

A philosophical mood apparently taking hold of me, I glanced at a family near me, smiling at the tree. A little girl jumped up and down with glee as a baby sat in the stroller babbling to himself. It seemed overdramatic, even to myself, but I began thinking about life and how sometimes, like the tree, things didn't always work out exactly the way we hoped. Sometimes malfunctions happened, bulbs blew out, and mistakes were made. Sometimes we felt like saying "Oh well," and moving on to the next thing. But sometimes it was worth hanging in there. Look at the joy a simple thing like the lights had brought to so

Voice of Innocence

many.

Turning to Corbin, I again thought about our future. I thought about how there would probably be many malfunctions in our lives, too. Like the lighting crew, we would face burnouts and faulty wiring on our journey together. We would face bitter cold that threatened to overturn the warmth of our relationship. But it was at that moment, staring at the tree and the crowd cornily roaring at the sight, I realized there was always hope—even when things got tough, you had to keep trying, because in the end it was worth it. It was at that seemingly meaningless festival I realized Corbin and I could make it last if we just didn't give up.

Corbin, too, seemed lost in the atmosphere, deep in thought. We turned to head back to my house before the entire crowd dispersed, walking hand in hand slowly.

"That was fun," Corbin announced again, truly meaning it.

"Yeah. I have to admit, it's pretty neat seeing everyone around that single tree," I begrudgingly conceded.

"We should make this our tradition," Corbin proclaimed. I looked up into his eyes.

"Yeah, I'd like that," I grinned.

"Just think, a few years down the road, we could be like those families, chasing kids at the petting zoo and listening to them whine about their hot chocolate," he laughed.

"A few years?"

"Okay, maybe not a few. But eventually?"

"Eventually. Let's just enjoy a few years to ourselves, though, okay? I don't want to have to share my hot chocolate, not yet anyway."

"Deal," Corbin grinned, squeezing my hand.

It had been a long year and a half, but we still had a long way to go. We were young and carefree. We hadn't been tested yet. But on that night, huddled in the warmth of his hand and his heart, I felt like the Christmas spirit would carry on for years and years to come. I felt like the peace we felt standing with our community around the tree lived within our relationship. I felt like I wanted to live there, too. For the first time since I met him, I entertained the possibility that this could be it, this could be what people search for all of their lives. *How lucky I am*, I thought, *to have found it so young. I have so much time to appreciate it now.*

* * * *

If only I had been right, I think, rolling over under the covers. If only I had time to appreciate the peace I found in Corbin. If only we could have had our own miracles to work out the broken connections and dilapidated bulbs. If only we could have found a sense of that Christmas spirit to carry us through the bad times, to help us stay strong.

If only we could have kept the tradition alive, returning with our own family to celebrate at that silly festival.

If only time had been on our side.

I think about time and drift into the netherworld between sleep and alertness, seeing Corbin's face against that winter backdrop as I fall into a gentle reprieve.

Chapter Thirty-Nine
Hello Again

~ Emma ~

My heart pounds as my mind brings me back to the present. For a split second, my mind trudges to an unreachable, impossible place. I lift the icy fog of the winter air from my brain, shaking off the sluggishness that accompanies the winter months. Hank's barking at the front door snaps me back to reality. *Get real, Emma,* I scold myself. There's no way. Stop it. It's probably your annoying mother returning for the rest of her bottle of wine.

Glancing at the clock, I realize it is nearly midnight. Normally, a sense of alarm would have encroached upon me at the sound of a doorbell this late at night. Visions of serial killers and men in black masks would lead my fingers to the familiar emergency numbers of my cordless phone. The strains of the day numb my mind to any potential fear, however. Too tired to ponder the possibility of an unsavory person being behind the ringing of the doorbell, I slowly rise to my feet. My slippers trot across the floor with a scraping sound as I reach the stairs. I rub my eyes, trying to bring consciousness back to them, as I approach the final step. Hank is still woofing, warning away whomever has encroached on our property at this hour. I finally reach the front door, extending my hand toward the handle. I look at my feet as I slowly inch the door open. When I look up through the crack, my stomach plummets as if I have just rocketed down the biggest hill on the biggest roller coaster in the world. A serial killer with a machete would have been less shocking and perhaps less painful. It is not my mother returning for her wine bottle, although at this moment, she would be wishing that she had.

For a seemingly eternal moment, I just stand in silent reverie with the door slightly ajar. My chest tightens into a knot and my composure threatens to unravel. Hank keeps barking while wedging himself between me and the "stranger." A car alarm piercingly honks in the distance, a coincidental symbol of how we both must feel. I marvel at the randomness of both the honking and the fact that I notice. When faced with traumatic and shocking events, the human mind will find the oddest focal points. However, my heart eventually overthrows my brain's defense mechanism as everything blurs together in the background. The only thing I see is him.

    He hesitates cumbersomely as well, standing on the doorstep with his eyes locked on me. He has changed over the years. In the dim, flickering porch light, I can tell that his brown hair is shorter and showing signs of greying. Rugged stubble slightly hides the jawbone that had been so prominent in his youth. The ruggedness that now denotes him is foreign to me, but it seems to fit him. He has stoicism about him as well that is far removed from the carefree boy I had once known, had once kissed. His stance seems automatically and irrevocably defensive, like he is waiting for someone to throw a direct punch at him. Maybe it's life he is waiting to deflect. Who could blame him? Despite all of the variances in his character, his are the same eyes that had locked on that fifteen-year-old girl so long ago. They are the same eyes in which I saw my life reflected when I sat at that art table or underneath the span of that majestic Oak tree. They are the eyes that reflected back my own soul, even when I wasn't sure what that soul looked like. They are the eyes that had haunted my dreams, driven me forward, taken me backward, and filled my thoughts in all of the in-betweens. They are the eyes that I had longed to see but hadn't realized how much until this moment when they were right in front of me. They are the eyes that had offered me refuge and salvation. They are the eyes that had condemned me to a life of want and longing, of regret and sorrow. They are the eyes, I felt certain, that would save me from myself and would promise me something no one else could.

    I slowly push the door open just a hint more. "Emma, I'm...I'm sorry...I just had to come. I can leave if you want. I just had to see...see that you were doing okay," his gravelly voice offers slowly. He tastes every word as I soak each one in. His words come out like a question instead of a statement. I can feel the doubts he has suffered over the past hours at coming here, maybe even the past few months.

For a minute, I feel myself drifting back. I am not a forty-seven-year-old housewife with a dog named Hank and a husband who is out at the ER. I am sixteen again, looking into those familiar, soft eyes that seem to make everything okay. I find myself mindlessly walking toward him with confidence and falling into his arms. I realize that this time I'm not reminiscing. It's happening.

The embrace is soft yet hungry, tender yet sensuous. He wraps his arms around me, nuzzles his jaw into my hair, and squeezes as though his arms will stay locked on me forever. His familiar cologne wraps around me, engulfing my body in its sweet temptation. His breath hits my neck and sends chills down my spine. Electricity stuns my body, awakening me so much that I realize I have been asleep for many years. Life singes through my fingers, to my toes, to my heart. I am home.

In our embrace, everything else that has transpired dissipates. Things are right again in our worlds because we are where we were supposed to be all along. We are where we should have been decades ago and never had the chance. All of the what-ifs and if-onlys evaporate into the night sky as our hearts again find each other. If this weren't such a momentous occasion, I would probably start spewing about how corny this scene would be in a movie and how ridiculous this would seem. To a heart iced for decades, to a dream stomped into the ground, to a connection severed from external and not internal forces, though, these comments do not have a chance to surface. These comments are lodged in the back of my brain while my heart takes the lead.

"Emma, I've missed you," Corbin whispers into my hair. I pull back to look at him, to see the tears running down his face. This time, the tears are not awkward. They are the tears of a lost dream being found again, of a lost woman being rescued from the depths of her unrecognizable loneliness.

"I'm so sorry," I mutter up at him as I drink in his eyes again.

He shushes me ever so gently. He draws my face to his and caresses my lips with a hunger I have forgotten. I feel the kiss pulsate through my body, through my fingertips and toes. It loops through my core, through my heart, through my soul. It rights all of the wrongs that had been ever so present in my life until this point. It quiets the regrets, it assuages the sorrows. It softens the tremors of the past. My lips feverishly respond to his electricity as my hands find his hair.

When he finally pulls away, gently tugging at my bottom lip one last time, I start crying. He tows me back into him as the tears flow freely. We stand on the porch in silence, our connection felt and not spoken. My chest heaves with the weight of the moment. Breath seems to escape me as his mere presence exudes my life force out of me. I am, for the first time in decades, fully aware of the wants of my body and the needs of my ever-present soul.

I cry for what had been, for what could have been. I cry for what life has taken from both of us. I cry because I don't know where my life will go from here, where it should go. I cry for everything we have lost, and yet, I cry for everything we have gained. Life, working in its mysterious way, has given us a sort of second chance. We have a chance to forgive and to let go. We have a chance to relearn who we are and who we could become. I do not know where this embrace will lead or what possibilities our electric kiss has foreshadowed. I shudder at the prospect of his being here and what it could mean. So many lives could be turned upside down, not the least of them, John's. I grasp Corbin firmly, not wanting to let go and face life's harshest decisions and complexities. For now, I just want to soak up Corbin himself and feel his strong arms around me again. Maybe things will end the same way they did when we were younger. Maybe fate is simply against us. But maybe…

All I know is that he is back. Free and clear with new promises ahead of him, he is back. There will be no more talk of innocence or guilt, belief or disbelief. For now, we will hold onto each other and the promise of tomorrow. No matter what happens, tomorrow has to be brighter and fuller than yesterday. With the future spread in front of us and uncertainty clouded over us, we again bathe in each other's eyes. In those sparkling brown pools, I see myself as I was when I was a young girl and I see myself now. I see everything in between. But above all, I see his love for me, a love that has been to hell and back and has survived. For now, that will be enough for me.

THE END

About the Author

After graduating from Accounting at Mount Aloysius College in December of 2009, I realized that I wasn't pursuing my true passion in life. Thus, I earned a second Bachelor's Degree in English/ Secondary Education. I am currently a high school English teacher in my hometown and love the opportunity I have to foster an appreciation for literature in my students. Besides teaching, publishing a novel has always been one of the top items on my "bucket list." I started writing *Voice of Innocence* while still in college. Recently deciding that I should follow the advice I give to my students, I realized it was time to share my writing with others. I currently live in my hometown with my husband Chad (my Junior High sweetheart); our cats Arya, Amelia, Alice, and Bob; and our Mastiff Henry. Besides being an avid reader and writer, I love spending time with Henry and shopping.

Contact Lindsay at:

lindsayanndetwiler@gmail.com.
lindsaydetwiler.wordpress.com
https://www.facebook.com/voiceofinnocencebylindsaydetwiler